INCREDIBLE PRAISE FOR *LONG UPON THE LAND* AND MARGARET MARON'S DEBORAH KNOTT SERIES

"Maron proves as adept as ever at melding a central mystery with an involving family story...Maron emphasizes the close relationships of Deborah's extended family and the way their rural lifestyle connects them to the land, which makes for an especially heartwarming read."
— *Booklist*

"Bestseller Maron's 20th Deborah Knott mystery (after 2014's *Designated Daughters*) combines strong plotting, a superb cast of recurring characters, and a rare sense of place that transports readers to rural North Carolina. District court judge Deborah and the huge Knott clan headed by Deborah's father, reformed bootlegger Kezzie Knott, become involved in a murder investigation when Kezzie finds Vick Earp bludgeoned to death on the family farm. Vick and his Earp relatives have had an ongoing feud with the Knotts. When Deborah's lawman husband, Dwight Bryant, is appointed lead investigator, the victim's uncle, Joby Earp, is quick to stir up charges of favoritism. Providing counterpoint to the murder case is the backstory of Deborah's mother, Sue Stephenson, and Sue's relationship with the mysterious Capt. Walter Raynesford

McIntyre, of the U.S. Army Air Corps, whom she meets in 1943 at a USO club. It all adds up to another sparkling chapter of the Knott family saga."

—Publishers Weekly (Starred Review)

"Sprinkled with the low-country vernacular and the wonderful characters of Colleton County, NC, this title is a worthy addition to Maron's series."

—Library Journal

"There's nobody better."   —Chicago Tribune

"Maron writes with wit and sophistication."

—USA Today

"As always, Maron skillfully layers an absorbing plot with the doings of Deborah's large extended family."

—Booklist

"Opening a new Margaret Maron is like unwrapping a Christmas gift."

—Cleveland Plain Dealer

"Of today's series writers none has been more successful at weaving the bond between star and audience than Margaret Maron."

—San Diego Union-Tribune

"Maron has a pleasant, easygoing style that's smooth, generous, and perceptive…a delightful, thoughtful, good-natured series."

—Providence Journal

LONG UPON
THE LAND

LONG UPON THE LAND

THE LAND

Margaret Maron

GRAND CENTRAL
PUBLISHING

NEW YORK   BOSTON

Grand Central Publishing
Hachette Book Group
1290 Avenue of the Americas
New York, NY 10104
grandcentralpublishing.com
twitter.com/grandcentralpub

Originally published in hardcover and ebook by Hachette Book Group
First Mass Market Edition: March 2016

Grand Central Publishing is a division of Hachette Book Group, Inc.
The Grand Central Publishing name and logo is a trademark of Hachette Book Group, Inc.

The publisher is not responsible for websites (or their content) that are not owned by the publisher.

The Hachette Speakers Bureau provides a wide range of authors for speaking events. To find out more, go to www.hachettespeakersbureau.com or call (866) 376-6591.

ISBN 978-1-4555-4531-5 (mass market); 978-1-4555-4530-8 (ebook)

Printed in the United States of America

OPM

10 9 8 7 6 5 4 3 2

Here's to the ladies with whom I lunch and who know more about Colleton County than I do: Claudia O'Hale, Belle Allen, and Mary Nell Ferguson.

ACKNOWLEDGMENTS

Once more I give my heartfelt thanks to the three who have been with me almost from Deborah Knott's beginning: District Court Judges Shelly S. Holt and Rebecca W. Blackmore and the Honorable John W. Smith, director of the Administrative Office of the Courts. I truly could not have done this without your patient and generous help.

DEBORAH KNOTT'S
FAMILY TREE

(stillborn son)

Annie Ruth Langdon (1)

(1) Robert — m.
- 1) Ina Faye
- 2) Doris > Betsy, Robert, Jr. (Bobby) > grandchildren

(2) Franklin — m. — Mae > children > grandchildren

(3) Andrew — m.
- 1) Carol > Olivia > Braz, Val
- 2) Lois
- 3) April > A.K., Ruth

(4) Herman* — m. — Nadine > *Reese, *Denise, Edward, Annie Sue

(5) Haywood* — m. — Isabel > Valerie, Steven, Jane Ann > grandchildren

(6) Benjamin — m.

(7) Seth — m. — Minnie > John, Jessica, Richard

(8) Jack — m.

m. — **Kezzie Knott**

(9) Will — m.
- 1) Patricia ("Trish")
- 2) Kathleen
- 3) Amy > at least 2 children, including Jackson

(2) Susan Stephenson

(10) Adam* — m. — Karen > sons

(11) Zach* — m. — Barbara > Lee, Emma

(12) Deborah — m. — Dwight Bryant > stepson Cal

*Twins

LONG UPON
THE LAND

*Honor thy father and thy mother,
that thy days may be long upon
the land which the Lord thy God
giveth thee.*

— Exodus 20:12

*Let's close our eyes and make
our own paradise…*

— "Let's Fall in Love"

1943

She first notices him because he always sits at a table off to the side of the USO club and he usually sits alone. For some reason, he reminds her of her father, the only person in Dobbs that she misses. Not her mother, not the friends she had gone to school with, and certainly not the boys who joined up as soon as they turned eighteen and who think she is counting the days till they return.

KEEP UP THEIR MORALE! the posters urge; and to do her part, she writes weekly letters that give them news from home yet promise nothing, no matter what they might think. If they survive the war—and one has already died in the Battle of Corregidor—they will come back and become doctors, lawyers, or bankers like their fathers before them. They will be good men, pillars of the community, and they will live in big houses and buy their wives fur coats or take them to Europe every three or four years once things settle down over there, but she never plans to become one of those wives herself. Turn into her mother? Devote her life to maintaining a perfect home, to keeping up appearances?

No—NO—*NO*!

She drops out of Saint Mary's after one semester. "It's a debutante school!"

"So?" says her mother. Ever since Sue and Zell were toddlers, Mrs. Stephenson has dreamed of seeing her daughters make their debut together and she will never forgive the Germans for a war that has cancelled all debutante balls for the duration.

"You keep saying what you don't want," her bewildered father says. "What is it you *do* want, honey?"

"I don't know," Sue cries. "I don't *know*! I just want to live a real life," which is the closest she can come to articulating this nameless yearning to be needed, to make a difference.

"Do you want to teach?" he asks.

In his world, teaching is the most popular choice for women who do not immediately marry. "What about music?"

The organist at their church is a woman, a woman so pale and timid that he immediately searches for a more vigorous alternative and thinks of Margaret Mitchell, a distant cousin. "Or perhaps you could write?"

She is honest enough to know she has no true artistic talents. No desire to pour out her soul on paper and no deep interest in classical music. After years of piano lessons, she mostly plays Cole Porter and Irving Berlin by ear, while that one lackluster semester at

Saint Mary's only confirms that she is bright but no intellectual.

In eighth grade, a fiery and dramatic teacher reads them Longfellow's stirring call to action—*"Life is real! Life is earnest! And the grave is not its goal."* That's when a restlessness first takes root in her soul, a sense of time inexorably passing, a feeling that there is a life she is meant to lead, things she is meant to do, things that have nothing to do with the war, although it is the war that has let her mother be persuaded that they could contribute to the national cause. Mrs. Stephenson feels vaguely guilty that she has no sons to send to battle, which is why she finally allows Sue and Zell to go to Goldsboro in their stead.

Sue has pushed Zell to come with her, but she has no illusions that her job here at the airfield is vital to winning the war. Clerk-typists are at the bottom of the paper-pushing totem pole, and there is an endless stream of paper that must be pushed. Anybody who knows the alphabet can file. What raises her up an extra pay grade is her typing speed and accuracy. In the department where she and Zell work, every document requires four carbon copies. Make an error on the top sheet and each has to be carefully corrected with two separate erasers while all nine sheets—one bond, four carbons, and four onionskins—are still in the machine so as not to lose the alignment. Most of the girls in the typing pool average two errors a page; she averages one error per three pages and her slender fingers hit the keys so squarely and with such force that the fourth copy is almost as legible as the first.

The material itself is boring, though—reports and

requisitions that are as dull as the deeds and depositions she types for her father in the summer when she
fills in for vacationing clerks at his law firm.

After three months in Goldsboro, she tells her sister,
"Let's go to Washington. That's where all the fun is."

"*Washington?* Don't be a goop, Sue. Mother barely
agreed to Goldsboro and it's only sixty miles from
home. She'd never let us go three hundred miles away.
Never in a million years."

"We don't need her permission."

"Yes, we do," Zell says logically. "I do anyhow."
Zell is bookish. She shares none of Sue's troubling
doubts and looks forward to becoming Mrs. Ashley
Smith when Ash comes safely home. "Please stay
here. I couldn't stand it if you went and left me
behind."

"Who's leaving you behind?" asks Beulah Ogburn,
who shares the top floor of the boarding house with her
brother and the two Stephenson sisters.

"Sue wants to go to Washington."

"What's in Washington?"

"Life!" says Sue. "Excitement! People! Bright
lights!"

"With blackouts?"

Sue gives an impatient wave of her hand. "You
know what I mean, Beulah. Don't you ever get tired of
J.C. bird-dogging us?"

J.C. is their self-appointed chaperone and protector.
A slight deafness has kept him out of the army, so he,
too, works at the airbase. Night shift in the machine
shop. He'd rather be farming, but he adores his sister

and figures she'll be ready to go home as soon as he's saved enough money to buy a tractor.

Next day Beulah brings them a flyer calling for volunteers at the USO club. "They need girls to entertain the boys who'll soon be going overseas."

"Entertain how?" growls J.C.

Beulah reads the flyer. "Serve them coffee and doughnuts. Dance with them. Or just talk to them." Beulah is outgoing and gregarious and her feet were made for dancing.

J.C. disapproves, of course, especially as it means they'll be going out at night while he's working. Sue laughs at him. "Zell will chaperone us, J.C. She's practically an old married woman."

And indeed Zell would be quite happy to continue their quiet nights, reading a library book and writing long letters to Ash, but she's a good sport and Sue can talk her into almost anything. "At least it isn't Washington," she writes Ash.

They are popular additions to the club. Zell is a sympathetic ear for homesick young farm boys learning to fly, Sue augments the jukebox's outdated selections on the piano, and Beulah can convince the most uncoordinated left-footer that he's Fred Astaire. Like Sue, Beulah writes chatty letters to her brother's best friend, a boy who plans to marry her as soon as the war is over. "Not going to happen," says Beulah. "Footloose and fancy-free. That's me!"

(Except that she will go and fall head over heels in love with a boy from Nebraska who will be killed in action so that she winds up marrying J.C.'s best friend after all, but that's in the unknowable future. Right now, it's laughter and fizzy ginger ale and Friday night movies.)

But Captain Walter Raynesford McIntyre, US Army Air Corps, has the same sad eyes as her father and she wonders if he is unhappily married, too.

"He's too old for you," her sister Zell says the first time Sue meets him away from the USO club. "Besides, he's probably married."

"He's only thirty-four," she says. "And he's not married. I had someone take a look at his personnel file."

They go to a club at the edge of the airfield. He drinks bourbon on the rocks and she pours a little into her ginger ale. They talk about the war at first, then she tells him about Dobbs with its small-town social constrictions and suffocating standards. In return, he tells her about growing up in New Bern, down toward the coast. New Bern may be bigger, he says, but its people are just as narrow-minded and Raynesfords lead the pack, so he understands her frustration at not knowing what she wants from life.

Unlike most adults, he does not suggest possibilities.

"You'll know when you see it," he says. "I did." There's sadness in his voice and bitterness, too.

He's a flight instructor and she thinks he means that he wants to join the action, that he chafes at being kept stateside.

When he lights her cigarette, she takes the lighter from his hand. It's a brass Zippo with his initials engraved inside a frame composed of a vaguely familiar design.

"Greek keys," he says. "They're supposed to symbolize the flow of life...or love."

"Did your girlfriend give it to you?"

He slips the lighter into his pocket without answering. The sadness is back in his eyes and such a No Trespassing look on his face that she jumps to her feet as the jukebox plays a popular fox-trot. "Let's dance!"

She falls a little in love with him and he's sensitive enough to realize it. Nevertheless, it's two months before he tells her about Leslie's suicide and the dreams the two of them had of making a life together. He continues to badger his superiors—"I'm not a penguin, for God's sake. Let me fly!"—and orders finally come through. The night before he leaves for Europe, they drive out to the river to watch the moon rise. She drinks too much and starts crying because she's sure he won't come back.

He swears that he will and gives her his lighter to hold for him until he does. "But if I don't, promise me that you won't be afraid to break the rules if they get in your way. We only get one life, Sue. Don't waste it playing safe. Promise me that you'll have the life Leslie and I didn't get to have."

Her tears glisten in the moonlight and she holds the lighter between her two hands as if swearing on a Bible.

"I promise," she whispers.

CHAPTER

1

Now there are diversities of gifts.
— I Corinthians 12:4

I almost forgot," my brother Will said. It was only the first week of August, more than two weeks till my birthday, but he pulled a small, brightly wrapped box from his pocket. "Got another present for you."

"Aw, you didn't need to do that," I said. "The trellis was more than enough."

Will's an auctioneer and does estate appraisals, too. Somewhere or other, in his ramblings around the state, he had found a beautiful wrought-iron trellis that someone had scrapped. All it needed was a good sandblasting to get rid of the rust and Dwight had gladly taken it to a body shop in Dobbs. He and Will said it was a birthday present for me and yes, I would enjoy its beauty once it was in place, but we both knew who was the more enthusiastic gardener. This trellis was seven feet tall with graceful leaves and bunches of iron grapes and once it was set in holes filled with concrete, it would support the scuppernong vine that Dwight had already begun to root from one over at the homeplace.

When he's not digging trees out of the woods or transplanting flowering bushes to turn what once was a tobacco field into our own Garden of Eden, Dwight is Sheriff Bo Poole's second in command. I'm a district court judge and I should have been prepping for the heavy workweek coming up. Our benighted state assembly keeps slashing the court's budget, so in addition to my usual workload, I'd been asked to take a day out of my rotation and hear a case down in New Bern next week. Since the trellis was ostensibly for me, though, it was only fair that I help set it in place. Besides, helping Dwight erect a trellis was a lot more fun than reading depositions. But first Will and I had to wait while Dwight and another brother ran down the farm's posthole diggers. Seth thought Andrew might have been the last to use them when he expanded his dog run a few weeks ago.

Our son Cal and his Bryant cousins never miss a chance to ride in the truck bed, so they'd gone along, too.

We had wrestled the massive weight from the back of Will's van and while we waited for the posthole diggers, I took the little package Will had handed me and tore off the paper. Inside was a flip-top Marlboro box and inside that was something small and hard, wrapped in white tissue paper that fell away as my fingers fumbled with it.

A brass Zippo lighter.

I stared at it in surprise and my eyes filled with involuntary tears.

"Will?"

He gave a self-conscious shrug and his own eyes seemed to glisten for a moment. "Adam and Zach never smoked. You quit almost before you started and I quit last year. I thought you might want to keep it."

I could almost see our mother's strong slender fingers closed around it, cupping it in her hands to light a cigarette. She was never a chain-smoker—four or five a day was her limit, but I never saw her use a match. This lighter was always in her pocket, the brass smooth and golden. The engraved initials were almost worn off from the constant turning in her fingers whenever she was in deep thought. We should have hated it. After all, she died of lung cancer when I was eighteen. But it was so much a part of her that all the boys wanted it after her death. Not just her sons but her stepsons, too. Indeed Andrew was almost ready to fight the others until Seth stepped in and decreed that Will, as her oldest son, should be the one to have it.

It might have amused me had I been around at the time, because I was the only one who knew whose initials—W.R.M.—were engraved on the case inside a frame of Greek keys. By then, though, I was in such deep denial, so angry at the world, at my whole family, and at Mother for dying that I eloped with a sweet-talking car jockey, a man I almost killed with a rusty butcher knife, and didn't come home for a few years.

The first time I saw the lighter in Will's hands, I almost lost it, but for once I'd kept my mouth shut.

Now I opened the lid and flicked the little wheel

with my thumb. It sparked, but the wick didn't catch fire.

"Must be out of fluid," Will said and reached to take it back. "Who was Leslie?"

"Who?"

He pulled the lighter apart to show three lines of engraving on the inner casing: *11/11/1934—Happy 25th.* Below that was the name *Leslie* followed by four notes on a bar of music: *C, G, E, A*, a mixture of half notes and quarter notes.

"I never saw this," I said. "Mother told me that the man who gave it to her was a flight instructor at the airbase over in Goldsboro. I think the W stood for Walter, but I forget what the R was—a family name—Raynor, or something like that. His last name was McIntyre, though, and she called him Mac."

"Was he her boyfriend?"

I shook my head. "She said she could have liked him, but he was carrying a torch for someone who committed suicide."

"This Leslie?"

"Maybe. Mother never mentioned the woman's name."

"It would go with that scrap of music." Will hummed the notes and I recognized one of the old songs she used to play on the piano she had brought out to the farm with her when she and Daddy married. "Let's Fall in Love." When she was feeling sentimental or flirting with him or making up with him after one of their infrequent spats, this was the song she always played. What he used to play, too. I suddenly realized that he hadn't played it since she died. Not that I ever heard anyhow.

I looked at the date again. "He would've been in his early thirties when Mother met him."

"So why'd he give her a lighter his girlfriend had given him?" asked Will.

"I think she was supposed to hold it for him as a sort of guarantee that he'd come home safely from the war. Only he didn't."

"So she *did* like him."

"Not the way you mean. But she did say he changed her life."

"How?"

I shrugged. "It was one of those things she started to tell me, but then Aunt Zell or somebody came to sit with her for a while and we never got back to it."

There had been a terrible urgency about Mother's last summer. She had been too busy living to keep a diary and it was as if she felt that her life would be completely lost if there was no one who knew her stories. So between bouts of nausea and diarrhea, she told those stories to me.

Most of them anyhow.

Only later did I realize how much she had left unsaid. On the other hand, I'd be lying if I said I remembered all the details and nuances of the things that she *did* tell me.

"Would Daddy know?"

"We could ask him, but..." I didn't have to finish the sentence.

Will nodded. "Yeah," he said.

Daddy's never been one to talk about his feelings, but we know how deep the hurt goes. He'll smile with the rest of us when we talk about her—the house parties that lasted for days, the way she could play any song she'd ever heard, the time she lured his best looper away from the barn with better wages than he'd been paying, the way she teased that she fell in love with his eight little boys before she fell in love with him. But we knew not to probe deeper than those lighthearted family legends and anecdotes. Mother probably would have told me about their courtship had I been mature enough to ask, but I was as self-centered as any teenager back then. More interested in whether to go to a ball game with the team captain or with the coach's son.

The boys were all off starting their own lives that summer. College. New jobs. Marriage. Having babies. And all of them were unnerved by her losing battle with death. Daddy was in such fierce denial that he drove himself to exhaustion with farm work from first light to last dark. Even though Mother was dying, I couldn't help feeling sorry for myself. It seemed monstrously wrong that her day-to-day care fell squarely on me. I was supposed to be looking forward to college, not mired in bedpans and soiled bed linens and torn between grief and guilt.

I know now that those last two months were a gift and more than once I've wished that I'd listened closer or asked more questions, but she and Daddy were so right together that it never occurred to me to wonder how she could have married a roughneck bootlegger who barely finished grade school and who had eight little boys to boot.

She was a privileged town girl. Had it not been for

the war, she would have made her debut in Raleigh wearing long white gloves and a virginal white ball gown.

He grew up in rural poverty, the son of a small-time moonshiner.

Her father was a prominent attorney whose associates tried to get him to run for governor.

His father had died in a car crash while running from a bunch of revenuers.

She had studied Latin in high school.

He spoke the Queen's English—Queen Anne's English, as filtered through three hundred years of informal usage.

She was forever correcting our grammar. Although she never completely broke the older ones from using double negatives, none of us could get away with saying *ain't* in her hearing.

"It's not fair," Adam once grumbled. "Daddy says *ain't* all the time and you never correct him."

"When you're the man your daddy is, you can say whatever you like," she told him. "Till then, you're fixing to go to bed without your supper if you keep arguing about it."

At the sound of a motor, we looked up toward the house, but when the truck came into sight, it was Daddy's, not Dwight's.

"Speak of the devil and up he jumps," Will said with a grin.

I slid the lighter into a pocket of my jeans and went forward to greet him.

Without cutting his motor, he yelled, "Call the rescue truck! Somebody's been hurt bad and I'm scared to try and move him."

I patted my pockets, but of course I didn't have my phone on me.

Will already had his out, though, punching in 911. "Where is he, Daddy?"

"Down in the bottom, where Black Gum Branch cuts back from the creek. Somebody's smashed his head like a rotten melon. Where's Dwight?" He threw the truck in reverse and I scrambled to catch up with him.

"Wait! I'll come with you. Is he bleeding? Should we bring some ice?"

"Might help," he agreed and slowed to a stop by my back door.

I darted inside, scooped up some clean dishtowels by the refrigerator, emptied the whole bin of ice into a large plastic bag, grabbed my phone from the kitchen counter, and was back out to the truck in only seconds.

Will roared up in his van. "The ambulance is on its way. I'll go get Dwight," he said and dug off toward Andrew's house.

"Who is it?" I asked as we fishtailed through the sandy lanes that led down to Possum Creek.

"He was throwed down with his face in the dirt," he said grimly. "I won't sure if I should move his head, but I turned him so he could breathe. Leastways, I think he was breathing."

Our family farm is crisscrossed by lanes, some of which lead out to a couple of nearby roads that also cross the farm or serve as boundary lines.

"I was on my way to the food store," Daddy said by way of explanation, but I knew it was only a partial explanation.

A lane might be a shorter drive from point A (his back door) to point B (his destination) than the road, but the lanes also let him check up on parts of the farm he might not have visited recently. Most farmers still walk or ride their boundaries regularly, keeping an eye on crops, on fences, on drainage ditches that might need cleaning, or for a dozen other reasons. As a boy, he could have walked the family's hundred acres in an hour, but over the years, he and I and my brothers have added so much land to the original holding that wheels were a necessity. He's never cared much for what he calls "stuff," but let an acre of land come up for sale anywhere near the farm and he's right there with an offer, cash in hand. Last time my brother Seth totted up all the non-contiguous bits and pieces, too, we were surprised to realize that together we own close to twenty-five hundred acres.

We had been driving along the northern edge of Possum Creek. Now, as we neared the turn by the branch, Daddy put the truck in four-wheel drive and edged off the lane into the field.

"I probably already messed up any good tracks for how he got here," he said as he stopped and cut off the motor, "but you never know."

Mindful of his words, I was careful to step only on unmarked sand when I hopped out with my ice and hurried over to the body lying on the far side of the lane. Another two feet closer to the branch and he would have been hidden by a thick tangle of weeds and vines.

Blood had matted his hair and drawn flies and yellow jackets. I flapped them away with my dishtowel and gently laid the bag of ice on the wound, which was still oozing blood. Oozing meant his heart was still beating, didn't it? Or was it only gravity because Daddy had turned his head minutes ago? When I pressed my fingers against the side of his neck, I didn't feel a pulse and I couldn't tell if he was still breathing. It's been years since I'd taken a CPR course, but Daddy helped me move him onto his back and I started compressing his chest.

When Daddy relieved me, I used my phone to take pictures of the ground around the man where some tire tracks lay. No footprints and it looked like someone had used a dead branch to sweep the sand smooth. I walked a few more paces down the lane past where Daddy had stopped the first time and took more pictures.

Before I could kneel to take over again, Daddy sat back on his heels. "He's gone, shug. Ain't nothing more we can do."

We heard the sirens then and Dwight's truck barreled through the lane, a blue light clamped to the roof of the cab. One of our local rescue trucks followed and Will was close behind.

Three EMTs hurried over to the man who lay motionless on his back, his eyes closed and bluebottle flies circling his head.

CHAPTER

2

What man is this that walketh in the
field to meet us?

— Genesis 24:65

Any excitement on the farm can usually turn out several of my brothers who live here. Seth and Dwight had been at Andrew's when Will found them. Haywood was there, too, helping Andrew work on a malfunctioning burner at one of the bulk barns. Tobacco was ripening too fast to let a barn sit idle, so even a dead body wasn't enough to draw Andrew, but Haywood was too curious to stay behind and offered Seth a lift. Several nieces and nephews trickled in, alerted by the sirens. I looked around for the children, but Dwight had left them with Andrew.

By now, the ground around the dead man was so thoroughly trampled that there was no point in leaving him until more deputies arrived. Especially after Dwight sent pictures to the county's ME and said the

EMTs could detect no sign of life. "Looks like he was killed somewhere else and dumped here."

"Nothing to be gained by my coming out then," said Dr. Singh. "Just bag his hands and send him along to me."

All of us had taken a long hard look at the stranger's dirty, blood-streaked face. Ruggedly attractive, thin lips, and a nose that had probably been broken several years ago. He appeared to be between fifty-five and sixty, with thick brown hair that was beginning to go gray and a stocky build that would come in just under six feet. His jeans were well worn but his short-sleeved blue shirt looked fairly new. There was nothing in his pockets except a few loose coins. No wallet, no ID, but as they were loading him onto the gurney, one of the EMTs did notice that the sole of his left boot was about half an inch thicker than the right one.

"That should help us with an ID if no one comes forward," Dwight said. "Boots like that are usually custom-made."

As we waited for his backups, Dwight asked us to describe the scene when he first got there.

Daddy sat on the tailgate of his truck and fanned himself with the brim of his straw Panama. His white hair was damp with sweat and held the imprint of his hatband. "It was about ten-thirty, Dwight, and like I told Deb'rah, I was on my way to the grocery store. Didn't see nobody till I got to the curve here and seen his shirt in the weeds. I thought somebody'd throwed out some trash, so I pulled up and got out to see what it was. Sometimes kids park here and dump beer cans and stuff."

Teenagers often take advantage of isolated farm lanes and *stuff* was as close as Daddy could come to saying *condoms* in mixed company. (I know of at least one child that was conceived here back when I was in high school.)

"You recognize him?" Dwight asked.

"He was laying facedown in the dirt when I got here," Daddy said. "I seen how his head was all smashed in, so I turned it so he could breathe—*if* he could breathe. Couldn't really tell and then I went to fetch you. Got to say I didn't see no shoe tracks, but I might could've messed them up getting to him."

"What about you?" Dwight asked me.

"I was careful not to step where I saw any footprints or tread marks," I said, "but Daddy's were the only ones I saw. We turned him over on his back so we could try CPR, but it was too late."

"How was he lying?"

"Like Daddy said. On his face and all crumpled up, like somebody'd dumped some trash. We had to straighten him out to try CPR. I took pictures, though."

"Yeah?"

I couldn't blame him for looking surprised. I don't like being tethered to a phone and half the time I either forget to carry mine or to switch it on, a source of perpetual exasperation for him. This time I not only had it on, but had quickly taken pictures of the man's position and the ground around him before we moved him.

"I'll send them to Mayleen," I said.

Mayleen Richards—Mayleen Diaz in private life—is one of Dwight's best detectives and the department's computer whiz. He's already grumbling about how hard it's going to be to replace her when she goes on maternity leave.

Two deputies had arrived to make an inch-by-inch examination of the site, but they came up empty-handed. Not even a cigarette butt or gum wrapper. The body and a six-foot stretch of blurry tire tracks were all they would have for a starting point.

We'd had no rain in well over a week and the dry sandy soil barely held the tread.

Dwight was pessimistic about identifying the tire brand, but he sent one of the deputies to lift the man's fingerprints and put them online along with a physical description. "Ask Dr. Singh if he has any distinguishing marks or tattoos and don't forget to say that one leg's shorter than the other."

Until they got the ME's report or the body was identified, there wasn't much else Dwight could do, so I rode back to the house with him while the rest of the family dispersed. At least he and Seth had located the posthole diggers and they finished mixing the concrete and got the trellis set in place before Will headed back to town.

Haywood fetched the children home for us. Normally, he would have pushed his porkpie hat back on his head and stayed to offer unneeded advice or to speculate about the dead man. Today, he didn't even turn off his engine, just gave us a wave of his hand before driving off. Probably to go tell Robert, who had missed the excitement.

As I was undressing that night, Mother's lighter fell out of my jeans and landed on our bedroom floor with a *thunk*.

"What's that?" Dwight asked.

"Will gave it to me." I handed it to him. "Do you remember it?"

"Of course I remember it," he said. "I never once saw Miss Sue light a cigarette with a match."

"Do we have any lighter fluid around?"

"You're not going to start smoking again, are you?"

"Of course not, but I might as well get it working. Did you ever hear Mother say anything about it?"

He shook his head and, like Will, asked about the initials and the hidden inscription when he pulled the lighter apart. As we got into bed and turned out the lights, I told Dwight the little bit that I knew. A last-quarter moon shone through the windows, casting dark shadows in the room.

Lying close to him, I said, "Did I ever tell you what Mother said about you?"

"About me?"

"Well, she didn't know it was you. We were talking about marriage and she told me to try to marry someone I could laugh with the way she and Daddy could. She wondered if I'd met my future husband yet. I wish she could have known it was going to be you."

His arms tightened around me. "Me, too, honey."

"That lighter's got me wondering about them, though. Mother and Daddy were good together but they started off life so differently. How do you think they ever got together?"

I felt him shrug. "I don't even know how my own parents did."

"I do," I said. "Miss Emily said that their school bus

routes got changed when he was a senior and she was a sophomore."

"Yeah?"

"They already knew who each other was. He played basketball and she was a cheerleader."

"I did know that."

"Well, when the bus routes changed, they wound up on the same bus and got to see each other twice a day. He asked her out and they were married in the spring before she graduated. She always wanted to be a teacher, but you and Rob and your sisters came along so fast, she didn't go back to school until after your dad died."

"That was a rough few years," he murmured.

"Weird that I know more about your parents than my own."

"So just ask Mr. Kezzie," Dwight said. "Or ask Miss Zell. It can't be much of a secret."

He yawned and kissed me good night. A few minutes later, his breathing deepened and I knew he was already asleep.

He was right, though. There was no real reason not to ask.

Next morning—Sunday—after Dwight checked with his office and was told there was still no ID on the murdered man, we drove over to Dobbs, to the big white brick house where I'd lived after law school until I made peace with Daddy and built a small house out on the farm, the house that Dwight and I enlarged when we married and Cal came to live with us. Aunt Zell had invited us for lunch, so despite the heat, we left the car parked in the driveway and walked with her and Uncle Ash the few short blocks to the First Baptist Church. They never had children and they've always sublimated with Mother's brood.

Aunt Zell is only a year or two younger than Mother and it's bittersweet to think that she should still be with us. She would be white-haired now and perhaps look a little frail, but married more than fifty years and still as clearly in love with Daddy as Aunt Zell is with Uncle Ash. Dwight and I probably married too late to have fifty years but the two we've already had make me sure we could last that long if given the chance.

Mother's cigarette lighter had raised so many questions in my head that on the walk home, while Dwight and Cal talked fishing with Uncle Ash, who was too aware of Cal's young ears to ask about the body, I said, "Aunt Zell, what was Walter McIntyre like?"

"Who?"

"Walter Raynor McIntyre. I think that was his name. Mother met him while y'all were working over in Goldsboro. She made a point about his middle name when she told me about him. Like Raynor was a joke or something."

Aunt Zell's brow furrowed. "Walter Raynor McIntyre?"

"He gave her his cigarette lighter to keep for him when he was sent overseas."

"Oh. Mac. I don't think his name was Raynor, though." I could see her searching her memory. "Raymond? Rainier?"

"I'm not sure. She just called him Mac when she was telling me about him. So what was he like?"

She shook her head. "I didn't really know him. He was a flight instructor who used to come to the USO club. Real good-looking, as I recall. Sue went out with him a few times before he was reassigned. He was too old for her, but she said it wasn't really dating. What on earth made you think of him?"

"Will gave me that lighter for my birthday," I said, and back at the house, I pulled it apart to show her the inscription inside.

"I saw that lighter a million times," Aunt Zell said, "but I never knew anything about that engraving. Who was Leslie?"

"His girlfriend, I assume."

Aunt Zell hummed those four notes and frowned. "'Let's Fall in Love'?"

I nodded and she looked puzzled. "How odd. That was her and Kezzie's song."

"Looks like it was Mac and Leslie's song, too. Mother did say he changed her life."

"Really? How?"

"That's what I was hoping you could tell me."

"I'm sorry, honey. She didn't talk about him much after he left Goldsboro and I'm afraid I was too busy writing Ash every night to ever ask. Changed her life, she said? I wonder how? Did you ask your dad?"

"Not yet. He gets touchy when we ask too many questions about her."

While she brought the gravy back to a boil, I dished up the vegetables and took the biscuits out of the oven. Once we were seated, though, and Uncle Ash began to carve the roast chicken, I said, "Did Mother ever tell you exactly how she and Daddy met?"

Aunt Zell shook her head. "She didn't have to, honey. I was there. Ash, too. Remember, Ash?"

"I remember." Tall, with thin silver hair and hands knotted with veins, he carefully cut the wishbone away from the rest of the breast, put it on a plate, added some crispy skin, and passed the plate to Cal, who grinned in anticipation of pulling that bone with him. "I also remember how you didn't approve."

"I didn't disapprove," she protested. "That was Brix Junior. And I knew he'd tell Mother."

December 15, 1945

Sue Stephenson! Thank the Lord!" says the bald-headed man selling tickets at the door of the American Legion Hall. "I hear you and DeEtta really tore up the piano at her party last week. If you'll play till our fiddler gets here, I'll let y'all in for free."

Ash Smith puts his wallet back in his pocket as if it is a done deal that his future sister-in-law will save him the cost of their tickets. "Don't tell me Simon's drunk again."

"Not this time. Naw, he went and broke his arm. Fell off a chair while he was trying to stick a star on top of their tree. His wife says he's got somebody good to come take his place, but folks are here and wanting to dance right now."

Beyond the ticket table, the hall is crowded with merrymakers. All white, of course, except for the bartender and the dishwasher behind the bar.

Fun-loving middle-class couples mingle with junior members of the country-club set, the women in
their brightest colors since before the war, the men
in jackets and ties. Several are still in uniform because their discharge papers have not come through
yet, but rationing has finally ended and people are
more than ready to put the war years behind them
and get on with their lives—*the lives they lived before the war*, thinks Sue. The same comfortable lives
their parents and grandparents live. Working at the
same jobs, going to the same parties, shopping at
the same stores, worshiping in the same churches
with the same people they've known all their lives.
Mac said it would be different, that things would
change—*had* to change—yet here they are. Except
that everyone seems to have more money, it could be
1935 not 1945.

On this raw December evening, the windows are
draped in garlands of pine and cedar tied with big red
bows, and a tall Christmas tree casts a festive glow
over the shabby room. A double row of chairs and
small round tables line the side walls of what is basically a wide empty hall with hardwood floors and a
low wooden platform at the far end. To the left of the
platform, doors lead out back to a kitchen and rest-
rooms; to the right is a bar.

Although Colleton County is technically dry, private clubs like this are exempt even though "trial"
memberships can be bought at the bar for a small fee.
Real members bring their own bottles of liquor that are
labeled and kept on shelves locked behind wire doors
to which only the bartender has keys. Men tell him

their names, point to their bottles, and pay him for set-ups—the ice and mixers.

"Just ginger ale," Sue says when Ash asks what she wants to drink. She has developed a taste for bourbon on the rocks while working at the airfield, but here in the Bible Belt, few "nice" women drink more than a single shot spaced over the evening and well cut with a soft drink. If she asks for a real drink, her mother will surely hear about it and she herself will never hear the end. Instead, she hands her red wool coat to her sister Zell and heads for the upright piano that stands on the dais. In truth Sue is glad for the diversion. She hadn't wanted to come, but their mother disapproves of either daughter going out alone in cars with men, even a man as honorable and trustworthy as Ash Smith.

Never mind that Sue and Zell spent the last two years of the war living in a boarding house in Golds-boro so they could work at the Seymour Johnson Air-field. The war is over now and men need their jobs, so here they are back in Dobbs, ready to marry and settle down.

Or so Mrs. Stephenson thinks.

Zell is halfway there. Ash slipped a diamond ring onto her third finger two days after he came home in November and a May wedding is planned. Her whole life seems laid out before her, a life like her mother's and grandmother's. There will be book clubs, teas, meetings of the Daughters of the Confederacy or the DAR, Bible study groups, and occasional trips to New York and Washington until the babies start coming. (They are hoping for at least three.)

After that, it will be PTA, Cub Scouts or Brownies,

and dinner parties for Ash's bosses and fellow buyers at one of the large tobacco companies.

Not me, though, thinks Sue as she sets her drink on the scarred piano and speaks to the drummer, who is older by a good ten years. The guy on bass was three or four grades ahead of her in school. They are not part of her crowd, but they know who she is, just as she has a clear sense of their social standing as well. Not that she cares, but her mother's judgmental voice is always in her head: "*Not quite our kind of people, are they, dear?*"

They hand her a playlist that consists mostly of swing band standards for the older dancers mixed with boogie-woogie tunes for the young and agile. Only one is unfamiliar. She can read sheet music, but mostly plays by ear. "If your fiddler doesn't get here by the time you're ready for this one, one of y'all will have to hum it for me."

She runs exploratory fingers over the keyboard. B-flat wants to stick and the G feels spongy, otherwise it is in surprisingly good shape. The drummer hits his high hat to get the crowd's attention, the bass player gives her the key, and they launch into a lively version of "In the Mood." Toes tapping and fingers snapping, a dozen or more couples immediately spill onto the dance floor. After some slower tunes—"Begin the Beguine," "Who Am I?" and "Once in a While"—they clear the floor of gray-hairs with "Jukebox Saturday Night." Among the younger set, Zell and Ash are almost as good as Ginger Rogers and Fred Astaire as they jitterbug down the length of the hall and back. His legs are a blur when he spins her in and out, and the

skirt of her swingy new dress swirls so high that Mrs.
Stephenson's lips would be clenched in a tight line,
embarrassed that a daughter of hers would show that
much thigh in public.

Near the middle of that first long set, Sue hears
the sound of a fiddle behind her and glances over her
shoulder to see a tall skinny man in a cheap blue suit
and a string tie. He looks like someone who would
be more at home on the stage of the Grand Ole Opry
than playing pop songs for this crowd. A worn fiddle is
tucked beneath his chin and his fingers fly up and down
the strings as he works his way into the song they are
playing. At first he follows their lead, but by the second chorus, they are following his.

The set ends with Ash swinging Zell over his head,
giving nearby dancers a flash of white lingerie. Sue
closes the piano, smiles at the other players, and stands
to join her sister and their friends.

"Hey," says the drummer. "You're not quitting on
us, are you?"

"I was only filling in," she says. "You don't need me
now."

"Sure we do," says the bass player. He props his tall
instrument against the back wall and they move off the
platform where he pulls out a crumpled pack of cigarettes, then slaps his pockets in a fruitless search for
matches. Sue hands him her lighter. He immediately
reads the initials engraved on the front of it. "Your
boyfriend?"

"No." How to explain that complicated relationship? "No, just a friend who didn't make it back from
Germany."

"Sorry," he says and offers her one of his cigarettes.

She starts to refuse. Movies are making it more acceptable that women smoke, but her mother still thinks it "common" for women to do so in public. What the hell, though? "Thank you," she says, and bends her head to accept a light from him before he lights his own and passes the Zippo back to her.

The drummer and the fiddler are lighting cigarettes of their own and they sit on the edge of the platform. With her skirt tucked around her knees, she perches on the step beside the bass player, chatting with friends who come and go with song requests and, in Sue's case, asking for a dance before the evening was over. No one seems to be saying much to the fiddler, so she turns toward him and says, "I'm Sue Stephenson. I don't believe we've met?"

"Kezzie Knott," the man says.

His name is vaguely familiar, but she can't think in what context. "Here in Dobbs?"

"Over near Cotton Grove," he says brusquely and walks away toward the bar.

"Don't mind him," says the drummer. "He's had it pretty hard."

The bass nods. "First time I've seen him play since Annie Ruth died."

"His wife?" Sue asks.

"Yeah," says the bass. "Childbirth fever. Weird when you think about it. To die like that after kicking out such a bunch of babies." He shakes his head at the irony. "They let him out of prison six months early so he could come home and take care of them."

"Prison?"

"Surprised you don't know," says the bass. "I believe your daddy was the one got him that early release."

"Really? What was he in for?"

A sly grin appears on the drummer's lips. "Income tax evasion, won't it?"

That means a federal prison, thinks Sue.

Puzzling.

This Knott man doesn't look as if he has enough income to make evading taxes an issue.

They finish their cigarettes and start to return to their instruments when her sister Zell hurries up. "C'mon, Sue. Brix Junior wants to dance with you."

Sue rather doubts that. Brix Junior is their father's much younger half brother who's due to join Stephenson and Lee when he finishes law school. As usual, he is surrounded by a mix of college girls and Junior Leaguers and seems slightly surprised when Zell pulls on his arm.

"Here she is, Brix. I told her you wanted the next dance."

"Thank you, darlin'," he drawls and hands one of the girls his glass as the fiddler launches into "Easy to Love."

"Why did Zell say you wanted to dance with me?" she asks as he sweeps her expertly across the floor.

"I always want to dance with you," he says. "You know how to keep your feet out from under mine."

"Be serious, Brix."

"I guess we didn't think you ought to be up there playing with those guys."

Sue frowns. Brix might be a bit of a snob, but

Zell isn't. She hadn't said a word against her playing when it was just the drummer and the bass. Which must mean—?

"Who's Kezzie Knott, Brix? Why was he sent to prison? And don't say income tax evasion."

"But that's what it was. What the government said it was anyhow. Said he was selling something he didn't pay taxes on."

"White lightning? He's a bootlegger?"

"And a pretty successful one on the whole. Prison was a bit of a setback, but they say he's back supplying shine to distributors all up and down the East Coast. Father says he sends a lot of business to the firm. Anybody that works for him, if they get caught, he pays their legal fees and takes care of their families if they get jail time, which isn't as often as you might think. Any money left over, he puts it in land. He's getting quite a spread out from Cotton Grove. Wanted to buy that farm your grandmother left you and Zell. His land touches it now."

"Really? I never heard about that."

"Catherine was sure y'all wouldn't be interested."

For once her mother is right, thinks Sue, but she and Zell should have heard the offer and made that decision themselves. The tenant house that once sheltered sharecroppers back when her mother was a girl has long since fallen to ruin. A hurricane took half the roof before she and Zell were born and no one thought it worth replacing. For years now, the land has been rented out to a neighboring farmer and the rent money put into a savings account for the girls. It suddenly occurs to Sue that they might have a tidy little nest egg.

Maybe even enough to travel. To see the world now that the war is over. To find the life she is meant to have, the life she promised Mac she *would* have.

"Have to say I was surprised to see him here tonight. It's not like he needs the money. But I've heard he loves to play the fiddle and he's pretty good, isn't he?"

"Hmm?"

"Knott," says Brix, bringing her back from sudden dreams of New York. Paris. Rome.

She matches her steps to his and realizes that Brix is right. The fiddle player really is good. He weaves the melody in and out between the bass and drums, never straying so far that the dancers lose the rhythm, but never completely predictable either. When the song is over, she lets Brix go back to the girls clustered at his table and she spends the rest of the evening dancing with several young bachelors in their set.

All are perfectly nice young men, men her mother approves of.

All eligible.

All boring.

CHAPTER

3

Remember the sabbath day, to keep it holy.

— Exodus 20:8

As we were leaving Aunt Zell's, Dwight's phone rang.

"We've got a hit on the victim's prints," he said, so I dropped him at his office and Cal and I drove on home alone.

When we neared the farm, Cal said, "Can we go by Uncle Robert's?"

He and Robert, my oldest brother, have forged a bond over the farm's old Cub tractor. I learned to drive on it when I was Cal's age and now Robert is teaching Cal. They've been talking about disking in our spring garden to get ready for a fall crop of leafy greens. Dwight had already bought some cabbage and collard plants and was keeping them in a cool shady spot till time to set them out.

"I don't know, honey. It's Sunday," I reminded him,

"and you know how Aunt Doris feels about working on Sunday."

"We won't be working, Mom. He's just going to show me how to hitch up the discs. That's not work."

When it comes to males and machinery, the line between work and play is so narrow not even an angel could dance on it. Or so it seems to be in my family.

"First, we'll go home and change clothes," I said, "then you can call him and see what he thinks."

As I expected, Robert said for Cal to come on over. When we got there, we found him out under the shelter with the Cub. "You can stay, too, Deb'rah, but Doris has gone shopping with her sister."

It doesn't bother Doris that Sunday play for her means Sunday work for others.

"That's okay," I said. "I've got some stuff I need to do."

Cindy Dickerson, the trial court coordinator down in New Bern, had emailed me the pleadings for tomorrow's court and when I finished with those, I spent another hour reading up on family law.

Our chief district court judge has proposed that we subdivide our court into specialty areas: civil, criminal, and family. He's asked if I'd like to hear the family cases—the divorces, custody disputes, contested child support, etcetera. With its monotonous round of DWIs, assaults, rubber checks, and petty crimes, criminal court has begun to bore me. Yes, domestic situations can be heartbreakers, but those situations interested me more and more these days and I think I've done some good work there. And let's not overlook a side benefit: Dwight and I wouldn't have to be so careful about discussing his work in case it proved to be something I'd have to rule on.

Decision made, I called Judge Longmire and told him yes.

By late afternoon, the sun had moved around to the other side of the house and a light breeze tempted me out to our shady screened-in porch to finish reading the Sunday paper. I had gone back inside to pour myself a glass of tea when I heard a car door slam and glanced out in time to see the taillights of a gray patrol car leave the yard.

Dwight looked hot and tired, but he smiled when I opened the door. "Is that for me?"

"Absolutely," I said.

He had drained my tea in three deep gulps. "Thanks, shug. That really hit the spot."

He followed me back into the kitchen for more and while I poured a second glass for myself, he loosened his tie and hung his jacket on a doorknob. "The guy's name was Vick Earp. Ring a bell for you?"

"The only Earp I know is our dentist. Any kin?"

He shook his head. "You issued a domestic violence restraining order on him last year."

"I did?"

We took our tea out to the porch and settled into lounge chairs while Dwight tried to refresh my memory. "He lives on the far side of Cotton Grove. Drives an oil truck for Dexter Oil and Gas. Wife Rosalee, two daughters, both grown and both living out of state."

"Because they were tired of watching him beat up on their mother," I said. "I didn't recognize him yesterday and I can't quite put a face to her but I do remember her saying that about her daughters. Yet she never divorced him, did she?"

"No."

"Have you talked to her?"

He nodded and swirled the ice cubes in his glass with a deep sigh. Telling the relatives is the hardest part of his job. "Even with a black eye, a cut on her chin, and a big purple bruise on her arm, she still says he was a good man till he wrecked their first car and one leg wound up shorter than the other."

"Always somebody else's fault," I said. "Never his own sorry doing. As I recall, he'd been drinking when he crashed. Did she kill him?"

"Who knows? We caught up with her at her cousin's house. She claims she's been there since around six Friday evening and her cousin backs her up. Says she doctored the cut on Mrs. Earp's chin and then put her to bed with a sleeping pill."

"Is that when his head got bashed in? Friday night?"

"Hard to say. Singh puts the actual time of death about a half hour before Mr. Kezzie found him yesterday. That would make it around ten o'clock. No way to tell when Earp got hit or when he was dumped, though. He was hit at least three times and he had bruises on his knees like he'd fallen. What did him in was probably the blow to the back of his head with something straight and narrow. Like a thin but heavy four-inch-wide board. Ray and Tub and I went over to the house. There's blood on the back steps. Looks fresh. No sign of whatever was used to hit him with, though."

"A man that violent must have enemies," I said.

"You'd think so, wouldn't you? Mrs. Earp said no when I asked her, that he was pretty much a loner. Her cousin did say he was on the outs with his brother. She also said somebody took a shot at him last weekend through the windshield of his truck. I'll go back and talk to them tomorrow."

"If he lived on the other side of Cotton Grove and if that blood's where he was struck down, why do you reckon he was brought out here?"

"Well, Mr. Kezzie did say that kids have been known to park there on a Saturday night. Maybe someone remembered it as a fairly isolated spot." He suddenly grinned. "You ever park there with anybody?"

I laughed. "You have to be kidding."

"You telling me you never made out with anybody in the backseat of a car?"

"No. I'm just saying I never did it within five miles of the farm. Daddy seemed to have eyes everywhere in those days. Still does, for that matter."

"You gonna name names?"

"Right after you do," I said. "Seems like I remember hearing that you and Will got bogged down in that branch one night on your way home from a ball game. Not that the branch is on the way to your house from the school gym. I believe one of you had to sneak past our house without Daddy knowing so you could wake up Seth to pull you out with a tractor."

He laughed. "Those girls never went out with us again."

Before I could tease him for their names, the sound of a motor made us look around to see that little red Cub putt-putting down the lane in second gear. Cal was in the driver's seat, a big grin on his face. Robert stood behind him on the tow bar and he was beaming, too.

"Show us where you want it cut in," Robert called to Dwight, "and we'll get 'er done tomorrow."

We walked out to the garden, which seems to have grown exponentially this season. You can give a country boy a town job, but he's never going to buy all his food in town. Not if he has a square foot of dirt to play with.

Dwight pointed to the rows where garden peas, zucchini, and potatoes had grown and been harvested. Field peas, tomatoes, and okra would bear until frost, but the rest could be cut in and rows run for the fall planting.

Robert came back to the porch with us and allowed as how a glass of tea would taste real good and did I still have some of those sugar cookies I'd baked last week?

I did.

I brought out the cookie jar and he took a handful. Dwight and Cal helped themselves, too.

"I always think of Mama Sue when I eat one of these," Robert said. "She'd wait till it was almost time for us to get home to start making them. Us boys would get off the school bus of a cold winter day and we could smell them all the way out to the road. Ain't nothing like a warm sugar cookie and a cold glass of milk." He munched reflectively. "Unless it's warm chocolate cake. She said when she was a girl, their cook would make one on a Saturday morning and it'd smelled so good she couldn't stand it, but her mama wouldn't let it be cut till Sunday dinner. After her and

Daddy got married and she came to live with us, she always sliced us off a piece of chocolate cake while it was still warm. These days I heat mine up before I put on my ice cream, but that was before microwaves."

Cal's only been in our family two years so he hasn't heard all the familiar stories, but because he'd been fascinated when Aunt Zell described how my parents met, I asked Robert to tell him about his own first meeting with Mother. It's one of our more dramatic family legends and I never get tired of hearing it. Too bad Frank wasn't here or I'd make him tell his Mama Sue story, too.

"How old were you then, Robert? Nine? Ten?"

"Something like that," he agreed. "She saved our lives," he told Cal. "Me and Frank's. Won't for her we'd've been long dead by now."

He took a swallow of his iced tea and leaned back in the chair with Cal sitting cross-legged on the floor in front of him. "I forget why she come out to the farm."

"To cut a Christmas tree," I reminded him.

"That's right. It was getting on toward Christmas, 'cause her and Aunt Zell come out next day and brought us some Christmas candy. We'd had a real cold snap and Possum Creek had near 'bout froze solid, something we hadn't never seen before..."

December 18, 1945

Oh, for heaven's sake, Zell," Sue says impatiently. Despite boots, wool slacks, and heavy jacket, she's starting to shiver and her words leave little puffs of steam on the frigid air. "What's the big deal? Go. I'll be fine."

Zell looks from her sister to her fiancé. The icy wind has reddened her cheeks and ruffled the wisps of fair hair that escaped from beneath her blue scarf hat. Her pretty face is torn with indecision. "You sure?"

With manful chivalry, Ash Smith says, "If you'll wait till after lunch, we can all go and I'll cut the tree for you."

Sue shakes her head. "I'm perfectly able to cut a Christmas tree by myself." She glances up at the dark sky. "Besides, they're predicting sleet this afternoon."

"I could maybe change our appointment," says Ash.

Zell gives him an anxious look. "But didn't Mr. Clark say we have to decide this morning?"

With one gloved hand on the door handle, Sue gives an exasperated shake of her head. "Make up your mind, Zell. It's too cold to stand here in the middle of town arguing about it. I'm going."

"Well...if you're sure you'll be okay?"

"Ash, will you please put my sister in your car and go buy her dream house before I turn into an icicle?"

The big white brick house has come on the market only that morning. As soon as he finished dealing with the owners, the real estate agent immediately called Ash. Jim Clark is an old friend of the Stephenson family and over the years, he has heard Zell speak wistfully of the Hancock house. When Ash visits Clark's office to check out possibilities for their first home, Clark says, "Too bad the Hancock heirs can't agree on a selling price."

On the off chance that those quarrelsome siblings are finally ready to deal, he phones the oldest Hancock son after Ash leaves and bluntly tells him that the longer the house sits empty, the greater the chances of vandalism or deterioration.

It's a timely push. The very next day, they agree on an asking price.

"I've been working on them two years, and now they want the money yesterday," Clark says when he calls Ash and sets up an appointment to view the place. "I hear the Hancock daughter's already ordered a brand-new 1946 Cadillac. It's a fair price, though, and I'll have to list it in tomorrow's *Ledger*, so if you want it, you'd better get your offer in today."

It's really more than Ash can afford, but Zell reminds him of the rent money from her half of the farm and she's sure their fathers will help them.

Only two blocks from First Baptist Church of Dobbs and the shops on Main Street, the location is so desirable that it will not stay on the market long. While less imposing than the Stephenson residence a few blocks farther from Main Street, the house has a warm and welcoming charm that their more formal childhood home lacks and Zell has fantasized about living there ever since she was a little girl.

It's too big for them now—"Four bedrooms," Zell says, happily visualizing the children who will fill those rooms. "We'll grow into it, though."

Sue knows it will break her sister's heart if the house slips away when it is almost in their grasp, so to end the argument, she slides into the car, firmly slams the door, and heads toward Cotton Grove and the farm they inherited from their grandmother. The car is ten years old, the tires are worn, and the heater no longer works, but it lasted the girls through the war and Sue suspects that they will find the keys of a new one under the Christmas tree she plans to bring home today.

In truth, she's glad to be going alone. As much as she loves Zell, she is tired of hearing about bridesmaid dresses, whether the word *obey* should be left in the vows, the reception menu, and endless dithering over the honeymoon. New York and Broadway shows or a picturesque mountain inn?

Now with a house to furnish, it will be carpets and curtains and whether to paint or paper those four bedrooms.

If she were honest, Sue tells herself, she would admit that there's a touch of jealousy in her impatience with Zell's wedding chatter. Zell knows what she wants out of life and is diving into it headfirst, while she has nothing. Nothing she can put into words anyhow.

When her parents ask about her plans after she and Zell come home from Goldsboro, all she can say is, "I want to *live*! I want to make a difference. To *matter*!"

"You're not planning to become a missionary, are you?" asks an alarmed Mrs. Stephenson. Not that she thinks missionary work isn't noble. After all, they *are* Missionary Baptists. But *Baptists*, not—God forbid!—Catholics. (At thirteen, Sue briefly toyed with becoming a nun and going to Africa to work in a leper colony.)

"Why not try the law?" suggests her father. He will never admit that he favors one daughter over the other, but he worries that her restlessness might take her away from Dobbs. Even though Goldsboro is only fifty miles away, gas rationing has not allowed frequent visits and the big house felt lonely without their lively debates over the dinner table. "Women can do almost anything these days and the way you like to argue, you could do very well in a courtroom."

Mrs. Stephenson frowns. "Please, Richard. It's bad enough that you keep defending every piece of trash in the county. Don't encourage our daughter to join you."

"Now, Catherine," he teases. "We'd give her nothing but respectable civil cases."

Sue laughs at that. "Oh no, you wouldn't. It's murderers and rapists or nothing."

"Really, Sue!" In a perfect world, no child of hers would even know that word, much less utter it over dinner.

Sue smiles as she remembers that conversation. Tempting as it is, annoying her mother is not worth the price. Go back to school? Sit in airless classrooms for another three or four years? Even a leper colony would be preferable to that. At least she'd be outdoors and there would be zebras and elephants and maybe a lion or two.

Dad is right, though. More and more opportunities are opening up for women, but she cannot think of a single nine-to-five job that appeals to her. She isn't lazy and she doesn't mind hard work but it's silly to think of New York, Paris, or Rome if it means she'd still be in an office doing the same boring thing over and over. For the first time in her life, she wishes she were more creative. Dad says she has good common sense, but what's the good of common sense if she can't find a sensible use for it? She can't go on drifting like this.

"Life is real! Life is earnest! And the grave is not its goal."

For more than six years, those words have echoed in her head, yet here she is, six years closer to the grave and still no goal in sight.

"You only get one life," Mac had said. "Don't waste it."

Maybe Zell has the right idea. Marry someone nice, raise a family, and do good works. Zell has joined a book club that plans to raise enough money for a library truck that will give farmers and their families easy access to books, which could change a child's life, broaden his horizons.

She turns off the highway onto a rough dirt road that curves through pines and tall bare-branched oaks, then into a narrow lane surrounded by fields planted in winter rye. Under a gray and leaden sky, the rye has a dull, pinched look, as if hunkering down to wait out the cold before turning bright green again. Sue realizes that she doesn't know who currently rents the farm nor even what these fields will grow come springtime. Tobacco, yes, but what else? Corn? Soybeans? Sweet potatoes?

The lane ends up at the ruins of the abandoned tenant house surrounded by pecan trees. Half the roof has fallen in and all that's left are some foundation stones that still support the wooden floor and a fire-blackened stone chimney. Shortly after she learned to drive, she and Zell came out with hot dogs and camping gear. They built a fire in the old hearth and planned to spend the night until a puff adder slithered out from behind one of the stones in the fireplace. Normally she could talk her sister into anything, but Zell drew the line at snakes. She went back to the car and refused to get out again until they were safely back in Dobbs.

Patches of bright yellow daffodils once grew on either side of the door and huge gardenia bushes still flower there in the summer with fragrant white blossoms. The girls and their grandmother used to come pick flowers for the church and Grandmother would tell them of driving out from town in a horse and buggy with her father to check on the crops and speak to the family that worked the land back then.

"Every fall, the farmer would give us a big bag

of pecans," she tells the girls, "and in the summer,
his wife always sent us home with sweet corn, tomatoes, and the best piccalilli you ever tasted. Not too
vinegary. Mama never could get her to give the pro-
portions. I guess everybody needs something special of
their very own."

Sue is ten years old and the idea of making memo-
rable piccalilli so seizes her imagination that she asks
their housekeeper to teach her how.

"Why you want to do that?" Mary asks, but for once
Mrs. Stephenson encourages her daughter's fanciful
notion.

"In fact, it's time both you girls learned how to cook
a little so that you can manage if your housekeeper
suddenly gets sick or quits," she says, and she asks
Mary to let them help her in the kitchen.

Zell takes to it enthusiastically and begins to collect
cookbooks and recipes, but Sue loses interest once she
learns the basics.

Now, she switches off the engine and lets momen-
tum carry the car further down the slope, past two
dilapidated tobacco barns, to a stand of cedars amid
tall longleaf pines that stretch up toward the low-lying
gray clouds. Beyond the barns, hidden by a tangle of
wax myrtle, grapevines, and briars, lies the creek. She
gets out of the car and lets the silence wash over her. A
crow caws in the distance and somewhere a dog barks,
but the only other noise is the wind in the pines, a gentle swishing that sounds like waves softly breaking on
a sandy shore. She has not realized how tense her muscles were until she feels them begin to relax.

With a saw in one hand and a rope in the other for

dragging the tree back to the car, she wanders down among the cedars looking for a perfectly shaped tree, rejecting this one as too short and that one as too scraggly. Eventually, she finds one that will do. It's full and bushy on the front and the flatter side can go next to the wall in their living room. As she stoops to clear away the weeds from the base so she can saw through the trunk, she hears voices coming from the creek bank.

She moves quietly through the bushes and two little towheaded boys come into view. Both wear overalls and jackets, but no hats or gloves. The creek is frozen over and they are out sliding on the ice. It looks like fun and half thinking she might join them, Sue steps out of the bushes.

"Hey!" she calls.

Like deer startled by a hunter's gun, they immediately bolt for the opposite bank and, to Sue's horror, crash through the ice into the cold, muddy water.

Both boys sink below the surface, but just as quickly, they bobble up again, clutching for the edge of the ice nearest her. Each time one of those half-frozen little hands reaches for safety, though, the ice breaks off and leaves them floundering in the water.

Sue drops the saw and steps onto the ice. An ominous crack warns her of the danger and she quickly lies down on her stomach to spread out her weight. Still clutching the rope, she crawls toward the frantic boys, but halfway there, she knows the ice will not support her.

With one end of the rope looped around her wrist she slides the other toward the children. It stops just out of their reach. She pulls it back to her, fashions a hasty coil, and heaves again with all her strength.

This time the older boy is able to grab it. Treading water, he gives the end to the younger one and both hold on tightly.

Gingerly, Sue backs toward the creek bank and when she can stand, she hauls the rope hand over hand till they, too, reach the bank. Both are white with cold and shock.

"Come on!" she says. "I'll drive you home."

One boy starts to turn away, but he still clutches the rope blindly and Sue herds them up the slope and through the trees to the car, where she wraps them in one of the blankets she and Zell keep for cold winter drives.

"Where do you live?" she asks as she scrambles in and slams the door.

They stare at her mutely, their teeth chattering as they huddle together, too cold or too scared to answer.

Running on adrenaline herself, Sue turns the key, stomps on the accelerator, and promptly floods the engine. She tries the starter again and again. It's hopeless. The car is going nowhere for at least twenty minutes and those little boys are chilled to the bone and shivering uncontrollably.

She jumps out of the car and uses her gloved fingers as a rake to pile up some pine straw several yards away. Mac's Zippo is in her pocket and she soon has a blaze going. Pine cones and dead twigs join the straw, followed by dead limbs.

"Now then," she tells the boys. "Let's get you out of those wet clothes."

They try to resist, but she will have none of that. "You can keep your underwear on, but you're going to catch your death if you don't get next to the fire and dry out so don't be silly."

She leads them over to the fire and wraps the second blanket around them once they have shed their drenched outer garments, then forages for more wood until the flames leap up. A large oak branch serves as a drying rack for their wet clothes and as the warmth begins to thaw those little faces, the younger one stops crying.

"My name's Sue," she says. "What's yours?"

"Frank," the smaller boy whispers.

"You're brothers?"

"Yes, ma'am."

"What's his name?"

"I'm Robert," the other boy says shyly.

"Well, Robert, is your house very far away?"

He shakes his head and gestures toward the creek. "Just over yonder. Daddy'll come looking us if we ain't home for dinner."

As it isn't quite eleven, Sue knows that could be at least an hour away.

"You think he'd hear if I blew the horn?"

"Maybe."

Worth a try, thinks Sue. She piles more dead limbs on the fire, then goes over to the car and blows the horn three times, waits a few beats, then blows it three more times. She repeats the sequence twice before returning to the fire.

"Let's hope he notices," she says.

"He will," says Robert, and little Frank keeps looking up past the old ruined house as if he expects their father to suddenly appear.

She has just stood to go try starting the car again
when she hears an engine. A moment later, a battered
old pickup truck comes down the slope and skids to a
stop nearby.

"Daddy!" the little boys cry and they drop the
blankets to run to the tall man who emerges from
the truck.

He scoops them both up in his arms. "Here, now.
What's happened to y'all? How come you're so wet?"

Sue retrieves the abandoned blankets and drapes
them around those small bare shoulders.

Frank is sobbing into the safety of his father's chest
and words are tumbling from Robert. "We was larking
on the ice and it broke and she pulled us out but then
her car wouldn't start. We near 'bout drowned, Daddy."

Sue realizes that this is the fiddle player from last
Saturday night. "Kezzie, is it?" she asks. "Kezzie
Knott?"

She sees his blue eyes widen in recognition but now
her own reaction is setting in and she is suddenly shak-
ing with anger.

"What sort of father lets little boys like this play
around a creek with no one watching them?"

In a voice cold with matching anger, he says, "A
right sorry one, I reckon, Miss Stephenson."

He carries the boys to his truck and sets them down
inside with the blankets still tucked around them.
"Where's y'all's clothes, son?"

"I'll get them," Sue says and goes over to the branch
for them.

The man follows. "What's wrong with your car?"

"Flooded."

"I'll start it for you," he says.

"Don't bother. I'm sure it'll start by the time I've finished cutting a tree."

He frowns. "Tree?"

"A Christmas tree. That's what I came out here for and I'm not leaving without one."

"And what was you planning to cut it down with?"

Sue looks around blankly. "I had a saw. I must have dropped it when I saw them fall through the ice."

"Show me."

"No. You need to get them home to warm dry clothes."

"They'll be fine. I left the heater running." He sees where their footprints had left the bushes and heads toward the creek.

Reluctantly, Sue follows and soon finds the saw where it has fallen.

Kezzie Knott stares out at the broken ice for a long moment, then takes the saw from her. "Which tree you want?"

Wordlessly, Sue shows him the one she decided on earlier. Minutes later, it's tied to the top of her car and he's poking around under the hood.

"Try it now," he says and to her relief, the engine catches.

"What about the fire?" she asks through the rolled-down window. A fine rain has begun to fall.

"I got a shovel," he says. "I'll throw some dirt on it. You better get on back to town 'fore this rain turns to ice."

As she takes her foot off the brake and starts to roll up the window, he puts his hand on the glass and looks her straight in the eyes. "My boys? They was real lucky you come along when you did. I thank you."

That night, Sue opens the door of her father's study. The lamps are turned low and soft carols play on his radio.

"Dad?"

Mr. Stephenson glances around and motions for her to join him. A tall man, he stands in front of the blazing hearth, his slender frame sharply silhouetted against the flames, and Sue realizes with a sudden pang that his shoulders have begun to stoop. His hair is completely white now and age spots blotch the back of his hands. She knows that her parents delayed having children until several years into marriage, but seeing him clearly like this makes her aware that he is no longer young. Is indeed well into middle age.

"Finished decorating the tree?"

Sue closes the door and smiles at him. "You know Mother and Zell. They're still making sure every strand of tinsel's just so. Poor Ash. He just wants to sling it on in clumps."

"Wise man," her father says, crossing to his desk.

"Wise?"

"How do you think I've gotten out of having to drape tinsel one strand at a time all these years? If you do something badly, your wife won't expect you to do it well. She'll just decide you're hopeless and do it herself."

"Someone should tell Ash." She pulls a chair up near his. "Can I ask you something, Dad?"

His eyes twinkle behind his smudged glasses. "Has saying no ever stopped you?"

"I'm serious." She lifts his glasses from his face, breathes on the lenses, and begins to polish them with a clean handkerchief from her pocket.

Her father massages the bridge of his nose and leans back in his chair. "Very well then. Seriously."

"Tell me about Kezzie Knott."

"Knott? Why do you ask about him?"

Eyes on her task, Sue says, "He was one of the musicians at the dance Saturday night. They said he'd been in prison and Brix Junior said you were his attorney."

"So?"

"Brix Junior says he's a moonshiner. Is he?"

Mr. Stephenson shrugs. "Probably, but that's not what sent him to prison. He was charged with tax evasion. He owned a little crossroads store out from Cotton Grove and he was buying a lot more sugar than he could prove he sold in the store." A small smile appears at the corner of his mouth. "I believe the store is no longer in his name."

"But he owns it?"

"Not that anyone can prove."

"Brix Junior said you got him released early."

He nods and his smile disappears. "His wife died and there was no one else to take care of his children. I was able to persuade the authorities that he wasn't a danger to society."

Sue holds his glasses up to the light, polishes away a final smudge, and hands them back. "Brix Junior says he asked about buying Grandmother's farm."

"I didn't realize Brix Junior was so interested in Knott's business," Mr. Stephenson says as he settles his glasses into place. "Why are you?"

"No reason. I just wondered why he wasn't drafted. Making moonshine isn't exactly a vital industry, is it?"

He chuckles. "Depends on who you ask." When he sees that she isn't smiling, he says, "He had too many people dependent on him, honey. A widowed mother who was dying, a wife, and five or six little boys."

"*Five or six?* Are you serious?"

"You said you wanted me to be. Last I heard, there were actually eight. All boys. He married young and they started making babies right away."

"Kept her barefoot and pregnant?" Her scornful voice turns to pity. "That poor woman."

"Hard to know what goes on between a husband and wife," her father says mildly. "Could be that's what she wanted."

Something in his tone makes her wonder if he was the one who put off having a family, or was it her mother?

"Did you want a son, Dad?" she asks.

"Now, Sue—"

"Someone to come into the firm with you like Brix Junior?"

He leans over and pats her hand. "Every man wants a son, honey, but I wouldn't trade either of my girls for ten Brix Juniors."

When Zell comes downstairs next morning, she finds her sister in the breakfast room. A roll of red ribbon lies beside a half-eaten biscuit and Sue is filling small paper bags from a bowl of hard Christmas candies. Zell pours herself a cup of coffee and joins her at the table.

"Who are those for?" she asks.

With Ash hovering at Zell's elbow all day yesterday, there had been no chance for Sue to talk to her alone. "Promise you won't tell Mother or Dad?"

Zell listens wide-eyed while Sue tells how she pulled two small boys out of Possum Creek. "You could have drowned yourself. I *knew* we shouldn't have let you go out there alone."

"Then come with me this morning. I want to see if they're okay and I thought I'd take them some candy. I doubt if their father does much for Christmas."

Yet even as she says it, she remembers how eagerly those little boys had run to him and how he'd scooped them both up in his arms. She cuts lengths of the ribbon and begins to tie bows on the eight bags.

Hearing their voices, their housekeeper opens the kitchen door. "You want me to scramble you an egg, Miss Zell?"

"No, thank you, Mary. Just a biscuit and some jam, please."

Sue looks up from tying the last bow and says, "Do we have anything festive I can put these bags in, Mary?"

"Might be something in the pantry," the older woman says.

Sue follows her out through the kitchen and there on a top shelf of the pantry are several tins that had held fruitcake and cookies from her father's grateful clients.

"That one's right nice," says Mary, pointing to a slender white canister painted in a Currier and Ives winter sleighing scene. The lid pictures seasonal greenery and the tin is big enough to hold all eight bags of candy.

Last night's freezing rain petered out before bedtime and the morning sun is rapidly clearing the pavement, but there are patches of treacherous ice the sun has not yet touched and the car fishtails more than once even though Sue drives slower than usual.

As they near Cotton Grove, she turns off onto the dirt road that leads to their farm and stops at the first house to ask directions.

"You got to go back around and get across the creek and come in from the hardtop," says the farmer who is crossing the yard to his barn when they drive up. "You can't see the house from the road, but there's a mailbox at his turn-in with a big cedar tree on one side and a magnolia on the other. On the left like you was going Cotton Grove. It's at the bottom of a wide curve when you get to the creek."

They thank him and retrace their route till the dirt road intersects with the highway.

"Bottom of a curve?" Zell asks as both scan the passing woodlands,

Sue nods, concentrating on the road's icy patches. "Cedar tree, magnolia, mailbox on the left."

They are beginning to think they must have gone too far when the road curves down and they see the landmarks the farmer described. The lane rises up from the bottom land and when they crest the rise, they see an old two-story wooden farmhouse with outbuildings behind. Like most of that time and place, the house is built of unpainted heart pine that has weathered into a soft silvery gray. Down the slope and off to one side is a family graveyard. Some of the stones are just that—big rocks dragged up from the creek—but one is a black marble obelisk. It has to be at least ten feet tall and must have cost a fortune.

As they drive into the yard, little boys tumble off the porch and out of the barn. A colored woman comes to the door with a toddler in her arms. A dark blue shawl protects both of them from the biting wind.

"Mr. Kezzie ain't here," she calls as soon as Sue steps out of the car. "Won't be back till dinnertime."

"That's okay," Sue calls back cheerfully. "I came to see how Robert and Frank are after their swim yesterday."

White teeth flash in that dark face. "You the lady that pulled them out?"

Before Sue can answer, the door of the wash house is flung open and a blue-and-white enameled dishpan sails into the yard, where it hits a tree with such force that flakes of enamel shatter to the ground. It's followed by two boys who flail at each other as they careen through the door. The taller child is Frank. His face is red and distorted with anger and grief as he hurls himself at a slightly smaller one who tries to run.

"Frank! Andrew! You young'uns stop that this minute!" the woman calls, but they pay her no mind.

Sue rushes over and is sent tumbling to the ground herself when she pulls them apart. The younger boy runs for the safety of the house. Frank tries to go after him, but Sue wraps her arms around his furious little body. He struggles for a moment and then collapses in long shuddering sobs against her shoulder.

"He took Mama's dishpan!" the boy wails.

"Oh Lordy!" says the woman. With the toddler perched on her broad hip, she bends down to comfort him. "Oh, honey baby, Aunt Essie's so sorry. She forgot all about that."

The woman looks at Sue in consternation. "I told Andrew to fetch me a pan so I could soak some real sandy collard greens. I meant the one hanging on the wall." She turns back to the boy whose first wild cries have dwindled into hopeless sobs. "Don't be blaming Andrew, honey. Blame Aunt Essie."

A ring of little boys now circles them. They stairstep up to the one she recognizes from the day before. Robert.

Still sitting on the chilled ground, she pulls a handkerchief from her pocket and wipes the child's nose. "What happened, Frank?"

His voice is a misery of hopelessness. "They're gone. Andrew messed all through them."

"Messed through what?" Sue asks. "Show me. Maybe we can fix it?"

He shakes his head and fresh tears stream down his cheeks.

"Come on, honey," the woman coaxes. "We need to get this baby back in the house where it's warm before these nice ladies freeze to death." She offers a free hand to help Sue stand up. "I'm Essie. I take care of these young'uns."

"I'm Sue. Sue Stephenson." She gestures to Zell, who has gotten out of the car with the bright canister in her hands. "And this is my sister. Zell, why don't you show these young men what we brought them while Essie and I go see what's got Frank so upset?"

"No!" says Frank. "I'll show you by myself." He glares at his brothers through tear-reddened eyes. "And the rest of y'all better stay away."

Taking Sue by his cold little hand, he leads her into the wash house. A brick firebox has kindling laid, all ready to build a fire under the deep iron tub set into its surface. Two large zinc tubs stand upside down on a ledge of rough planks that runs the length of the small structure, and a second blue-and-white enameled dishpan hangs from a nail in the wall. The 2x4s that support the countertop stand directly on a dirt floor. A window at the far end lets in light and probably helps keep the place bearable in summer.

"There," says Frank and his lower lip quivers again as he points to a spot beneath the window, just under the edge of the counter.

Sue can see the outline of where the round pan must have been pressed into the dirt before it was dragged from its resting place. Multiple footprints of all sizes crisscross the dirt floor but that spot under the counter is wiped smooth.

"It was Mama's footprints," he says, his voice quavering again. "Last time she did the wash, right 'fore she went to the house to have Jack." His blue eyes bore into hers, searching for understanding. "I come in here after the burying and there was her footprints and I put the dishpan over them so I'd always have them and then Andrew went and— I hate him! I *hate* him! And I'll hate him forever!"

"Oh, Frank," she whispers and hugs him to her as grief overcomes him again.

"Now she's really all gone," he moans and her heart breaks for him.

When he has cried himself out, she says, "Listen, Frank. Her footprints may not be there exactly as she left them, but they aren't really gone."

"But they is, Miss Sue. See?" He points to the smooth dirt that the pan had once covered.

"The shape, maybe, but not the substance."

"What's substance?"

"What things are made of, honey. Your mama's footprints were made in the dirt and that dirt's still there. See where the pan piled up a little ridge of dirt before Andrew lifted it off?"

He gives a doubtful nod.

"That's where your mama's footprints still are. Not in the same shape maybe, but still the substance that she stood on. Wait right here and don't touch it yet, okay?"

He looks at her in mute hope and nods.

She darts out to the yard and is back a moment later with the now-empty Christmas canister. "If we put that little pile of dirt in here, you can keep it safe for as long as you want."

Wanting to be persuaded, he watches as she pulls the lid off and kneels down beside that smooth spot.

"I'll do it," Frank says, so she sits back on her heels and holds the canister while he gently scoops up the dry dirt as solemnly as if something of his dead mother really is being poured into the tin.

When he is satisfied that he has saved all the dirt her

feet had touched, Sue snaps the lid back on and hands the canister to him.

"And if Andrew touches it, I'll kill him," he says fiercely.

The hired woman invites Sue and Zell into the big, shabby, and blessedly warm kitchen. She wants to hear about Robert and Frank's near drowning in more detail. While the children are distracted by the Christmas candy and the pretty lithographed scene on Frank's can, she thanks Sue in a low voice for comforting him. "That baby took Miss Annie Ruth's passing the hardest."

The two older boys seem to regard Sue as their own personal property, but she soon charms the others. While the younger boys chatter and tussle, Essie puts together a big pot of beef stew and gets started on fried apple pies for the midday meal.

"Come see our tree, Miss Sue," Robert says and leads the way into the unheated front parlor. Somehow Sue hasn't expected such a big tree nor one so festive with tinsel and lights.

Or that eight small socks would be hanging along the mantelpiece. The older boys point out theirs.

"Santa Claus don't come for grown-ups and Jack's too little for candy," says Robert, "so can we give his to Daddy?"

The kitchen fills with smells of cinnamon and apples and the hearty aroma of beef stew. Four-year-old Benjamin volunteers to sing "Jingle Bells," and Sue teaches them how to click-click-click their fingers for the chorus of "Up on the Housetop."

By the time they drive away, Sue knows all eight boys by name and can even distinguish between the two twins.

"I didn't know you were so good with children," Zell says as they turn back toward Dobbs. "If you don't want to go to law school, maybe you could be a teacher or something."

"Or something," Sue says thoughtfully.

CHAPTER

4

*But brother goeth to law with
brother...Now, therefore, there is
utterly a fault among you, because ye
go to law one with another.*

— I Corinthians 6:6–7

Next morning, I was up before the noisy wrens who are raising a second or third brood under our bedroom window, and by six-thirty, I was on the road with a cup of coffee and a cold sausage biscuit left over from yesterday's breakfast. The weather report had mentioned the possibility of rain, which we badly needed, but the sky seemed indecisive about it. For the first hour, I drove east under gray clouds, listening to the morning news. Shortly before Goldsboro, though, the bright morning sun broke through and made me reach for sunglasses.

A couple of jet fighter planes suddenly appeared off to my left, coming in at such a steep angle that I gave an involuntary tap on my brakes even though reason immediately reassured me that they did not intend to crash. I'd almost forgotten that Seymour Johnson Airfield was here in Goldsboro and it set me thinking about Mother again. This was where she met that man who gave her his lighter and somehow changed her life.

Or so she'd said.

By Kinston, the NPR station from Chapel Hill had faded out and I'd had enough of the grim Middle East news and reports of a congress that only wants to block the president and further the stranglehold of the rich instead of focusing on what could help the country. I slid a new Red Clay Ramblers CD into the player and tried not to match the speed of Bland Simpson's fingers on the keyboard. Highway 70 between Kinston and New Bern is almost a straight four-lane shoot along the border between Jones County and Craven. The speed limit is 70, but without cruise control, I'd have been ticketed many times over in the years I've driven this road to Harkers Island.

Harkers Island?

Combined with thoughts of Mother and anticipation of New Bern, a flashbulb went off in my head.

I had stayed on the island a few years back while holding court in Beaufort and someone invited me to a large noisy cocktail party with skeet shooting down by the water. I had spotted an old boyfriend I hadn't seen since the winter I lived in New York, so I didn't pay much attention to the people I was meeting for the first time. But an elderly white-haired man had given me a warm smile when we were introduced.

"Judge Knott? Colleton County? You any kin to Kezzie Knott?"

I always get that sly grin when people mention him. He'd once run a network of whiskey stills all through eastern North Carolina.

"My father," I'd said and that had gotten me an even warmer smile.

"Married Sue Stephenson, didn't he?"

"You knew her."

He picked up on that past tense and a fleeting shadow crossed his still-handsome face. "We both worked at the airfield in Goldsboro during World War Two."

I should have nailed him to the ground right then, but as I say, it was noisy and there was this guy I had unfinished business with, so I said, "Do you live here? Could I come and talk to you some time?"

"I'm just up the road in New Bern. But don't leave it too long or I may not still be around," he'd said.

What the devil was his name?

Adams? Ashworth? Austin?

It's a trick a fellow judge taught me. When he can't remember a name, he starts at A and works his way down the alphabet.

Baker? Bowman? Bradley?

I was to the L's before I finally remembered Livingston, as in Doctor, I presume? One of the guests had even made a joke of it and he had given the pained smile of someone who'd heard that joke a million times because he was indeed a physician.

Surely I could find him if he was still alive. How many Dr. Livingstons could there be in New Bern?

*   *   *

The westbound lanes on 70 were thick with campers and boat trailers and people heading home after a weekend at the beach, but traffic was light in my direction. I reached New Bern and the old red brick courthouse on Broad Street in time to have another cup of coffee with Cindy Dickerson, who met me at the door. She introduced me to a Gina Cruz, who would be my clerk for the day, and Gina in turn guided me through the maze of halls and locked doors of this much-remodeled courthouse. Back of Courtroom 5 was a small office and lavatory where I put on my robe and freshened up, then Gina told the bailiff to notify the attorneys that we were ready to start.

The courtroom was a smallish nondescript chamber similar to so many others across the state. The case, a civil suit between two elderly cousins, wasn't.

Wade Mitchell and Caleb Mitchell. Both quite wealthy. Both prominent, civic-minded businessmen who wielded enough power and enough political connections to make it easy for the local judges to recuse themselves and let someone outside the district hear the case and make what was bound to be an unpopular decision on one side or the other.

At stake were two plots in Cedar Grove Cemetery. Their Mitchell grandfather had bought a ten-grave plot a hundred years or so earlier, close to an eight-grave plot where his own grandparents, parents, and siblings rested. Edward Mitchell was buried there alongside his wife, as were his two sons and their wives, parents of Wade and Caleb. That left two empty grave sites and each grandson wanted them for himself and his own wife.

There were other newer cemeteries around the edges of New Bern, but except for an older one at Christ Church, I soon learned from the opening arguments that Cedar Grove was the oldest and most prestigious. It became the town's principal burying place during a devastating yellow fever epidemic in 1798 that took close to a thousand lives, a tenth of the population back then. The last family-size plot was sold several years ago for more than a thousand dollars.

A friend of mine from Brooklyn tells me that in New York, the coffins can be stacked one on top of the other, three or four deep, and that each stack can be considered empty twenty years after the space was last opened. "But you don't want to look too closely at that pile of dirt under the blanket when they dig a new grave," he says. "That may be your great-grandmother's thighbone. It's the only way you can bury seventy-five relatives in a ten-by-twelve plot." He once showed me a picture of his great-grandfather's marble funeral marker, a weeping angel atop two graduated blocks of marble. So many names and dates have been engraved on those stones over the last hundred years that they look like pages from a telephone directory.

Unfortunately, nothing like that could happen in New Bern.

As the only child of the oldest Mitchell son, Wade Mitchell claimed both spaces by right of primogeniture. Caleb Mitchell's attorney snorted derisively at that.

"Their grandfather's will specifically left his entire

estate to be divided equally between his two sons and
that estate included the deed to this cemetery plot."

I was shown a copy of the will and of the original
deed, which remained in their grandfather's name.

"You never asked your fathers to change the deed to
reflect their dual ownership?"

"When you're young, you don't think about where
your body's going to go," said Caleb.

"I just took it for granted," his cousin said.

"What's the current value of these two remaining
plots?" I asked.

"That's hard to say for something this historic," said
one of the attorneys and the other chimed in. "Assum-
ing a willing seller and a willing buyer, it might be in
the neighborhood of a thousand dollars."

"Each?"

They nodded.

Two thousand dollars for a piece of dirt that probably measured no more than six-by-eight feet?

I addressed the two cousins directly. "Would either
of you gentlemen consider selling to the other?"

"Absolutely not!" exclaimed Wade.

"Never!" said Caleb. "The first Mitchell was buried
there in 1801. There's not enough money in New Bern
for me to sell my birthright."

Wade bristled at that. "It's my birthright, too."

"What about cremation?" I asked.

They frowned at me.

"If you and your wives were to be cremated, each
grave could hold two urns."

I should have known that solution wasn't going to
fly either.

They wrangled on and on, dredging up family history to back their reasons, and airing old and irrelevant grievances. Sometimes it's best to let the combatants get it all out of their systems, but I was beginning to feel like Solomon with that baby claimed by two different women, only I didn't have a sword. Looking at it as a problem in logic, I did have fair and equitable options. I could award each of them a plot. I could give one cousin both plots and order him to pay his cousin the full value of the other, or I could order them to sell both plots and split the money.

From the passion they had displayed, though, I knew that none of those options would satisfy both. It reminded me of a case I'd had over in Asheboro a few years back where two divorcing attorneys both wanted to keep possession of the office they shared. I might have to go the same route with these two.

I thought of our family graveyard out at the homeplace. Right now the fence surrounds enough space for all of Daddy's twelve children and their spouses, but what if there weren't? How would I feel to know that I'd be cut off from my family for all eternity? With the cheerful innocence of a ten-year-old, Cal had already picked out a corner for the three of us, but there's no way his whole generation of cousins could fit in as well. If the land stays in the family, the fence could be moved to take in another quarter acre or two. But if the farm's been sold and divided and developed by the time death comes for them? Would some of them be sitting in a future courtroom passionately arguing for the right to join their forebears?

By the clock over the rear doors, it was now 11:30.

"We'll recess for lunch," I told them, "and I'll give my ruling at one."

The bailiff gave me directions to the cemetery and recommended that I stop by a café called The Country Biscuit for the best shrimp salad sandwiches in town. They added a go-cup of strong iced tea to the bag and I drove over to Cedar Grove Cemetery, where I parked in front of the main entrance. Heavy black iron gates were supported by columns of marlstone thick with petrified seashells. Just inside the gates was an informational plaque that gave a bit of the history and marked the resting places of New Bern's more important citizens. Caleb Bradham, the pharmacist who invented Pepsi, was pictured, but no Mitchells. Using the map one of the cousins had brought to court, I did locate the disputed plot just east of the central square.

Crushed oyster shells lined the drives and huge ancient cedars draped in curtains of Spanish moss offered welcome shade as I walked past grave markers that ranged from simple clean stones to weeping angels and somber saints. Disintegrating granite tablets were engraved with lines of overly sentimental poetry and after two hundred years, many were illegible.

> *I hear your death knell o'er and o'er—Good-bye,*
> *good-bye forever more.*

On a stone that dated back to the yellow fever days: *Weep for an infant too young to weep much / When death removed this mother.*

Except for slightly newer headstones and an angel that looked rather amused, the Mitchell plot was much

like the others, bounded by a low brick wall and
shaded by one of those ubiquitous cedars. The whole
cemetery seemed deserted except for a caretaker mow-
ing grass at the far end, and I enjoyed the peace as I sat
on the wall to eat my sandwich.

After reading all the names on the stones inside this
enclosure, my eyes drifted over to surrounding plots.
To my surprise—although it shouldn't have surprised
me, given that it had been mentioned in court—I noticed the Mitchell name on an older monument two
plots away. Still munching on my sandwich, I walked
over to read the names and dates. The earliest was
1803. Theodore Mitchell and his beloved wife Amelia.
The latest was a plain flat stone for an Edward Guthrie,
who died in 1967. The black iron fence seemed to
mark off the same amount of space as the disputed
plot, yet it held only seven graves if I could trust the
tombstones.

I was walking back to my car, considering possibilities, when a stone near the path jumped out at me:
Raynesford. That was the name Aunt Zell and I had
tried to remember! The name of the man who'd given
Mother that cigarette lighter. The stone was behind a
fence too high for me to step over and I had to go
around to the gate. I found a Walter Raynesford buried
amid several others of his clan, but no Walter Raynesford McIntyre.

The two elderly Mitchell cousins seemed a bit weary
when I took my seat and faced them. Indeed, they both
looked as if they could use a nap.

"I went out to the cemetery during my lunch break,"

I told them. "It's a beautiful spot and I can understand how both of you would want it. I guess it would be a comfort to know that would be your final resting place."

Both men nodded and started to speak, but I held up my hand. "Who was Edward Guthrie?"

Blank looks.

"He died in 1967 and is buried in a Mitchell plot close to your family's."

"Uncle Ned?" asked Wade Mitchell.

Caleb Mitchell nodded. "He was the son of Grandfather's sister."

"So y'all are kin to Theodore Mitchell?"

Two more nods. "He was our grandfather's grandfather."

"Who owns that plot where he's buried?" I asked.

Shrugs and more blank looks.

"It seems to me that there are at least two unused spaces in that plot," I said.

The cousins looked at each other in dawning comprehension of where I was going.

"Uncle Ned's widow remarried and she was buried with her second husband in Cove City," Caleb Mitchell said slowly. "But didn't he have a sister?"

"They moved to Morehead City years ago," said Wade Mitchell.

"It seems to me," I said, "that if this is in your family line and no one's used it since 1967, whoever owns it might be willing to sell."

One of their attorneys said, "If you'll continue this case, Your Honor, we'll search the records and find out who the current owner is."

"How long would you want?" I asked.

"A week?" said one.

The other nodded. "That should give us time to trace the owners."

Wade Mitchell turned to his cousin. "You know something? It could turn out that we already own it through Grandfather. He could have inherited it."

"Does that mean you'd be willing to go there?" asked Caleb.

Wade frowned. "No, I meant it would be a good place for you and Jenny."

"Like hell!"

"Gentlemen!" I said in my most authoritarian voice and they subsided but still glared at each other like resentful schoolboys. "This has already taken up too much of the court's time. I'm willing to continue this matter for another few days, but if you can't come to an agreement, then I'm going to settle the matter for you."

I looked at my calendar and set the court date for the following Monday.

To get started on my own research, I spent an hour in the Special Collections Room of the library, where a helpful Victor Jones gave me a quick orientation and let me look at an inventory of the cemetery that had been made back in the nineties. There were several McIntyres but no Raynesford McIntyre. Not that I'd really expected to find him that easily. He was probably buried somewhere in Europe, where he died. A whole slew of Raynesfords, though.

Mr. Jones showed me the Raynesford genealogical records that took up a good six inches of manila folders in a file drawer. Raynesfords had evidently arrived in New Bern shortly after the Revolutionary War and they had flourished and multiplied for a hundred years, then had gradually begun to dwindle until he knew of only two of that name left in town. Josephine Raynesford was an elderly spinster who still lived in the family home a few blocks from the library. Her nephew, another Walter Raynesford, had turned the house into a bed-and-breakfast and gave guided tours for their guests in a shiny black 1956 Cadillac convertible.

"The name may be almost gone, but I'm pretty sure Raynesfords linger on through the female side."

"Is there any way to find out if a Raynesford female married a McIntyre man?" I asked, thinking that if I found some of his relatives, they might could tell me more about this man in Mother's past.

"You could search the marriage records, but it'd probably be quicker to just ask Miss Jo. She's the one who gave us most of this Raynesford material." He wrote out her name and contact information for me.

When I asked about a Dr. Livingston, I was told that he was retired. "But he still maintains an office for some of his old patients over on Pollock Street and you can often catch him there in the afternoon."

A small nameplate attached to the porch railing of a large clapboard house that backed up to the grounds of Tryon Palace identified the office of Dr. Grover Livingston. There was no one at the reception counter when I walked in through the unlatched screen door.

An inner door was open, though, and a man called from the next room, "Jasper? Come on in."

"Sorry," I said, following his voice. "I'm not Jasper."

"Would you like to be?" asked the chubby little man who sat behind a large cluttered desk. His hair was white and his eyes twinkled with mischief as he looked at me over his rimless bifocals.

"No, I'm good with being me," I said.

He laughed. "And you are—?"

"Judge Knott. Deborah Knott." I realized that I had never seen this man before. He looked nothing like the tall handsome man I'd met in Beaufort. "Sorry to interrupt you, but I was looking for a Doctor Livingston."

"That's me."

"Is there another Doctor Livingston in town?" I asked. "The one I wanted would be about eighty."

"Actually, he'd be about ninety-two if he was still alive. My dad. He died last year. Did you say judge? Is this a legal matter?"

"Not at all, Doctor. I met your father down in Beaufort three or four years ago. He said he knew my mother back when she worked at the airbase in Goldsboro and I was hoping to ask him a few questions."

"Too bad you didn't come sooner. He loved to talk about his war years and his mind and memory stayed clear right up till the end."

("*That's what you get for chasing after an old boyfriend,*" said the preacher who lives in my head and never misses a chance to lecture me on my shortcomings. "*Carpe diem.*")

(*"Give it a rest,"* said the pragmatist who usually cuts me a little slack. *"How was she to know?"*)

Dr. Livingston saw the disappointment on my face. "When was she there?"

"Only two years so far as I know. Maybe 1943 till the war ended."

"She must have made an impression on him if he remembered her after all that time," he said. "What's her name?"

"Susan Stephenson," I said. "Her sister was there, too. Ozella Stephenson. Zell."

He gestured to a bookshelf behind him and to a row of small red leather-bound books. "I've been reading his diaries, but I'm only up to the beginning of the war. Give me your card and if I see their names, I'll let you know. I'm afraid Dad was a cross between a workhorse and a billy goat. Tires me out just to read all the work and women he got through."

I dug a card from my purse. "I doubt if my mother was one of them. She never mentioned him that I can remember."

He gave a wry laugh. "He never mentioned any of his women to us, either. And he made damn sure my mother never saw these diaries. Kept them locked in a cabinet in his office."

"There was one man, though," I said slowly. "A Walter Raynesford McIntyre. From New Bern. Did you ever hear of him?"

Dr. Livingston frowned. "McIntyre?"

"Walter Raynesford McIntyre. He was a pilot. I think he was killed during the war."

"Sorry. I know the Raynesford name, of course. But

McIntyre? Doesn't ring any bells, but I'll keep an eye out for his name, too."

I thanked him and said I expected to be back in New Bern next Monday.

"Good," said Livingston. "Maybe I'll skip ahead in Dad's diaries and see what I can find."

CHAPTER

5

*Give strong drink unto him that is
ready to perish.*

— Proverbs 31:6

DWIGHT BRYANT—MONDAY, AUGUST 11

Shortly after Deborah left for New Bern that morning, her brother Robert drove the Cub tractor into the yard and Cal was out the door before Robert could cut the motor, leaving behind a half-eaten bowl of cereal. Amused by his son's enthusiasm, Dwight walked out to the garden behind them to move the sprinkler hoses out of the way while his white-haired brother-in-law showed Cal how to lift and lower the set of discs attached to the tow bar.

Even though they went over the area designated for the winter garden twice, cutting the old vines and dead plants into the ground, the whole operation was completed in less than fifteen minutes, to Cal's disappointment.

"Tell you what, Dwight," said Robert. "How 'bout I take him on back with me and we'll do Seth's garden and maybe Andrew's and Daddy's, too."

"Can I, Dad? Please?"

Dwight glanced at his watch. "Sorry, buddy, but I need to drop you off at Aunt Kate's and get on in to work." He and Deborah split the cost of the live-in nanny that his sister-in-law had hired to care for her three while she created fabric designs in her studio, a remodeled packhouse at the far edge of the backyard.

"I can take him over when we're done," Robert said. "Maybe they got something needs cutting in, too."

Now that his daughter Betsy and her husband had moved to Raleigh, Robert and Doris didn't see as much of young Bert as when they lived in a trailer next door and it was Deborah's impression that Cal helped fill part of that void for her brother.

"Please, Dad?"

"Okay, but you mind Uncle Robert and don't go trying to do something he hasn't checked you out on."

"I won't," Cal promised.

As they trundled away, the tractor in its lowest gear, Dwight put the sprinklers back on the tomatoes, okra, and field peas, then called Kate to say that Cal probably wouldn't be getting there much before lunchtime. "And if you and Rob have forty or fifty acres you want cut in..."

Kate laughed. "No, but if he wants to give the kids a ride around the farm, I know mine would love it. Mary Pat's so jealous that Cal gets to drive."

Next Dwight called the office and sent two detectives to Dexter Oil and Gas to see if Earp's boss and co-workers could tell them anything useful.

Lastly, he talked to Detective Mayleen Richards to say that he planned to question Mrs. Earp and her cousin again before heading for Dobbs, which was in the opposite direction from Cotton Grove.

"They called," Mayleen told him. "At least her cousin did. Marisa Young. She asked if it was all right for Mrs. Earp to go back to the house? I told her you'd let her know. Ray's on his way over there right now. He thought maybe y'all might want to take another look at the house before you let her in?"

"Thanks, Mayleen. Give me twenty minutes, then call her back and ask her to meet us there."

"Sheriff Poole wants to see you when you get in and so does Ashworth."

As expected. Bo Poole would naturally be wanting an update on this murder, and Melanie Ashworth, who handled the department's public relations, probably needed a statement she could give to any media inquiries.

Fifteen minutes later, he parked in front of a modest white frame house that sat on a half-acre lot at the edge of Cotton Grove. It had green shutters and a narrow porch that ran the full width, and it seemed well cared for. Thick rows of azaleas and rhododendron separated the houses along this street, dogwoods and willow oaks shaded the front yards, and pines rose up in back. No garage on the Earp house, but the empty carport had space for two vehicles and there was a metal storage shed in the backyard.

Yesterday, he had given the place no more than a cursory look before learning that Mrs. Earp was at her cousin's house on the east side of town. She had tearfully handed over her keys to Ray McLamb, his chief deputy, who then came back here to examine the house with the department's crime scene techs. They had found no blood inside the house, just what was left on the porch steps. The hot August sun had baked it to such a crust that only a few ants were still interested. No flies or wasps. Nevertheless, they scraped up a sample for the ME.

One of the department's cruisers slid in behind Dwight's truck, and McLamb joined him under the carport. When Dwight left Washington and joined the Colleton County Sheriff's Department, Ray was one of his first hires and the department's first African-American detective. Looking cool and trim in khaki trousers, a tan short-sleeved shirt, and mirror sunglasses, he sported short hair and a dapper pencil mustache.

They had run Vick Earp's name the day before and several incidents had popped up. Beginning when he was sixteen, there had been an open container citation, several aggravated speeding violations, a couple of DWIs, and a felony assault from six years earlier that had landed him in jail for two days. The restraining order Deborah had issued last year was his second one in four years.

"Her cousin said someone put a bullet through the windshield of his truck," Dwight said. "Wonder why he didn't report that?"

Ray shrugged. They had put out the word yesterday, but so far the truck was still missing. "Notice anything

about this?" A sweep of his arm took in the whole carport, which had none of the usual clutter. "Come look
at his tool shed."

Dwight followed him to the backyard and
watched as Ray unlocked the double doors of the
ten-by-ten metal structure. Floor-to-ceiling shelves
on the left wall held the usual assortment of paint
cans, automotive oils and fluids, insecticides and
weed-killers, each grouped according to use. Peg-
boards filled the other side plus the wall above a
workbench at the back and each tool was outlined
to fit on a specific hook. A push lawn mower had its
space under the workbench.

Ray shook his head in wonder. "The guy was a
neat freak. A place for everything and everything in its
place."

"Depressing," Dwight agreed, thinking of his own
garage.

They walked around the house, seeing no signs of
violence other than the blood on the back steps. Ray
unlocked the front door of the house and the interior
was as organized and tidy as the tool shed. Each corner
of the blue couch had a geometrically positioned decorative pillow. No scatter of newspapers, no empty cups
or saucers on the polished coffee table in the living
room. Indeed, no sign of normal living at all until they
moved into the kitchen, where a pan of burned bacon strips sat on the stove. The fixings for BLTs were
on the counter along with a sliced lemon on a cutting
board. On the floor were shards of a blue ceramic sugar
bowl and sugar was strewn from the sink to the back
door, along with bits and pieces from a broken glass

tumbler. A crumpled dishtowel was wadded up on the counter.

"Nothing out of place in the rest of the house. The bed's made and the bathroom's spotless, so this must've been where he hit her," Ray said.

Dwight nodded. "She said she was making sandwiches for their supper since it was too hot to turn on the oven. He knocked the glass out of her hand and punched her in the eye. That's when she grabbed her keys and ran. He tried to come after her, but he slipped and fell—probably on the sugar—and that gave her enough time to reach her car and get away."

"You reckon that's her blood or his out there on that step?"

"Offhand, I'd say his. She had a black eye and there was a cut on her chin, but it didn't look very deep."

Five empty beer cans, each crushed flat, were in the trash can beneath the sink, along with larger pieces of the sugar bowl and some glass. "Doesn't look like he ate supper here, does it?"

"More like he drank it," said Dwight. "And see? Three of those cans are on top of the glass."

"Like he started to clean up and then decided to have a couple of beers instead?" said Ray.

"Maybe." Dwight lifted the trash bag out of the can and tied the top. "Let's take this back to Dobbs. See if it's only his fingerprints on these. Someone might have interrupted his cleanup and they had a beer together."

As they walked out onto the porch, Ray paused. "Wonder where the cat is?"

"Cat?"

His deputy pointed to two small bowls on a wooden table at the end of the porch. One held water, the other a few bits of dry kibble. "Must be a cat. They wouldn't feed a dog up there."

While they talked, Mrs. Earp drove up in a white Toyota and parked in the carport. She was followed by her cousin in a gray minivan with a bike rack on the back.

Both women looked to be in their early fifties. Both had brown hair lightly streaked with gray. Rosalee Earp's was shoulder length, Marisa Young's was short and parted down the middle. Mrs. Earp was thin and fragile looking in pale blue slacks and a sleeveless cotton tunic in a flowery print with ruffles at the neck. The bruises on her arm and around her eye were a dark purple, and a flesh-colored Band-Aid covered the cut on her chin.

She got out of her car with a tentative, tremulous air that Dwight had seen too often in victims of domestic violence.

Her cousin was a different matter. More sturdily built, she wore jeans and a loose, man-styled lavender shirt with three-quarter-length sleeves. He had a feeling that if any man ever raised a hand to Miss Young, he'd probably draw back a stump.

She clearly intended to run this interview and put herself in front of Rosalee Earp when Dwight stepped forward to meet them. "Have you found Vick's killer yet?"

"Sorry. No." Dwight reached past her to take her cousin's hand. "How are you this morning, Mrs. Earp?"

"Okay," she said weakly. "It still seems unreal that Vick's really gone."

He led her to one of the molded plastic chairs on the back porch and, once everyone was seated, asked her to tell them again exactly what had happened the last time she saw her husband.

"He hit her," said Marisa Young, who had taken the next chair. "That's what happened."

Dwight held up his hand. "Please, Miss Young, I need to hear this in Mrs. Earp's own words. You say you last saw him Friday evening?"

"Friday, yes," Mrs. Earp said shakily. "I work part-time at Wal-Mart. After work, I tidied the house and washed the kitchen windows—Vick can't stand looking through a dirty window."

Miss Young gave a soft snort of indignation but subsided when Mrs. Earp laid a gentle hand on her knee.

"Be fair, Marisa, he did just as much around the place as I do."

"But he got to set the agenda, didn't he?"

"Oh, Marisa." She withdrew her hand and turned back to Dwight and Ray. "Vick came home a little after five and was going to cut the grass, but he couldn't get the mower started and he was already mad because the new windshield for his truck—and where *is* his truck?" she asked fretfully. "Wasn't it with him?"

"We're looking for it, ma'am," Ray told her.

"Well anyhow, the windshield didn't come in even though they'd *promised*, so when the mower— he had it worked on last month, see? They told him whatever they'd done wasn't going to hold and that he needed a new one, but he was sure it would've lasted out the season if they'd done their work right."

Marisa Young rolled her eyes, but didn't speak.

"It was really hot and he had a couple of beers. Usually he doesn't have one till supper time, but with all that…" She gave a helpless wave of her hand toward the tool shed. "I was frying bacon for BLTs and I'd made some lemonade. When he came in for another beer, I tried to give him a glass and that's when—when—" She touched the bruise on her cheek. "It spun me around so hard, I knocked the sugar bowl off the counter and he went ballistic. Like I'd done it on purpose. I knew he was going to hit me again even harder. There was sugar all over the floor and he slipped on it and fell and that's when I ran out the door and drove over to Marisa's."

With tears in her eyes, she reached for her cousin's hand. "I knew I'd be safe there. He's scared of her. Six years ago, she shot the hat off his head and told him that next time she'd aim a little lower."

"Not that I really would," said Miss Young, "but after that, he never came around till after he'd cooled off and was ready to sweet-talk Rosy."

"He never meant to hurt me," said Mrs. Earp. "And he was always so sorry. He brought me roses last time and this ring." She touched a silver band set with three small stones. "Topazes. He said they matched my eyes. And the time before that, he took me to Wilmington for a week. A second honeymoon."

"While her ribs healed," Miss Young murmured.

"His temper would get the best of him and then his

leg bothered him a lot. It didn't heal right after his accident and—"

Miss Young could not let that pass. "A lot of men have it a lot worse, Rosy, and they don't punch out their wives."

"What time did you leave?" asked Dwight.

"Around six?" She looked to Miss Young for confirmation.

She nodded. "You got to my house about a quarter past. I was watching the six o'clock news."

"Did he come over after he cooled off?"

Both women shook their heads.

"The bed doesn't appear to have been slept in," said Dwight, "and it doesn't look as if he fixed a meal. Any idea where he might have gone?"

"You said someone hit him over the head," said Miss Young. "Where?"

Dwight started to touch a place on the back of his head, but she chopped the air with an impatient hand.

"I meant where was he?"

"We don't know yet."

"But when did he actually die?" Miss Young persisted.

"Around ten o'clock Saturday morning, around the time he was found, but we don't know when he received the blow that ultimately killed him. We're not even sure he was still alive when he was found."

"Who *did* find him?" Mrs. Earp asked. "And where?"

"Out near Possum Creek on a deserted lane off Grimes Road."

Something flashed in her eye. "Black Gum Branch? How'd he get out there?"

Dwight was surprised. "You know it?"

She nodded and tears welled up in her eyes. "Thirty years ago. That's where we courted on moonlit nights after the movie. On our way home from Raleigh. It was so quiet and peaceful back there. The creek broadened out where the branch joined it, and when the moon came up..." Her voice dwindled off. "He used to live out that way. We even picnicked there a few times." She sighed. "He was so loving back then. But after the babies came and he hurt his leg, everything started going wrong. He always wanted to farm, but we couldn't afford to buy land or equipment. His family lost their land when he was a boy and my family never had any...he still liked to drive out there, though."

She shook her head sadly. "Poor Vick."

"Rosalee?"

Unnoticed by them, an attractive woman had emerged from the bushes behind the tool shed. Her red hair, styled in a pixie cut, blazed like polished copper in the morning sun and she wore a short-sleeved coral jacket over a black dress that seemed a little formal for walking through bushes. She hesitated as she took in the badge dangling from Dwight's belt. "Is everything all right?"

"Not really, Rusty." Mrs. Earp stood to motion her forward. "This is my neighbor," she told them. "Rusty Reynolds."

"What's wrong?" the woman asked.

"It's Vick," Mrs. Earp said, tearing up again. "He's dead. Somebody killed him."

"Killed? Oh, Rosalee, how awful! Who? When?"

Dwight stood and introduced himself and Ray. "Where exactly do you live, ma'am?"

"Over there. Our yards back up on each other." She gestured to the trees and bushes behind the tool shed before turning back to Mrs. Earp. "What can I do, Rosalee? Let me take Diesel back to my house. Get him out of your way."

"Diesel?" Mrs. Earp looked around helplessly. "He must be inside."

"Who's Diesel?" asked Dwight.

"My cat," both women said, which made Mrs. Earp smile for the first time.

It lit up her thin face and hinted at the youthful beauty she must have had. "He was a stray," she said, "and we both adopted him. Or rather he adopted us. For a long time we didn't know that he was splitting his time between us and we were both feeding him."

"My son named him Diesel," said Rusty Reynolds.

"Because he's got a purr like a diesel truck," Mrs. Earp said, reaching for the knob on the back door. "Built like one, too. The poor baby must be scared and hungry if he's been shut in the house all weekend."

As soon as she walked inside they could hear her calling the cat with coaxing noises. Rusty Reynolds followed.

The two-bedroom house was too small and too compulsively tidy to offer many hiding places for even the smallest of cats. "And Diesel's pretty big," the women told Dwight.

They looked under the beds, behind the couch, and inside all the closets and base cabinets.

No Diesel.

Back out on the porch, Mrs. Earp checked the bowls on the wooden table. A light skim of dust and pollen covered the water and a steady stream of ants was working on the few bits of kibble. "I fed him Friday when I got home from work, but I don't think he's touched this bowl since," she said and dumped the remains over the edge of the porch onto the grass. "When did you feed him, Rusty?"

"Not since Friday morning." She gave a wry smile. "Do you suppose he's somebody else's cat, too? No wonder he's so fat."

Dwight knew how concern for a pet or a child could ease the enormity of murder, but there were still questions that needed answering. Before he could tactfully ease Rusty Reynolds back across the yard, though, she glanced at her watch. "Rosalee, I'm so sorry, but I have to go back to work. I only came home to see about Diesel, but if there's anything I can do—anything at all…"

"Thanks, Rusty," said Mrs. Earp.

While Ray followed Mrs. Reynolds out into the yard to get her work address, Dwight turned back to Mrs. Earp and her cousin.

"You say he had no enemies, Mrs. Earp, yet someone put a bullet through the windshield of his truck."

"On the passenger side," she murmured.

"To scare him, not hit him?"

"Maybe. I don't know."

"Who did he think did that?"

She shook her head. "He never said. Just that whoever did it was going to pay for it. It wasn't going to go on his insurance."

"Let me rephrase that. Who do *you* think it was?"

"Maybe Tyler?" She looked at her cousin for confirmation. "His brother?"

Miss Young nodded. "Probably. Tyler's a good shot."

"So it was to scare your husband, not hurt him? Why?"

Mrs. Earp looked away, shamefaced. "He owed Tyler money for painting the house but he wasn't going to pay it because Tyler did such a sloppy job. Vick was always real particular about how things ought to be done and Tyler didn't take the shutters off, so white paint got on them and then some green paint dripped on the siding. He didn't caulk around the doors and window frames and he didn't tape the windows, so they had to be scraped with a razor blade."

"And guess who got *that* job in ninety-five-degree weather," Marisa Young muttered.

"Your husband's pockets were empty when we found him," said Dwight. "Did he have a phone?"

Mrs. Earp nodded and gave him the number.

"And I believe you mentioned an uncle?"

"Joby. He and Earla raised Vick and Tyler. She's sweet, but Joby…" Her voice trailed off. "Vick blamed him for losing their land. I forget how it happened, but Joby's got a mean temper and he used to beat on the boys till they got big enough to hit back."

"Apples didn't roll far from that tree," said Miss Young.

Mrs. Earp just sighed.

Dwight took down both names and told her that they would be in touch.

"What about the funeral?" Mrs. Earp said. "Where is he now?"

Ray handed her a card with the ME's number. "If you'll call here, they'll tell you when they can release the body to a funeral home."

"Cremate him," said Miss Young.

CHAPTER

6

Am I my brother's keeper?

— Genesis 4:9

No one was home in the houses on either side of the Earp house. Mrs. Earp had told them that most people in this neighborhood worked full-time jobs, so Dwight and Ray were not surprised that no one came to the door when they tried the houses across the street.

"Guess we'll have to come back later," Dwight said. "Right now, let's hear what the Reynolds woman can tell us and go from there."

As they walked back to their vehicles, Dwight's phone rang and the ME's name popped up on the screen.

"What's the game, Major?" Dr. Singh sounded amused. "Stump the chump?"

"What do you mean?" Dwight asked.

"That blood sample you sent me. It's feline, not human."

"*Cat* blood?"

"Unless you've got a tiger out there. Tigers have the same blood type as *felis domesticus*. Did you know that? And for what it's worth, the blood on your victim's pants and shoes came from a cat, too."

"The hell you say!"

"Was the cat black?"

"Yeah, how'd you know?"

"A black hair in the blood and more black hair under his nails."

When Dwight relayed what Dr. Singh had found, Ray said, "Diesel?"

"Probably."

Ray shook his head. "Poor lady. First her husband, now her cat. Want me to check around the edge of the yard? See if it crawled off to die under a bush? That much blood, it couldn't have gone far."

"Okay, but make it quick."

While Ray walked down the row of azaleas and dogwoods that lined the backyard, Dwight called Melanie Ashworth and brought her up to speed on the murder.

"I'm glad you called," she said. "I'm getting questions about how and why Vick Earp's body wound up on your father-in-law's farm."

"Did you release that location?"

"I did not," she said crisply.

Melanie Ashworth was the department's recently hired public information officer. She had an associate degree in communications from Colleton Community College and had worked for several years as an off-screen reporter at one of the Raleigh television stations before coming to them. That experience made her well aware of the dangers of disengaging tongue from brain when briefing the media.

"Must have been one of the EMTs," Dwight said.

"The thing is," said Ashworth, "I think the *Clarion*'s implying that Mr. Knott—Mr. Kezzie Knott— had something to do with the murder, but will probably get a pass on a real investigation because his daughter is a judge and his son-in-law is Sheriff Poole's chief deputy. Now the *News and Observer* wants a statement about that aspect."

The *Cotton Grove Clarion* was a small local weekly whose editor had supported Bo Poole's opponent in the last election. It was barely read outside the county, but the *News and Observer* was read statewide.

Dwight groaned. "Keeps coming down to politics, doesn't it?"

"I'm afraid so, Major."

"Thanks for the heads-up," he said.

Ray McLamb joined him a few minutes later and reported no sign of the missing and now presumed dead cat. "No sign of fresh digging for a grave either," he said.

They drove over to the bank on Market Street where Rusty Reynolds was a loan officer.

She was just stepping out of the restroom off the lobby as they entered and when she recognized them, she showed them into her office. Her eyes were almost as red as her hair, the tip of her small nose was bright pink, and her voice had a slight wobble. "Diesel's dead, isn't he?"

"What makes you say that?" Dwight asked.

"I just remembered the blood on the steps. Vick finally did it, didn't he? He kept threatening to, but Rosalee was sure it was just his temper talking. And it's all my fault." She reached for the box of tissues in her desk drawer and blotted her eyes. "I forgot that I was going to get home late Friday and I didn't leave any food out for him, which means he would've gone back to Rosalee's and if Vick had been drinking—" She reached for a fresh tissue.

"He'd threatened to kill the cat before?" asked Dwight.

She nodded. "Poor ol' Diesel thought everybody loved him. But every time he twined around Vick's legs, Vick would...well...not flat-out kick him, but the next thing to a kick if he'd been drinking. Diesel never seemed to learn. Vick kept saying he was going to stomp the daylights out of him." She sniffed and looked at them sadly. "So he finally did it, didn't he?"

"We're not sure what happened, but yes, that was cat blood on the steps."

As more tears welled up in her eyes, Dwight said, "Did you see either of the Earps Friday afternoon?"

His routine question seemed to steady her. She blew her nose, then took a deep breath. "No. I told you. I came home late. Around eight-thirty. I called for Diesel, but he never came."

Dwight looked at his notes. Mrs. Earp had said, and her cousin confirmed, that she had fled the house around six. "There's still plenty of daylight at eight-thirty. Did you happen to look over their way and notice his truck? Hear any voices?"

"The trees and bushes are so thick back there that I

can't see through them even in the dead of winter. I did go out to water my flower beds, but I didn't hear anything."

"You mentioned your son. Was he there that evening?"

Mrs. Reynolds shook her head. "He and my husband have gone down to visit relatives in South Carolina. They left Friday morning and won't be back till this evening."

After more pointed questions, she admitted that the Earp marriage was violent. "When you've been neighbors this long, you can't help knowing about each other. Not that Rosalee would ever say, but I could see the bruises and she did call the cops on him last year and got a restraining order, but then he talked her into coming back. Except for Marisa, she doesn't have any family to go to. They're like sisters, though. Both of them are only children. Their parents are dead, Marisa doesn't have kids, and as for Rosalee's daughters, they live up near Washington. On the Maryland side, I believe."

"Did Earp hit them, too?"

"Rosalee always put herself between him and the girls." She sighed. "But it's not like it happened every day or even every month, Major, and to be fair, he was a hard worker. You saw what their place looked like. Neatness was almost compulsion for him. He detailed her car and his truck every Saturday morning, kept the grass cut and the leaves raked. On the other hand, he was always finding fault. Cutting her down, criticizing her. If he was at home and she let Diesel in, he complained the whole time about cat hair and he wouldn't hear of keeping a litter box. He just couldn't stand any kind of mess or anything out of place."

"And yet he didn't put away the lettuce and mayonnaise and he left most of that mess on the kitchen floor," Dwight said when he and Ray were back in the parking lot. "Why?"

"The cat?" Ray suggested. "Or maybe he was interrupted. If we do find different prints on one of those beer cans, we'll know somebody else was there, somebody who maybe asked him to step outside so they could bash his head in."

"Either one's possible," Dwight agreed dryly. "See if you can run down his brother and get a statement. And while you're at it, see if he's ever registered a gun and ask if he's the one that put a bullet through Earp's windshield. I'll go talk to the uncle."

Back in the fifties, before the county got serious about zoning, any landowner could dig a well, put in septic tanks, and start renting spaces for mobile homes. The address Dwight had for Joby Earp was located in Rolling Vista, one of those informal trailer parks a few miles out from Cotton Grove. Rolling Vista might have seemed an appropriate name for a treeless field fifty years ago. Today, tall oaks and maples spread deep shade over a cluster of older singlewides and all the vistas were blocked out by overgrown azaleas and privet. A bank of mailboxes stood at the entrance of an unpaved U-shaped drive that led in from the highway, curved past the mobile homes, and exited back out a few hundred feet further down the road. There was no rental office, only a homemade sign that gave the name and phone number of a management agency. The trailers themselves were weathered and shabby but the grounds were neatly kept and summer zinnias and tubs of petunias brightened more than one dooryard.

Dwight slowed to a stop by one of them and called through the window of his truck to two old men who sat on an old wooden bench under a magnolia tree in full bloom. "Can you tell me where Joby Earp lives?"

Both pointed to a faded green trailer two doors down. "He ain't home, though. Saw him drive out about an hour ago. Him and his wife, too."

"Either of you know his nephew Vick Earp?"

One man shrugged, the other said, "Didn't know he had one."

"Didn't they use to have two boys living with 'em?" asked the first.

"So they did," said the second. "Ain't seen 'em around in years, though. Sorry, mister."

Dwight thanked them and circled past the green trailer to get back on the road. He called Deputy Mayleen Richards, gave her the number for Earp's cell phone, and asked her to see what information his phone company could provide about his recent calls. "Any word on his truck yet?"

"Sorry, Major."

"Tell Sheriff Poole I'm on my way in," he said.

Sheriff Bo Poole reminded Dwight of a bantam cock. His small body radiated confident energy and he walked as if there were springs on the soles of his feet. Six inches shorter than Dwight, he had an outsized personality and a good ol' boy folksiness, which hid a shrewdness that would probably keep him in office as long as he wanted to run because the citizens of Colleton County kept crossing party lines to vote for him. But the whole country was becoming more and more polarized and he knew such loyalty could no longer be taken for granted.

"Any leads in this murder?" he asked when Dwight tapped on his open door.

"Too early," Dwight said.

"You talk to Ashworth?"

"About the *Clarion*'s insinuations? Yeah."

"You know I got to ask, Dwight. Anything to it?"

"Did my wife conspire with her father, a man pushing ninety, to murder a stranger, dump him on his own land, and then lead us to his body?"

Bo leaned back in his big leather chair and laughed. "Well, yeah, put like that..."

"So far, the only connection to Mr. Kezzie is where the body was found, Bo. It's been a lover's lane for years and Earp's wife says he used to take her there back when they were courting."

"So is this somebody's idea of a joke? Who else would know him and know that place, too? What about Mrs. Earp herself? She do it?"

"I don't see how. She got to the cousin's house around six Friday evening, all beat up. Miss Young doctored her face and put her right to bed. Both of them say she never stirred from the house all night, which is probably when it happened. Not that Dr. Singh can tell us when the blow that killed him was actually delivered. But they were together all day Saturday and she was still there Sunday when I went to tell her Earp was dead. I've got people out talking to his co-workers and his brother. Sure would help if we could find his truck, though."

They batted it around for a few more minutes, then moved on to other incidents and lower-level crimes from the weekend. A house near Dobbs had mysteriously caught fire Friday night. It had been on the market for over a year. A spontaneous electrical fire or an owner looking to get out from under a mortgage?

"My money's on the owner," said Dwight.

Bo handed him the fire chief's report. "It seems to have started near the fuse box, so maybe the owner just got lucky."

"Or maybe the owner knows enough about electricity to rig a hot wire," Dwight said cynically.

A hit-and-run out at the soccer field Saturday morning had resulted in an arrest before sundown. They agreed that it was not a good idea to paint bright yellow flames on your equally bright red van if you're going to use it like a tank. At least six witnesses had described it to the responding officers.

A home invasion Saturday night in a Hispanic neighborhood would probably bring an arrest once Mayleen Richards had a chance to interview the terrified older woman who had been knocked around and was still in the hospital.

Also in the hospital getting checked out for any immediate harm was a four-year-old boy who'd been found in a meth house their drug team had busted the night before. DHS was hoping there would be no permanent brain damage.

The rest were routine brawls and disorderly conduct in the county's various clubs and bars.

"Let me know when Earp's truck turns up," Bo said.

Dexter Oil and Gas was located at the western edge of Cotton Grove, where Merchant Street petered out into industrial service yards. Cement blocks, rusty pipes, and piles of salvaged bricks were protected by chain-link fences overgrown with kudzu and honeysuckle. The smell of spent motor oil lingered on the warm humid air.

Earp's co-workers had heard about his death and none of them seemed particularly saddened that he'd been murdered. Nor could they offer a lead on who might have hated or feared him enough to do it.

Mrs. Dexter, his white-haired no-nonsense boss, was no help either.

"He didn't go out of his way to make friends," she told the detectives who questioned her. "I don't think he particularly liked it when I took over after my husband's stroke, but this isn't a touchy-feely place to work anyhow, and my employees don't have to like me as long as they do the work they're paid to do. I don't keep a pot of coffee going here in the office, and I don't encourage them to stand around and chitchat. My drivers get their route assignments every morning. They fill their trucks, they go out and deliver the fuel, and they hand in their invoices at the end of the day. Nine years Vick worked here and I couldn't tell you if he took cream or sugar in his coffee or if he even drank coffee. He was a good worker, though, and I'm sorry to lose him. He was first out the door in the morning and usually finished thirty-five or forty minutes before the others."

"He ever talk about his personal life?"

"Not to me he didn't. But then I never asked," she said briskly. "None of my business. Vick's route was mostly residential and nobody's ever complained about him running over their septic line or tearing up their yard. I can give you a list of them if you like."

"Let's wait and see if it's needed," said one of the detectives. Canvassing a long list of possible contacts was usually just busy work and not a fun way to spend a hot August day. No point giving the boss ideas, he decided.

Deputy Ray McLamb was having only marginally better luck with Vick Earp's brother Tyler, who shared a rental house on Old 48 with two other guys. Two small brick houses were wedged in between a filling station and a tire repair shop. One of them had a FOR RENT sign in front and looked empty. The other house made it immediately obvious that Tyler Earp didn't share his brother's compulsion for order. No manicured lawn and pruned shrubbery here, just a fringe of weeds next to the foundation and around the edges of a dirt yard that served as parking space for a Honda Civic that looked as if it'd been towed there after a serious wreck. It was missing a bumper and a right fender. A sheet of clear plastic had replaced the right front window on the passenger side. Next to the Civic was a red Ford pickup with a couple of ladders, two long-handled paint rollers, and a clutter of paint cans, buckets, and tarps in the bed.

A man in a dirty white tank top came to the screen door when Ray knocked. Through the screen Ray saw several deer antlers mounted on the far wall.

"Hey, Ty!" the man called. "Somebody here to see you."

When there was no immediate response from further inside the house, the man said, "You a cop? This about Vick?"

Ray nodded and showed his badge. "And you are?"

"Cully Lamb. Hell of a note, idn't it?"

"Did you know him?"

"Oh yeah." He did not elaborate and he did not open the screen door, but he did point to the metal lawn chair on the porch and said, "Take a seat."

"You here Friday night?" Ray asked.

"No. Sorry."

"What about Tyler?"

"What about me?"

Lamb turned back into the house and a beefy man with a beer belly took his place in the doorway. He was barefooted and his jeans were streaked and speckled with paint of different colors as was his dark green tee. His left arm seemed to have come in contact with some wet white paint.

Ray flashed his badge again and identified himself. "I need to talk to you about your brother Vick."

"What about him?"

"You know that he died Saturday?"

"Yeah, I heard."

"I'm sorry for your loss, but I—"

"Nothing to be sorry about," Tyler Earp said. He pushed open the screen door, stepped out into the yard to light a cigarette, and sat down on the edge of the low porch. "Tight-assed SOB. Not much of a brother. Cheated me going and coming our whole life and died owing me fifteen hundred dollars for painting his house."

"That why you shot out his windshield?" Ray asked.

"Who said I did that?"

Ray shrugged. "You have a gun, don't you?"

"Who says?"

"I see a gun rack in your truck. And I saw those antlers on your wall. One of 'em looks to be an eight-pointer."

"Nine," Earp said proudly. "Ought to've had a taxi-dermist mount it, but I couldn't afford it. Took him down with one clean shot right through the heart."

"So if you'd really been meaning to shoot Vick, he'd've been dead two weekends ago, not this past one?"

"Hey, no, man! That's not what I said."

"Isn't it? Where were you between Friday afternoon at six and Saturday noon?"

"Cully and me and Rocky were at the Lillie Pad."

Named for the original owner, a Lillie Hunsacker, the club had figured in more than one official report over the years. Cotton Grove didn't have too many places that welcomed the sort of people the Lillie Pad attracted, so it was a popular hangout for the town's less desirables.

"Then Cully got lucky, so me and Rocky came back here."

"Rocky's your other roommate?"

"Yeah."

"And he can vouch for you the rest of the night?"

"I reckon. He was pretty wasted, though. Me, too, for that matter." He finished his cigarette and crushed the butt out in a large clamshell that served as an ashtray.

"Rocky have a last name?"

"Capps. Rocky Capps."

"He here now?"

"His car's gone so he's probably at work. In Fuquay. He sets tile." He gave Ray the name of the shop.

"Did you see Vick anytime that night?"

"Nah. He does his drinking at home."

"His truck's missing. You happen to know where it is?"

Tyler Earp shrugged. "Probably in a shop somewhere getting a new windshield."

Back in Dwight's office, after the others had given their report, Ray said, "He wasn't happy about me bringing his gun in, Major, and it's a twelve-gauge shotgun, not a rifle. I know his brother wasn't shot, but I thought we'd better do a test firing before it goes missing in case we need to prove he was the one who shot up that windshield."

"Good thinking," Dwight said. "Right now, the only one with a solid alibi is Mrs. Earp. Ray, how 'bout you run down this Rocky Capps and find out if he can vouch for the brother. I'll swing back by Rolling Vista tomorrow, see if I can catch up with the uncle. We'll try Mrs. Earp again tomorrow, too. Maybe she's had time to remember who else had it in for her husband."

And maybe, he thought to himself, he'd also go have a talk with his father-in-law.

CHAPTER

7

In the mouth of the foolish is a rod of pride.

— Proverbs 14:3

I made good time driving west that afternoon. Going with the flow put me about eight or ten miles over the speed limit. Even at that, though, cars were regularly passing me. Times like this I feel like a gazelle, running with the herd. Yes, an occasional lion (i.e., patrol car) might bring one of us down but as long as I stay in the middle of the pack and don't make myself conspicuous by cutting in and out, I'm safe.

Dwight laughed the first time I told him my herd philosophy. "You think a few poor schmucks get ticketed so the rest of the herd can run free?"

"Works for me," I told him.

I put the car on cruise control and automatically kept two lengths behind the car in front. Running with the herd left my brain running free to puzzle over Walter Raynesford McIntyre and to wonder if he and

Mother were mentioned in those diaries. It was not surprising that Dr. Livingston connected me to her when he heard my name. People say I look a lot like her so my looks must have reminded him of her, especially when he heard I was a Knott. Daddy still has a high name recognition around this part of the state and Dr. Livingston probably knew who Mother had married.

All of which led me once again to wonder how they wound up together. Surely he didn't propose to her simply because she pulled Robert and Frank out of that icy creek?

And how did she find the nerve to disregard the social barriers?

I have only dim and disconnected memories of my Stephenson grandmother and they are not warm and fuzzy ones. Certainly my brothers never took to her. They say she acted as if they were slightly dirty. She never cuddled any of us and she terrified Benjamin the one time she came out to the farm. Mother always shrugged whenever the little twins and I asked what she actually did. The older boys could only say that she looked at them meanly. "Like the Wicked Witch of the West," says Seth.

Although Aunt Zell and Uncle Ash were fine with Daddy and his sons after they got over their surprise, she admitted to me years later that Grandmother never did. "She was a snob, honey. Pure and simple. A product of her time and her social standing. Try not to blame her."

But I did blame her. How could anybody look down on Daddy and my brothers? But now that I'd begun thinking about it, I realized that he never brought her up on his own. My grandfather was a different matter and Daddy always spoke of "Lawyer Stephenson" with warmth and respect. But then Grandfather had defended Daddy and several of his workers more than once in court and he was the one who got Daddy's federal prison record expunged.

"That was Dad's wedding present to Sue," Aunt Zell once told me, back when I was living in her upstairs mother-in-law suite. "But your grandmother—"

The memory had made her laugh. "Did you know that Kezzie bought our piano as *his* wedding present to Sue? He wanted to surprise her so he came over to the house when Sue wasn't there to ask if Mother would sell it. Mother named her price and I could tell that she didn't think he had two nickels to rub together. She was going to be the gracious grande dame and just give it to him but he pulled out a roll of bills big enough to choke a horse and peeled off what she'd asked without blinking an eye. She was so startled that she automatically took the money he was holding out to her. Then he winked at me and said, 'You might want to wash your hands after handling this, Miz Stephenson. It might have chicken shit on it.'"

"He didn't!" I said.

Daddy knows all the words, but he never uses strong language in front of a woman if he can help it.

"Well, maybe he didn't phrase it quite like that, but that's what he meant."

I shook my head in wonder. "She must have hated having him in the family."

"Mother never did have a sense of humor," Aunt Zell said dryly.

December 21, 1945

She emerges from the larger of Dobbs's two department stores with two full shopping bags. The store will deliver the linen tablecloth for her mother and a place setting of the Royal Doulton china pattern Zell and Ash picked out last week, but Sue has opted to carry her lighter gifts: a dark red dress for Mary, monogrammed handkerchiefs for Dad and Brix Junior, gloves and scarves for her friends. She has always been popular and several girls claim to be her best friend, so she feels obliged to give them all the same presents to avoid hurt feelings.

She has spent the afternoon running last-minute errands for her mother. Usually the Stephensons entertain at the country club, but once a year they hold an open house for friends and important clients. Extra hands have been hired to help Mary, who's had them polishing silver candelabras and serving trays, washing the crystal, and making sure that everything is spotless for tomorrow night. Roses for the centerpiece will be delivered first thing in the morning and Zell has wired garlands of holly and cedar to the staircase.

One of Sue's shopping bags holds a five-pound fruitcake dense with pecans and candied fruit that an impoverished cousin has made for them, the first since before the war. It will be sliced into little squares and tucked into the tiny fluted paper cups Sue bought at the dime store. Now that rationing has ended, there will also be trays of butter creams and pralines to go with after-dinner coffee.

At the corner crossing, someone calls, "Miss Stephenson?"

She turns to answer. The street is busy with Christmas shoppers and children coming home from school, but none of them seem to be looking her way.

Then a tall, loose-jointed man steps from the truck parked at the curb and walks around the front of it to join her on the sidewalk. Kezzie Knott. He carries two folded blankets and holds them out to her. "I was coming to give these back to you. My hired gal washed 'em and—"

Belatedly he realizes that her hands are already full.

"Here, let me," he says and, ignoring her protests, he opens the truck door and lays the blankets on the bench seat. He puts the shopping bags under the dash and holds the door for her. "I'll take you home."

She keeps telling him she is perfectly capable of managing by herself, then realizes how silly that sounds because clearly she cannot carry the blankets, too, so she thanks him and steps up into the cab, tucking her skirt around her legs so that he can close the door.

When he slides under the wheel and starts the engine, she says, "I live over on South Third."

"I know."

The truck is old and shabby, with dented fenders, but the motor purrs smoothly and she senses it has more power under the hood than one might think.

"I met the rest of your sons," she says brightly.

"Yeah, they said you come out to see 'em." His voice is curt. "Brought 'em candy."

"I hope you don't mind."

"They don't need no charity. I can buy candy for 'em myself."

"I'm sure you can, Mr. Knott, but it wasn't charity. It was for friendship, or don't they need that either?"

He doesn't answer, just keeps his eyes on the road.

It's only a few short blocks to her home and when he parks at the curb, she jumps out of the truck with her shopping bags before he can come around. She opens the front door, sets the bags inside, and turns to take the blankets. She cannot decide if he's angry or merely shy. Not that it matters.

"Is that you, Sue?" her mother calls from the living room. "What on earth took you so long? Philip Johnson's called at least four times. Did you get the fruit-cake?"

Sue grabs the blankets and quickly stuffs them into the coat closet before Mrs. Stephenson can reach the hall, where she pauses in the archway. "I didn't realize we had company."

Had he been one of Sue's usual crowd, Mrs. Stephenson would not have hesitated. She would have expected an introduction and she would have invited him to come in and stay for a few minutes. Instead Sue sees her mother's eyes turn cold as she notes his scuffed brogans, his overalls, and the worn cuffs on his brown barn jacket. Her smile becomes slightly less cordial.

"Were you looking for Mr. Stephenson?" She assumes he's one of her husband's clients who has coincidentally arrived just as Sue was returning. "I'm afraid he only sees clients at his office."

Her tone is so dismissive that Sue says, "Mother, may I introduce Mr. Knott?"

He takes off his brown Stetson and gives a formal nod. "Ma'am."

"Mr. Knott was kind enough to drive me home with all my packages."

"Drive you home? I don't understand."

"Won't you let me thank you with a cup of coffee, Mr. Knott?" Sue says sweetly.

Cold air is blowing through the open door, but Mrs. Stephenson's lips tighten as if she expects him to track manure on her carpet if he should step across the threshold.

"No, ma'am. I got to get on back. I just come to—" He catches himself, realizing that Sue doesn't want him to mention the blankets. "I just thought them bags looked too heavy for her to carry this far."

He puts his hat back on and turns to leave. Sue follows him out into the chilly air and closes the door behind her.

"Mr. Knott? Wait. I want to apologize for what I said out there at the creek. I was so frightened by what almost happened to Frank and Robert that I spoke out of turn. I had no right to question the way you take care of them or to assume they're neglected because they wandered off."

He keeps walking. "They ain't town boys, Miss Stephenson, and they ain't yard dogs to be kept on a chain. They didn't wander off. They got the freedom of the whole farm and they know where the boundaries are."

"They could have drowned."

He turns at that and his blue eyes bore coldly into hers. "They said you scared 'em into bolting. Was they lying to me?"

Her own eyes drop as she realizes that she probably did startle them. "But what if I'd been a bear?" she argues. "That would have scared them even more."

He suddenly grins. "Would've scared me, too, 'cause they ain't been no bears in Colleton County in forty years."

Chuckling, he continues toward the street. Then, without looking back, he suddenly thrusts one arm in the air, snaps his fingers, and sings, "Click, click, click!" as he gets into his truck and drives away, leaving her both smiling and confused.

But when she returns to the house, her mother is not smiling.

"What on earth possessed you to let that roughneck drive you home?" she asks angrily. "And in such a vehicle! What will people think?"

"Sorry, Mother."

"What if he'd been a criminal or—or—"

"Tried to molest me?" she asks innocently.

"Really, Sue!"

She's saved by the telephone bell. It's Philip Johnson. Friends are putting together a caroling party tonight and he invites her to go with him.

"I'd love to," she says.

Philip never confuses her.

Later that night, she asks her father about the farm and is pleasantly surprised to hear how much money she and Zell have earned from it since their grandmother deeded it to them. "With the new price support program, your tobacco quota makes those hundred acres more valuable than they would have been before 1938," he says.

"A hundred acres?"

"A hundred and fourteen, actually. Why do you ask? Don't tell me you and Zell want to start managing it?"

"If we did, could we make enough to live on?"

"Lots of men do, honey, but it's hard dirty work. You'd have to hire someone and buy equipment." He smiles. "You'd need a mule, too. Better to leave things as they are. I really don't think Ash would want Zell messing with it, do you?"

"Probably not," she agrees and goes upstairs to have a long talk with her sister.

CHAPTER

8

*The law is holy, and the commandment
holy and just and good.*

— Romans 7:12

Cal usually rides his bike down our long driveway to the road every morning and brings back the papers so that we can read them over breakfast. Dwight had warned me that the *Clarion* planned to make snide insinuations, so I was not surprised to read that the body of Victor "Vick" Earp had been discovered by "Kezzie Knott, a prominent local landowner. Mr. Knott is the father of District Court Judge Deborah Knott and father-in-law of Major Dwight Bryant, lead investigator in this case."

Melanie Ashworth was quoted as saying that Sheriff Bo Poole had ordered a full investigation, but somehow the *Clarion* made it sound as if the investigation might have been a little less full had he not specifically ordered it.

The *News and Observer* still leans Democrat and

Vick Earp's murder was given only a brief paragraph below the fold on an inside page, the same as any other incident of this sort. No mention of our names.

"They don't have a dog in this fight," Dwight said. "Unless the *Clarion* can come up with some real dirt or we make an arrest, this is probably the last mention."

"No sign of Earp's truck?" I asked.

He shook his head, drained the last of his coffee, and stood to leave. "What's on your docket today?"

"The usual," I said. "I'm scheduled for first appearances, whoever got themselves arrested this weekend."

"I thought you said you were going to be doing mostly family court."

"Soon as our calendars can be reconfigured," I said. "Maybe by Wednesday."

"What about you, buddy?" he asked Cal, who was absorbed in the comics page. "You and your cousins doing anything interesting today?"

"I think we're supposed to pick tomatoes for Grandma this morning. She wants to can spaghetti sauce." He frowned at the comics and then turned the page to me. "I don't get this one, Mom."

It took me a moment to get the esoteric pun myself and we both smiled as I explained it.

The house phone rang while Dwight was filling his travel mug and he paused to see who it was.

"Deborah?" I immediately recognized his sister-in-law's voice. "Oh, good. I was hoping to catch you before you or Dwight headed over with Cal."

"Something wrong, Kate?"

"Not really. Erin's dad was in a car wreck. He's going to be okay, but she wants to go be with him and her mom in Greensboro till he's out of the hospital."

Erin Gladstone is Kate's live-in nanny who aspires to write children's books. I immediately started running down a checklist of which niece or nephew might be free to watch Cal and his cousins for a few days, but Kate stopped me. "Rob left for Wilmington last night. He has to be in court first thing this morning for a client with a messy custody battle, but friends of ours have a condo at Wrightsville and they're not using it again till Labor Day, so I thought I'd drive down with the children. Cal, too, if that's okay?"

"You sure?" I asked.

She laughed. "Four bedrooms, two-and-a-half baths? Right on the beach? I'm sure."

Cal's eyes lit up when I relayed the invitation and I handed Dwight the phone to let him and Kate work out the logistics while I helped Cal pack his duffel bag.

He had to hunt for his bathing suit, which was drying on a line in the garage, and his flip-flops were so far under his bed that once he found them, he had to get a broom to fish them out.

"Don't forget your toothbrush," I said as I packed shorts, T-shirts, socks, underwear, and other odds and ends he might need for the rest of the week.

All this time, his little canine shadow danced around our feet and Cal gave me a hopeful look. "You think Aunt Kate'll let me take Bandit?"

"No, I don't," I said, "and please don't even ask her. Besides, do you really want to have to scoop his poop off the beach all week?"

He shook his head. "Forgot about that." He dropped

to his knees to pet the terrier, who doesn't have to be monitored out here in the country. Not with so many bushes and weedy places. "Sorry, boy."

He and Dwight had built a dog run out under some shady bushes so that Bandit wouldn't have to stay caged up in the house while we were gone during the day.

"Go ahead and put him outside," I said. "And make sure there's fresh water in his bowl."

I finished his packing and took the duffel to the kitchen. "Want to let's ride into Dobbs together?" I asked Dwight.

"Wish we could," he said, "but I have to swing over to Cotton Grove. See if I can catch up with Earp's Uncle Joby."

"Is that who his uncle is? Joby Earp?"

"Yeah. Why? You know him?"

"I don't think so," I said slowly, "but the name does sound familiar."

"Well, Earp's widow did say they used to live out this way somewhere."

"That's probably it," I said.

Still...?

The sheriff's department is located in the basement of the courthouse and when my morning session was over, I went down to see if Dwight was free for lunch. He was still out in the county, Mayleen Richards told me. Her baby wasn't due till Thanksgiving, but we were all beginning to wonder if she was expecting twins. She and her husband didn't plan to announce the sex before it was born, so her fellow officers had started a pool with fifty percent going to the baby.

There had been a lot of initial awkwardness between us in the past, but that had long since dissipated.

"Dwight told me about Vick Earp's record," I said, "but I didn't check to see if I handled any of his earlier cases other than that domestic violence order. Any chance I could look at it again?"

"Sure thing," she said and immediately pulled up a copy.

All were relatively minor offenses stretching back years—assault, driving while impaired, communicating threats, and, in a case that went back to when he was a teenager, felony speeding to elude arrest and, oh yes, possession of untaxed whiskey.

So *that's* what had triggered my unconscious to take another look.

(*"And that's probably when he used to live out there near the farm,"* said the pragmatist, my hard-edged internal voice of reason. *"Was he delivering some of your daddy's whiskey?"*)

(*"Now don't go jumping to conclusions,"* warned the preacher who shared headroom with him. *"Your daddy's not the only one who was making whiskey thirty years ago. And you don't know that he was still at it then either."*)

(*"Right,"* the pragmatist said cynically.)

Ten minutes later, I was sitting in my old office at the law firm of Lee, Stephenson and Brewer with my cousin and senior partner, John Claude Lee. Close as Portland Brewer and her husband Avery are to Dwight and me, I was glad that both of them were at lunch. No sign of my cousin Reid either. He's the current Stephenson of the firm.

Their receptionist and legal secretary was on her way out to lunch, too, but she's still nosy as ever and offered coffee or a soft drink in the hope of satisfying her curiosity as to why I wanted to talk to John Claude, who was having lunch at his desk. Sliced turkey on a china plate. Iced tea in a thin glass goblet— John Claude's idea of an informal lunch.

He thanked her with his usual old-fashioned courtesy, "and please pull the door to when you leave."

Back when I was still a partner, I had looked up Daddy's files. Contrary to what people might think, most moonshining arrests never end in jail time. Stills are destroyed, the whiskey and mash dumped on the ground, then the moonshiner goes to court, pays a fine, and goes on his way unless the feds get involved or some sheriff wants to make a point about law and order on his watch. Destroying a maker's copper still and dumping his mash was as punishing as jail time.

The files showed me that Daddy was never arrested again for making it after he married Mother. But more files indicated that he'd gone from maker to distributor—that he bankrolled others and he paid their fines. If one of his suppliers was convicted and did receive a sentence, he made sure the wife and children were taken care of while that man was away.

I remember being surprised by some of those names when I first read the files, men who are now pillars of the community. What I couldn't remember was if Joby Earp was one of those names.

When Sherry left us alone, I popped the top on the tomato juice I had picked up on my way over and inserted a straw.

John Claude winced. "Let me get you a glass, Deborah."

"This is fine, and I won't tell Miss Manners if you won't," I said, not wishing to waste time on formalities. "Are you still representing people for Daddy?"

"People?" he hedged.

"People," I said firmly. We both knew I meant people connected with white lightning, whether or not they were directly connected to Daddy.

He swears he hasn't made a drop since Mother died. But he's admitted to me that he used to lie to her about it and I have no illusions that he wouldn't lie to me. Besides, I knew for a fact that Robert and some of my brothers used to cut firewood for pocket money and that not all the wood got burned in residential fireplaces.

John Claude won't lie, but neither would he break attorney-client privilege.

"Then tell me about the Earps," I said. "Vick Earp."

"Who?"

"The man whose body was dumped out at the farm Saturday morning. He used to live near us and when he was fifteen he was convicted of driving without a license and trying to outrun a state trooper. He was transporting moonshine."

"I believe your grandfather handled that case," John Claude said carefully.

"And Joby Earp? Vick Earp's uncle?"

"What about him?"

"Did my grandfather represent him, too?"

"Not after—" He broke off abruptly.

"Not after what?"

"Really, Deborah. This is something you should be asking your father. Now unless there's something else, I have work to do."

Resigned, I stood to go. He stood, too, and even came around the desk to give me a warm hug. "We miss you here in the office, honey. Wouldn't be the worst thing if you lost your next election."

"Bite your tongue!" I said, hugging him back.

On my walk back to the courthouse, I couldn't help thinking back to Saturday morning. Dwight had asked us all if we recognized Vick Earp.

My brothers and I had said no, but Daddy had said, "He was laying facedown in the dirt when I got here."

Was that a denial or an evasion?

CHAPTER

9

The laborer is worthy of his hire.

— Luke 10:7

DWIGHT BRYANT—TUESDAY MORNING

When Dwight got to his brother's house, Mary Pat and Jake were waiting for their cousin on the wide planked porch, excited about spending a week at the beach. As Dwight set Cal's duffel bag on the wide wooden steps, Kate came to the door with R.W. in her arms. His nephew had Rob's red hair and green eyes along with Rob's penchant for sticking his nose into everything. Drawers were made to be opened and their contents dumped on the floor. Chairs were meant to be pushed over to tables, counters, and shelves so that he could climb up and explore.

The toddler struggled to get down from Kate's arms but she handed him, protesting and wriggling, over to Dwight. "He's into everything this morning. As soon as I put something in a suitcase and turn my back, he pulls it out. Miss Emily said she and Bessie would keep him while I pack the car and the kids pick her tomatoes, so would you?"

"Sure thing," Dwight said, slinging R.W. over his shoulder.

His mother's house was only a few hundred feet down the road, so he let the older children ride in back while he held R.W. on his lap to drive that short distance.

Miss Emily met them on her back porch. Her short hair was more white than red now but it still frizzed all over her head as she gave out buckets and pointed the grandchildren, even R.W., toward her tomato patch.

"Y'all gonna make enough spaghetti sauce to share?" Dwight asked.

"Don't we always?" his mother said. "Bessie and I plan to put up enough for us and you and Rob and your sisters, too. Hasn't it been a perfect summer for tomatoes?"

He followed his small mother into the kitchen where Bessie Stewart was busy at the food processor, mincing a pile of onions, oregano, and basil. She was as thin and neat in a summer print dress and spotless white apron as his mother was plump and exuberant in bright orange shorts and a stained orange top. When Emily Wallace married Calvin Bryant and moved to the farm, she found her childhood friend married to Cal's tenant farmer and already the mother of two. Bessie Stewart tried to teach her all that a farm wife needed to know, but after Cal was killed in a tractor accident and hail decimated the tobacco crop two years in a row, it was Bessie who pushed her back into teaching, "'Cause you never going to be no farmer, I don't care how long you live on one."

It was Bessie who delivered Dwight when a hurricane blocked the roads with fallen trees and downed power lines and she'd kept a soft spot in her heart for him ever since. "Come give me a hug," she said now, "but I can't hug you back because my hands have onions and garlic all over them."

Despite air-conditioning, the kitchen was steamy from pots of boiling water where the two women were sterilizing several dozen Mason jars. It looked like a lot of work to Dwight.

After half a lifetime as a teacher and then principal at Zachary Taylor High School, his mother had finally retired in June.

"I thought you were going to take it easy this summer," Dwight said. "Sit in a swing and catch up on your reading."

"I'm doing plenty of that," she said, gesturing to a stack of books on a chair next to the door. "Those go back on the bookmobile tomorrow and I've put a real hurting on that pile beside my bed."

"You getting close to finding out who killed the Earp boy?" asked Bessie.

"Did you know him?"

"Not to say *know* him, but we know who he is. Miss Earla raised him. Or tried to raise him. Always had a chip on his shoulder, didn't he, Em'ly?"

"Big as a woodpile," she agreed. "He and his brother both. Can't blame them, though. Not with Joby Earp as a role model and Earla Earp too scared to say boo to him."

"His wife said they used to live out here," said Dwight. "Where exactly?"

"Over off Grimes Road. Earps used to have right much land out there. In fact that might have been Earp land where he was found."

Bessie nodded. "Part of what Mr. Kezzie owns now. Used to be a hundred acres or more, I think, but Vick Earp's granddaddy started drinking it up years ago and his uncle finished it off when Vick and Tyler were just boys. They stayed on as tenants for a while, but Mr. Joby didn't like being told what to do and after Mr. Kezzie cut him loose, they moved over to Cotton Grove." She opened a cabinet door and gestured toward the top shelf. "Hand me down that box of jar rings, honey."

"Cut him loose?" asked Dwight as he turned to reach for the box. "Was there bad blood between them?"

"Well, you know how it is when men get to butting heads over the best way to do things," his mother said, cutting her eyes in warning to Bessie, who looked abashed as she realized how Dwight might think her words provided Mr. Kezzie with a motive.

"When was all this? I don't remember the Earp boys and they're only a little older than me."

"Oh, they were gone by the time you got to high school," his mother said.

"Sounds like he missed it, though," said Dwight. "Vick Earp's widow said he used to bring her out to Black Gum Branch when they were courting. She said he used to talk about trying to get back into farming but that they'd lost the family land and could never afford to buy more."

Bessie rolled her eyes and his mother made a soft scornful sound.

"What?"

"Just never saw any Earps really work at farming," Emily said, a slight emphasis on *farming* that passed over Dwight's head. As he opened the back door to let Cal in with the first bucket of tomatoes, she and Bessie exchanged a knowing look.

Out at Rolling Vista, no car was in the yard and no one answered his knock on the Earp trailer door, so Dwight drove on over to speak to Rosalee Earp again. He was not surprised to see Marisa Young's minivan parked under the carport. There was a spray of white carnations on the front door and several other cars lined the drive. He knew that Vick Earp's body had been released but he wasn't sure what sort of funeral was planned or when.

"This afternoon at two," Miss Young told him when she opened the door. Despite the heat, she wore a long-sleeved black silk shirt. Beyond her, Dwight could see that the small living room was crowded with somber-faced people similarly dressed.

"Where?" Dwight asked.

"At our church. Mount Sinai."

"Then I won't bother her now," said Dwight. "Tell her I'll come by tomorrow."

Back in his truck, he called Ray, who was still at the office. "You check out Tyler Earp's other roommate yet?"

"Sorry, Major. I called there a few minutes ago and he said Rocky Capps'd already left for work. I got the name of the tile shop in Fuquay, though. I was just leaving to go over."

"Give me the name," Dwight told him. "I'm in Cotton Grove and I can run on into Fuquay myself. In the meantime ask Mayleen if she's turned up anything useful from the phone company. Earp's being buried at Mount Sinai at two this afternoon, and I'd like both of you to be there. Get a feel for anyone else we might need to question."

At Portman's Floors and Tiles, the owner, a wiry little white guy with long gray hair tied back in a ponytail, looked at Dwight's ID and said, "What's that goof-up done now?"

"What's he done before?" Dwight countered.

"You name it, Rocky's probably done it. Backed into somebody's car in the Food Lion parking lot and left without giving his insurance information. Walked out of Wal-Mart wearing two pairs of sweatpants he didn't pay for. Ordered takeout at Wendy's and drove off without paying."

Portman reached for his wallet. "What's it gonna cost me this time?"

"You? Why you? He kin to you or something?"

"Naw, just the best worker I ever had. Even hungover, he's a real Michelangelo with tile. Not just setting it, but selling it, too. Colors and textures you think would clash—it's amazing. Customers come in here asking about an ordinary shower stall or kitchen backsplash and they tell me what they think they want—the basic meat and potatoes, you know? Then I send Rocky out to take the measurements and he comes back with an order for steak and caviar. He's got a notebook full of pictures of places he's done and once he tells them what he can do with their place, they'll wind up buying the high-end tiles, so hell yes I'm gonna pay his fines to keep him out of jail."

"You ever meet his roommate, Tyler Earp?"

"Yeah, I've let Rocky use him a few times when we're shorthanded or have a big rush job. He can mix the mud and help with the rough layout, but why? Oh, wait a minute. Is this about his brother getting killed? You think he had something to do with that?"

"We're just trying to eliminate him," Dwight said. "Capps is his alibi for part of the weekend."

"Well, good luck with that." That long gray ponytail swung back and forth as Portman shook his head dubiously. "Depends on how many beers Rocky had, don't it?"

He gave Dwight directions to where Capps was working that day.

Fuquay Springs and Varina used to be two sleepy little towns divided by a railroad track out in the middle of rolling tobacco fields. A mineral spring discovered in the 1850s brought in visitors from as far away as Richmond and Atlanta to take the waters, and the railroad helped make it a prosperous tobacco market. The two towns merged years ago and most of the tobacco warehouses are long gone, replaced by antique stores and trendy shops. Now the overflow from Raleigh and the Research Triangle has ringed the town with chain stores and shopping centers, and a profusion of housing developments cover the tobacco fields.

Despite the recession, new houses continued to be built and Dwight found Rocky Capps in the spa-like bath of a four-bedroom house in an established upscale neighborhood. The original large lots were being divided and infilled. Mature trees around this new house sported orange ribbons that had saved them from the bulldozer's blade and their branches cast welcome shade from the blazing August sun.

After Dwight showed his badge and introduced himself, Capps led him out under those trees where they could talk in private.

Late forties and showing every year of his age, Rocky Capps had the sallow skin of a habitual drinker. He wore a dirty ball cap with the Portman logo across the front and his long-sleeved plaid shirt was unbuttoned. An olive green T-shirt covered a barrel-shaped chest. His jeans were streaked with grout stains. He sat down on a stack of white bricks, took off his cap, and wiped the sweat from his face on the sleeve of his shirt as he listened to Dwight's questions.

"Friday night? Yeah. Me and Tyler were at the Lillie Pad till around ten. He's not supposed to drive anywhere but work for another week or so, so we were in my car and we both got pretty wasted." He gave a sour laugh. "I might would've blown a twelve if anybody'd stopped us. Lucky for me they didn't, huh?"

"Can't stay lucky forever," Dwight said mildly, "but that's not what I'm here for. After you and Tyler got home, did he leave again?"

"Not that I know anything about. He used the bathroom first and he was snoring in front of the TV when I came out and went to bed. Next thing I knew, it was ten o'clock in the morning and he was still asleep."

"In front of the TV?"

"Naw. In his bed."

"How'd he get along with his brother?"

He shrugged. "Okay, I guess." He fanned himself with the bill of his ball cap, then wiped his face again before putting it back on.

"We heard that he and Vick had a fight."

"Yeah, Vick owed him money but he wouldn't pay. Said Tyler did a sloppy job."

"That make Tyler mad?"

"Well, duh. Wouldn't you be?"

"Mad enough to shoot up Vick's truck while he was in it?"

"Hey, I don't know nothing about that."

"You know he's quick to use his shotgun, though."

"I don't know a thing about that, but he does like to hunt and he'll go out in the woods and do a little target practice once in a while. Really loves that gun. I've been to turkey shoots with him and he's pretty good. Got us a Butterball for Thanksgiving last year. We deep-fried it. If he gets another one this year, we're gonna spatchcock that sucker like we saw on YouTube."

Dwight laughed and let him get back to his tiles.

Back in Rolling Vista, the short driveway in front of the Earp mobile home was still empty yet there was something different about the place. Dwight couldn't quite put his finger on it but it was enough to make him get out of his truck and knock on the metal storm door one more time.

The old woman who answered was white-haired and stooped. She wore a long housecoat in a faded floral pattern that zipped up the front and a blue towel was draped around her shoulders. She had just washed her long hair and it fanned out over the towel like silvery dandelion fluff. Her face was lined and her eyes were red-rimmed.

"Mrs. Earp?"

She nodded mutely.

He held up his ID. "I'm Major Bryant. Colleton County Sheriff's Department. May I come in?"

She stepped back from the open door and gestured to a pair of recliners in front of the television. A brush and several hairpins lay on the coffee table between them.

"Sit down, Major. You're here about Vick, aren't you?"

"Yes, ma'am. He was your nephew, wasn't he?"

Her faded blue eyes filled with tears. "We're just getting ready to go over to his house. He's being buried today."

"I know," said Dwight. "And I'm sorry to have to bother you, but I need to ask you and your husband a few questions. Is he here?"

She shook her head and ran her fingers through her long hair, testing for dryness, and Dwight caught a whiff of rose-scented shampoo as she pushed her hair back from her face with both hands, twisted it into a coil, and secured it atop her head with those hairpins.

"He should be back soon, though. I told Rosalee we'd be there by dinnertime."

"When did you last see Vick?" Dwight asked.

"Maybe Mother's Day? Back in May? He sort of

thought of me as his mother. Him and Tyler both. We took 'em in when they were real little. He was four, Tyler was two. Their mama and daddy got killed in a car wreck and there was nobody else. I know some people say they turned out wild, but we did the best we could for them. Maybe if we could've stayed out in the country…"

Her voice trailed off in the silence of lost possibilities.

The silence was broken by the door opening and a truculent old man entered and glared at Dwight. "Who the hell are you?"

"Sheriff's Department," Dwight said. "Joby Earp?"

"I know you," the man said. "You're the one married the Knott girl, ain't you?"

Before he could answer, the old man held the door open. "I'll thank you to get out of my house. Knotts ain't welcome here."

"My name's Bryant," said Dwight, "and you can either answer a few questions now or I can have you hauled over to Dobbs. What have you got against Knotts anyhow?"

That got him a string of curses.

Mrs. Earp said, "Joby, honey—"

"You shut the hell up," he snarled. "You want to know who killed Vick? Go ask Kezzie Knott. He got somebody to help steal our land and now he's had our boy killed just because Vick got some of our own back."

"What do you mean?"

"Go ask him. And while you're at it, tell him I know who turned me in this last time and I'm not gonna forget it."

"Turned you in? Turned you in for what?"

But the old man just glared at him with his lips clamped tight. His wife was in tears.

"Please, Major Bryant. We need to go. Rosalee needs us to be there."

Dwight nodded. "We'll talk again later, Mr. Earp."

"Go to hell!"

Back at his office, Dwight pulled up Joby Earp's record and saw that he'd been arrested several times for possession of non–tax paid whiskey. As a repeat offender, he'd been sentenced to serve a year and a day in custody of the US attorney general, which meant forty-five days in custody, three years' probation, and a thousand-dollar fine. What surprised Dwight was that Earp had been released from Butner only two weeks ago.

Three minutes later, he was talking to Ed Gardner, the ATF agent who had signed the original arrest warrant.

"Oh yeah," Gardner said when Dwight told him why he'd called. "In fact, I meant to call you about that. Give you a heads-up after the *Clarion* piece. Seems to be a little range war going on out there."

"Range war?"

"Someone gave us an anonymous tip about Earp back in the spring, then this past month, we've gotten tips on a couple of small operations."

"And?"

"Can't prove it, but it looks like Kezzie Knott's involved."

"Huh?"

"His name's nowhere on record, but both those jokers were represented by Lee and Stephenson. We busted up their stills and they got the usual fines but you and I both know who pays Mr. Lee's fees in these cases."

Dwight sighed.

"Here's where it gets cute, though," said Gardner. "Both of those tips came from the same commercial phone number. Dexter Oil and Gas. Name mean anything to you?"

"That's where our victim worked. Joby Earp was Vick Earp's uncle and both of them seem to hold a grudge against Mr. Kezzie."

"Soon as I read ol' Joby's statement to the *Clarion*, I had a feeling. He must've picked up those two names while he was at Butner and passed them on to his nephew. Sorry, Dwight."

CHAPTER
10

Remember not the sins of my youth,
nor my transgressions.

— Psalms 25:7

DWIGHT BRYANT—TUESDAY EVENING

With Cal off to the beach and no need to rush right home after work, Dwight and Deborah had an early supper at a Tex-Mex place about three blocks from the courthouse, taco salad for her, beans and burritos for Dwight.

"Any progress on the Earp murder?" Deborah asked as she spooned extra guacamole on her salad and dipped her fork into the creamy green deliciousness.

"If you call eliminating another possible suspect progress," Dwight said gloomily.

"Who's been eliminated besides his wife?"

"His brother, for one. Tyler Earp. They fought because Earp owed him for a paint job and Tyler's prob-

ably the one who shot up his truck. He's alibied for
the first part of Friday night, though, and one of his
roommates says he was drunk and still sleeping it off
till midmorning Saturday. But the roommate was just
as drunk and probably passed out, too, so it's not rock
solid. And that truck's still missing. For all we know,
Earp's death might just be a carjacking."

"Killed when someone tried to steal it?"

"Men have been killed for less and it's only two
years old, according to his wife. We can't stop every
red F-150 on the road and ask to see the registration.
By now, it's probably headed for Florida with a different plate."

"You don't really believe that, do you?"

Dwight sighed. "No, not really. A carjacker would
leave him where he fell, not drive his body out to the
farm." He wet a corner of his napkin in his water glass
and dabbed at a spot of beans on his shirt. "I sent
Mayleen and Ray to the funeral this afternoon, but they
came up empty, too. They said it was a small turnout—
only twenty-three people, not counting the family. His
aunt and his wife were the only two who shed any tears
and Mayleen thinks most of the people came for them,
not Earp."

Deborah broke off a bit of her taco shell and dipped
it in the red sauce to gauge its spiciness. She liked a little heat, but what a waiter calls *mild* would sometimes
set off a bonfire on her tongue. This had just the right
amount of tang. "Did you know them when they lived
out near the farm?"

Dwight swallowed the bite of burrito he'd just taken
and shook his head. "I asked Mama about the Earp

boys when I dropped the kids off there and she said they moved over to Cotton Grove while I was still in grade school. They were enough older that we wouldn't have overlapped anyhow."

"What about Robert and Andrew?" Deborah wondered aloud. "They ever mention Joby Earp?"

He frowned. "Why're you asking about him?"

"Something John Claude said when I stopped by there at lunchtime. I wanted to know if my grandfather ever defended the Earps."

"Why?" he persisted.

"Just curious," she said, not quite meeting his steady gaze.

"Deborah?"

All three syllables. Serious.

"Vick Earp's arrest record," she said. "I must have read it when I issued that protection order for his wife, but it didn't really register because I didn't know he'd ever lived out there. I read it again this morning. You must have read it, too, Dwight. When Vick Earp was sixteen, he was charged with felony speeding to elude arrest. Also possession of untaxed whiskey. Back then, he was probably running it for Daddy because my grandfather defended him in court and he only got a light slap on the wrist. So I asked about Joby Earp, too."

"And?"

"John Claude wouldn't tell me but I sort of remembered that name from when I first looked through those files after I joined the firm. Something must have happened between them, though, because Grandfather dropped them before they moved to Cotton Grove."

Dwight frowned in hesitation.

"What?" she said.

"When I tried to question Joby Earp, he got belligerent. Accused Mr. Kezzie of stealing his land."

"What?"

"They didn't live *near* the farm, shug. They lived
on it. He just served forty-five days in Butner for possession of white lightning and he seems to think Mr.
Kezzie's the one who turned him in. He also thinks that
if Mr. Kezzie didn't kill Vick himself, he might have
had someone to do it for him."

Shocked, Deborah stared at Dwight. "You can't
possibly believe that."

He didn't answer.

"Can you?"

"Look, Deb'rah, I know you think he hung the moon
and you know how I feel about him, but there was a
time when he did ride roughshod over people. We both
know that. He would have had to. You can't run the
kind of operation he ran without some hired muscle to
back it up. He dealt with crooks and outlaws—hell, he
was a crook himself. Making and distributing untaxed
whiskey is a crime and you of all people know that."

"But that was back when times were hard for him.
He hasn't done that in years!" she protested.

"You sure about that, honey?"

They both knew she couldn't honestly say yes.

Her mother always said that was the one thing he
lied to her about and he had even admitted it himself
once. "It was the excitement. Running the risks. Knowing what I could lose if I got caught. That's something
your mama never rightly understood."

"Ed Gardner says John Claude defended two moon-shiners this month and you know what that means."

"Daddy may still bankroll some small mom-and-pop operations to keep his hand in," Deborah said. "That wouldn't surprise me. All the same, Dwight, he would never kill anybody. And he certainly didn't kill Vick Earp."

But she couldn't help remembering that he hadn't denied knowing him.

They finished their meal and Dwight signaled for the bill. "I'm going to have to tell him what Joby Earp said and ask him where their land was. That place where Vick Earp was found might well have been part of it."

Deborah nodded bleakly. "But just because they used to own it doesn't mean they didn't sell it to him. You know how Daddy is about land. He's spent his whole life pushing the boundaries of the farm further out from the homeplace."

"I know."

The sun was still high above the treetops when they walked out into the parking lot to her car and humidity wrapped itself around them like a hot damp blanket. As soon as she turned the key in the ignition, cool dry air flowed from the vents and she leaned forward to let the air blow on her face. "Are you going to talk to him now?"

"No point waiting," Dwight said.

"Can I come, too?"

He frowned.

"I won't interfere. I promise."

"Okay. Follow me out?"

Deborah nodded and drove over to where his truck was parked behind the courthouse. She would have preferred to get there first and give Daddy a heads-up, but she had promised not to interfere and like it or not, this was a murder investigation.

They stopped by the house first to let Bandit out of his pen and run around the yard while they changed into cooler clothes. With the little terrier on the seat between them, they drove through the lanes to the homeplace.

Her father's truck was parked by the back porch. He himself had just finished his own supper and was sitting on an old metal glider to hand-feed a few scraps to Ladybelle and Speck, the bluetick that Robert gave him after Blue died last year. Bandit hopped out and the dogs touched noses, smelled bottoms, and then wandered out into the yard when it was clear that there were no more scraps for them.

Kezzie tipped his straw panama back on his head and gave them a welcoming smile that turned to puzzlement as Deborah sat down next to him on the glider and took her fingers through his. Dwight sat down on the top step of the porch.

"Y'all are looking mighty serious," he said. "Something wrong? Where's your boy?"

"Kate took him with them to the beach for the week," Deborah said.

"It's about Vick Earp, Mr. Kezzie," said Dwight.

"The dead man we found?"

"Yessir. You recognized him, didn't you?"

"Thought it might be one of them Earps, but won't sure which one."

"Why didn't you tell us, Daddy?" Deborah asked, momentarily forgetting that she was supposed to be listening, not talking.

He withdrew his hand, reached into his shirt pocket for cigarettes, and struck a match to light it. "Me and the Earps never got along too good. Sammy Earp used to own that part of the land near Black Gum Branch."

"Vick Earp's grandfather?" asked Dwight.

Kezzie nodded.

"Sammy won't much of a farmer, but he knowed how to make good whiskey and we had an arrangement. Then he started drinking it, got into debt, owed me a lot of money. Land out here in the county won't worth much back then and he kept cutting me off a few acres till by the time he died and his boys got up in size, there won't but just a little bit down by the branch where I found Vick. Joby, he was Sammy's oldest. Me and him's about the same age. He didn't know Sammy'd deeded me so much of the land. I let them boys keep farming it after Sammy died and Joby thought the whole place was his. When I finally told him he owed me rent money, he got it in mind that I'd cheated his daddy out of their farm. He started bad-mouthing me around the community, but I let it ride till he—"

He broke off to take another drag on his cigarette.

"Till what, Mr. Kezzie?" asked Dwight.

He blew out a long stream of smoke and turned to look at Deborah. "You remember that time down by the creek after you lost that first election and you asked me if I ever killed anybody?"

She nodded. "I remember."

"You remember what I said?"

She didn't answer and he turned back around to face Dwight. "I told her that I wanted to a couple of times and meant to once, but never did. And that's as true today as it was then."

"Mr. Kezzie—"

He raised his hand to stop Dwight. "Hear me out, son. I know who it was stuck that pine cone up the *Clarion*'s backside, trying to make it sound like I killed Vick Earp. It was Joby Earp. Same man I meant to kill and didn't all those years ago."

The glider creaked on its rusty springs as he leaned back, took a deep drag on his cigarette, and let memory carry him back across the years.

December 27, 1945

For the second time in two days, Sue drives down the bumpy dirt lane to that abandoned tenant house and soon has a fire going in the old stone hearth. Dry pine cones, dead limbs, and pieces of the old collapsed siding all burn readily. The house had been built from heart pine, so the smoke billowing from the chimney is nice and black; and she is pleased to see it rise straight up in the still December air.

That end of the room still has part of the roof and three walls, and the fire soon warms the area around the hearth. She spreads one of those freshly laundered blankets on the floor in front of the fire, and settles onto the blanket with the legal documents she and Zell had registered at the courthouse first thing this morning.

She does not expect to wait long and sure enough, Kezzie Knott's truck soon trundles down the lane.

He pulls up beside her car and rolls his window down.

"I thought somebody'd set this place on fire," he calls.

Without getting up, she calls back, "Can't hear you."

He frowns at that, but gets out of the truck and walks over to the ruined house. "I thought this place was on fire."

"No, just keeping warm, but I'm glad you came. Maybe you can help me?"

"Help you do what?"

"The other day, you said your boys know your farm's boundaries. Could you show me mine?"

"Ma'am?"

"The boundaries of this farm. It's mine."

"Your'n? What about your sister? Ain't her name on the deed, too?"

She is not surprised that he would know that, but merely says, "Not anymore. I bought her half."

It has cost her all the accrued rent money and her half of the new car that was their joint Christmas present, but she doesn't tell him that.

"We registered the new deed this morning, but I can't decide where the corners are."

She spreads out the deeds that have passed down through the years from father to son and finally to a daughter. Her grandmother. The earliest one is dated 1764 and encompasses nearly 2,000 acres. By the end of the Civil War, the holding had been reduced to its present 114 acres and in addition to a written description of those final boundaries, there is a map hand-drawn by some long-dead surveyor. "I can see where it touches the creek, but where would that holly tree be?"

Reluctantly, Knott steps up into the ruined house and sits on his heels to look at the deeds. He turns the map to orient himself and while he studies it, she studies him.

A two-day growth of beard stubbles his strong chin and jawline and his deep-set eyes are a clear blue. A lock of wavy brown hair has escaped his hat to fall across his brow and she finds herself wanting to brush it back.

"That holly tree's the beginning of my land," he says. "Ain't nothing left of it now but the stump. I hammered in a iron pipe there when I got that piece from the Earps."

He picks up the 1764 deed. "Joseph Grimes? That must be why they still call it *Grimes land* on all the deeds. You come down from him?"

Sue nods.

The first Grimeses arrived in Virginia in 1703 and some of them eventually worked their way down to North Carolina. Her mother is a proud member of both the Daughters of the American Revolution and the United Daughters of the Confederacy. Sue herself has never seen the point of resting on an ancestor's laurels and rather suspects that Joseph Grimes might well have been one of those Englishmen who were given the choice between transport and debtor's prison.

"My granddaddy got our homeplace from this 'un," he says, pointing to one of the post–Civil War deeds.

"And you've added to it?"

"Figured I might as well since they ain't making no

more land." He sticks the deed with the map in the pocket of his brown work jacket and stands. "Come on then and I'll show you what's your'n."

"Are you sure you have time? I don't mean to take you away from your work."

He shakes his head. "I set my own hours."

She reaches up and after a slight hesitation, his hand takes hers to help her to her feet. She's wearing a short wool jacket and corduroy slacks tucked inside a pair of sturdy leather boots. As they pass the dilapidated curing barn, he reaches inside for a couple of tobacco sticks and hands her one. She did enough rough hiking yesterday to know a stick will come in handy for pushing aside briars and low-hanging branches.

At the creek, they turn east to follow its run to where her land ends at Black Gum Branch.

"Never knew that little branch had a name," she says. "Where's the black gum tree?"

"Probably blew down years ago." He points to a moss-covered stump. "I believe that might be what's left of it."

The branch peters out in a low marshy spot and after some poking around with his tobacco stick, he locates another iron stob. Due north from there, they come to the dirt road and cross it to walk along the western side of a cotton field. The dead stems hold empty bolls that still have wisps of cotton clinging to them.

"This ought to've been cut in last month," he said and she hears the disapproval of a good farmer.

"You really do farm, too?" she asks.

Till then, he's stayed a pace or two ahead of her. Now he turns. "What do you mean, *too*?"

She shrugs. "My father told me why you went to prison and you're still making it, aren't you?"

He glares at her, then heads south again without answering.

"Are you ashamed to answer?" she asks.

It's not a taunt, but it makes him face her again. "I ain't ashamed of nothing I do, Miss Stephenson, but that ain't none of your business."

"It is if you're making it on my land."

That stops him. "I ain't making it on your land."

"Maybe not right now, but you have in the past, haven't you? I was out here yesterday and I walked the creek over toward your line. Looked to me as if somebody had a still there back in the summer."

"And you'd know what a still site looks like?"

"I'm not stupid, Mr. Knott. I could see where a fire had been built. Bricks and rocks to hold the heat in beneath some sort of large vessel. A few pieces of firewood scattered around."

"Could've been some hunters looking to stay warm."

She laughs out loud at that and his own lips twitch before he turns. The field ends but he keeps on walking, breaking a trail through blackberry briars and wax myrtles out into a stand of longleaf pines new to her. A thick carpet of pine needles has smothered out the usual underbrush and there is nothing to block her view of this open expanse. She catches her breath at the way the morning sun streams through those high branches, sending down shafts of pure golden light between the tall, straight trunks of the pines, and he pauses to watch her.

"Is this mine?" she whispers, awed by the beauty. "Really, truly mine?"

He smiles at her. "Real pretty, ain't it?"

Impulsively, she stands on tiptoe, pulls his head down, and kisses his stubbly cheek.

Startled, he takes a step back and stares at her.

She laughs. "Don't think that means anything. That was just to thank you for showing me this."

"Yeah?" Without warning, he wraps his arms around her and kisses her full on the lips. "That's to say you're welcome."

Before she can react, the bark on the pine tree next to his head explodes in a shower of sharp chips that sting their faces. A split second later, the sound of the rifle reaches their ears.

He pulls her to the ground just as another bullet hits the pine trunk where their heads were only an instant ago.

"*Hey!*" he yells. "People here! Hold your fire!"

He looks down at her. "You okay?"

She nods.

"Fool hunter," he growls. "He could've killed us." He shouts across the clearing, "*Hey, you! Who's that shooting?"

No one answers.

"Stay down," he says, then sprints across the open expanse in the direction the shots came from and crashes through the bushes at the far side.

It's a good five minutes before he comes back. "Took to his heels," he tells her as he helps her to her feet. "You sure you're okay?"

"I'm fine," she says, "but your cheek—you're bleeding."

She reaches out with her handkerchief, but he moves away from her touch and pulls out his own handkerchief to blot up the blood.

"A tree branch caught me. Ain't but a scratch," he says. "We need to finish up here. Your south corner's down yonder." He turns and sets off at such a fast pace that she almost has to run to keep up with his long legs.

She's full of questions about that kiss, those rifle shots, and why he's suddenly so anxious to be gone. But she only asks about the shots.

"Somebody was hunting on my land without asking," he says. "Reckon that's why he took off."

"Your land? You own that?"

Past the stand of pines, he points to three slash marks on the north side of a huge old water oak. "That shows that your line runs on this side of the tree. Mine's on the other side."

She nods but doesn't speak and they finish walking the boundary in silence.

Back at the ruined house, he immediately heads for his truck.

"I brought sandwiches," she says, reaching for a picnic basket in her car. "Enough for both of us."

"Thank you kindly, Miss Stephenson, but dinner'll be waiting for me at my house and I got something that needs doing first."

"My name is Sue," she says.

"You're Lawyer Stephenson's girl. It ain't fitting for me to call you that."

"I kissed you, Kezzie. And you kissed me back."

"That won't fitting neither." He opens the door of his truck and steps in.

"I'll be here tomorrow," she calls.

"Well, I won't," he says.

And he isn't, even though black smoke rises from the chimney all morning.

Nor does he come the next three mornings.

On the fifth morning, he has the fire going before she gets there.

CHAPTER

11

*If it be possible, as much as lieth in
you, live peaceably with all men.*

— Romans 12:18

He was quiet for so long, that I touched his arm and said, "Why, Daddy? Why would you want to kill him?"

He sighed and seemed to pull himself back to the present. "Your mama and me'd just met and I was showing her the boundaries of her land out here when somebody took a couple of potshots at us."

"Joby Earp?"

His cigarette had burned down almost to his finger and he stubbed it out in the ashtray on the arm of the glider. "Come this close to hitting her."

He held his thumb and index finger less than an inch apart and I saw remembered anger flare in his blue eyes. "We never timbered that stand of pines 'cause your mama loved them too much, so I could show you the very tree. Still got one of Joby Earp's bullets in it.

He took to his heels when I ran after him, but I knowed it was him." His voice turned as harsh and cold as I'd ever heard. "Beat the tar out of him when I finally caught up with him that evening and yeah, I'd've killed him if somebody hadn't pulled me off so he could get away."

He held up his fingers again. "*This* close them bullets came, Deb'rah. Any closer and Sue—"

He took a deep breath, then fumbled in his shirt pocket for his Marlboros.

"Won't too long after that, the revenuers caught him. He couldn't pay a lawyer so he spent the next three months in jail."

I wasn't going to ask how Joby Earp got caught, but I realized that this must have been when my grandfather stopped representing him.

"I'd've run him off the land right then, but by the time he got out, me and Sue was married and Joby's wife come and begged her to get me to let bygones be bygones. Earla was a good woman with a hard row to hoe and Sue felt sorry for her. She'd took in his brother's boys to raise, so I backed off, even gave the oldest boy—Vick—a chance to work for me. He won't as good a driver as he thought he was, though, and didn't want to be told. Always picking fights with your brothers.

"Them Earps got to be such a thorn in my side that I offered Joby more than the land was worth to buy him out, but he wouldn't take it 'cause he knowed how it irked me to have them squatting there. So I just bided my time, waited till I heard he needed money real bad, then got somebody from the other end of the county to make him an offer. I got it for right much less than I'd offered Joby. Made him cuss me even more when he figured it out. Reckon Vick and Tyler grew up thinking they'd been cheated outten what was theirs."

He flipped back the top of his Marlboro box. One cigarette remained. No matches, though.

"I'll get you a match," I said and slipped into the kitchen for some. I had Mother's lighter in my pocket, but was still a little hesitant about letting him know that it was mine now.

He thanked me and the glider squeaked as he sat back and lit up. "First few years atter they moved, them boys used to sneak out here to fish in the creek, maybe shoot 'em a rabbit or two. Thought I didn't know. But I usually heard about it. Long as that was all they did, I never said nothing. It ain't easy knowing the land your people sweated over, maybe fought and died for, ain't never gonna be yours again. I felt sorry for 'em, but it was Joby and Sammy they needed to be mad at, not me."

"You have anything to do with him going to prison in June?" Dwight asked.

"Is that what he's saying?"

"'Fraid so."

"Guess that's why—" He broke off and took a long drag on his cigarette.

"Why what?" I asked. "Why some of John Claude's regulars have needed his services lately?"

Daddy turned to Dwight. "'Bout now's when you're gonna ask me if somebody can say was I here all Friday night and you know there ain't. Maidie'll say she'd of heard if anybody come up or if I'd gone somewhere in my truck. She says she don't sleep as sound as she used to, but it'd just be her word."

I almost had to smile. Maidie came to work for Mother when she was a teenager, met and married Cletus Holt, and had stayed on as Daddy's housekeeper after Mother died. Their house lay on the other side of the dog pens and garden, only a few hundred feet away, but Daddy could have driven his old truck past their house with a brass band playing in the back and both of them would swear he hadn't set foot off the place all night if they thought that was what he wanted.

"When's the last time you saw Vick Earp?" Dwight asked.

Daddy shrugged. "Might be six or eight years, at least. Saw Joby last year at a fish fry. He kept his distance, but I knowed he still held a grudge against me. Yeah, I was the one let the feds know where to find his still back when he shot at us, but that's the only time. If he's thinking I had aught to do with this last time, he's wrong. All the same, I reckon he's gonna try to sling as much mud on you and Deb'rah as he can."

"Don't worry about us," I said, patting his knee.

Had we been there alone, just the two of us sitting on the squeaky old glider watching the late afternoon fade into twilight, I might have seized the moment to ask about those days. "Your mama and me'd just met," he'd said before his voiced hardened with anger for Joby Earp.

Instead, Dwight whistled for Bandit and we left Daddy there alone with the two hounds and his memories.

CHAPTER

12

And the children of Israel came up to
her for judgment.

— Judges 4:5

The rest of the week passed quietly.

Dwight sent his detectives out again to question everyone connected to Vick Earp, but they could turn up nothing new. His were the only fingerprints on the beer cans and still no sighting of his truck. After examining his phone records, Mayleen Diaz reported that most of his calls were either to his wife or his customers. He had called his wife and his dentist around noon on Friday and those were all. No incoming calls had registered for that day.

"Mayleen thought that was a little odd, but I said that would be normal usage for you."

"Sticks and stones, Dwight," I said.

As for me, domestic court started with a permanent custody hearing. One of my fellow judges had awarded temporary custody to Ted Latham, the father of a three-year-old. Mrs. Latham had not contested that decision because they had agreed that she could have the little girl from five o'clock on Friday till five o'clock on Sunday and he was not asking for child support. Mr. Latham was back in court to petition for permanent custody on the grounds that his ex-wife, who lived with her own mother, was negligent and often went out partying both nights that the child was there. He had photos and affidavits to back up his allegations.

Mrs. Latham hotly disputed that and accused him of trying to turn their daughter against her. With tears in her eyes, she begged me not to take away those two precious nights. "I'm still young, so yes, I have a life and I do go out sometimes, but not until after Melody's gone to bed."

I looked over the affidavits. *Sometimes* seemed to be every Friday and Saturday night. "Who watches your daughter while you're out?" I asked.

"My mother." She gestured toward an attractive woman seated on the bench behind her. She appeared to be only five or six years older than me.

"Who gets up with her the next morning?"

"Mom. But she's always up with the birds anyhow, so for him to say Melody's neglected is a lie. My mother worships the ground she walks on and doesn't let her out of her sight the whole time she's here."

I had no doubt that she was telling the truth about her mother. I also had no doubt that it was the grandmother who was pushing to retain even that small amount of contact. My heart ached for her, but she was the one who raised a party girl and my first concern had to be for the child.

"There's no clear evidence that Melody's being harmfully neglected, but she certainly doesn't seem to have your full attention," I told Mrs. Latham. "Therefore, I'm going to award permanent custody to Mr. Latham and cut the visitation from forty-eight to twenty-four hours. That's from five o'clock Friday afternoon till five o'clock Saturday for as long as you are living with your mother and your mother is physically able to tend to your daughter's needs if you're not there."

I turned to the father. "If her current living circumstances change, you can come back to court and revisit the issue."

I granted two uncontested divorces before lunch, and after lunch, I terminated the parental rights of a couple who had pretty much abandoned their three children for the joys of methamphetamine. The youngest child would probably have permanent brain damage from being in the house while the parents were making it. I have no illusions about foster care, but at least the children would no longer be exposed to meth. Both parents had been notified. Neither parent showed.

As the week went on and other cases took precedence, the Vick Earp murder began to slide to Dwight's back burner.

"Ashworth says that the *Clarion*'s editor still calls her every day and there will probably be something more in the paper on Tuesday," he told me.

Kate and Rob had invited us to join them at the beach for the weekend—"That fourth bedroom's sitting empty," they said—so after work on Friday, we left Bandit with Daddy and drove down to Wrightsville Beach.

We hiked along the wide white sands, paddled past the low breakers to ride the swells, built sandcastles, and looked for sea glass and Scotch bonnets. For meals, we pigged out on shrimp and grits, fried oysters, and crab cakes at nearby restaurants. After supper, we played board games with the children. When they were in bed, we took our drinks out to the rocking chairs on the porch to rock and talk. It was the dark of the moon and without any streetlights to wash them out, stars blazed overhead and the Milky Way clearly swirled across the sky.

Except that she's a little taller and a half-size thinner, Kate and I look more like sisters than Dwight and Rob look like brothers. Dwight is taller and broader with brown hair and brown eyes, while Rob is built more like Miss Emily: small frame, red hair, green eyes. She always says that her four children split the genetic deck. Dwight and Nancy Faye look like their father, while Rob and Beth take after her. Dwight thinks that Rob is smarter and quicker on the uptake, but Rob thinks Dwight has more common sense, with a deeper understanding of the world and how it works. Rob and I talk law cases when we're together; Dwight and Kate talk about growing things.

It was a good weekend and we were all sorry to see it end when we had to pack up and drive back home on Sunday.

Monday morning took me back to New Bern to settle the dispute between Wade and Caleb Mitchell over the two grave sites in Cedar Grove Cemetery.

I had called the Raynesford House first thing that morning and was told that Miss Josephine Raynesford could see me at 1:30. Actually, I was told that she would "receive" me at 1:30.

"May I ask what this is in reference to?" asked the man who took my call.

I murmured something about genealogy and his voice warmed. "Aunt Jo loves talking genealogy. Which branch of the family are you? Caswell? Oliver? Henry?"

"Oh, I'm not related," I said. "I was hoping to learn about a family friend. A Walter McIntyre. Walter Raynesford McIntyre."

"That's my name!" the man exclaimed. "*I'm* Walter Raynesford."

"The one I'm looking for died in the Second World War. But before that, he was engaged to a girl named Leslie who killed herself just before the war."

"Really? What was her last name?"

"I'm afraid I don't know it."

"And this Walter was killed in the war, you say?"

"I think so. He was a pilot."

"That's not ringing a bell. Oh well. Doesn't matter. If he's one of us, then Aunt Jo will know. I'll tell her why you're coming so she can go ahead and look through her records. We go all the way back to the Isle of Wight in 1540, you know."

I didn't know, but I had a feeling I was going to find out.

Because New Bern was founded by some settlers from Bern, Switzerland, bears are a symbol of the town and fanciful bear statues dot the sidewalks in colorful clothes. My favorite is a British jurist in a scarlet-faced robe and curly white wig.

Inside the courthouse, any hope I might have had that the two elderly Mitchell cousins had reached an amicable agreement flew out the window as soon as I tapped my gavel to open the hearing. The only bright spot was that the Theodore Mitchell plot had been deeded to Edward Mitchell, their grandfather, which meant that they were the legal owners. No title search had been needed.

Unfortunately, neither man was willing to give up his claim to the two sites in the Edward Mitchell plot.

"This is what I can do," I said. "As you two are equal owners to the four plots, it is within my power to give each of you one grave in each plot."

Before they could jump in with objections, I held up my hand for silence. "Or I could give one of you both graves in your grandfather's plot and let your cousin have the two in the Theodore Mitchell plot."

Again they were ready to go at it hammer and tongs, but I rapped for silence with my gavel.

"Or," I said, "and this is my final offer. Each of you will write down what you are willing to pay the other for those first two plots and hand me your signed offer, which will be binding. Whoever offers the most will get both Edward Mitchell plots, the other will get the cash and the two Theodore Mitchell plots. You may go find a quiet place to confer with your attorneys, but if you do not agree to this, then I *will* split the lots. This is not an auction. You have one bid and one bid only and I don't care if the higher bid is only a penny more than the lower one. You have twenty minutes, gentlemen, and the clock starts now."

The attorneys wanted to argue that they needed time to figure out what was reasonable.

I shook my head and looked at my watch. "Eighteen minutes."

They scattered to opposite corners of the courtroom and there were indignant murmurs and much gesturing, but with three minutes still to go, both sides returned to their tables and I had their bids in my hand.

"Before I open these, I have one question," I said. "Before you started fighting over who's going to be buried where, were you two friends? Did you even like each other?"

"Of course we did!" said Wade.

"We had lunch together almost every day," said Caleb. "We were boys together."

I leaned forward. "And now you're going to let a little piece of dirt end a lifetime friendship? Never to be able to eat lunch together again, to sit and remember old times?"

They didn't answer.

"Both of you are wealthy men," I said. "Successful businessmen." I turned the folded papers in my hand. "No matter how much one of you bid, I'm sure the other could have bid more, but does it have to come down to this? Can't one of you do the generous thing and keep your friendship while you're both alive?"

I let the silence grow, then sighed and started to open the first bid.

"Wait!" said Caleb. "You're right." He turned to his

cousin. "You and Hope can go in with our parents. Jenny and I will take the other plot."

Sudden tears filled Wade's eyes and ran down his wrinkled cheeks. "You're sure, Caleb? Really?"

"Really. Your father was the oldest. You should have it."

A moment later, those two old men were hugging each other, almost giddy in their relief at saving what they had almost lost. I signed the documents that would make it official and as they left to go have lunch together, I heard Wade say, "You pick the place and I'll pick up the tab."

One of the attorneys paused as he was leaving. "Just out of curiosity, could you tell me what the other bid was?"

I shook my head and put the papers in my briefcase.

Wade might have thought he was more passionate about family ties, but generous-hearted Caleb had out-bid him by twelve hundred and two dollars.

The rest of the day was mine, so I drove over to Lawson's Landing, part of the North Carolina History Center at Tryon Palace, and ate outside under an umbrella while overlooking the river. The salad was good, but the coffee was nectar for the gods. Better than anything I've ever gotten at Starbucks.

With time to kill before meeting Miss Raynesford, I stopped by Mitchell's Hardware, an old-fashioned store founded by a distant cousin of Wade and Caleb Mitchell. Or so I was told. It still sells loose nails and screws by the pound plus dozens of other items you can't find at a chain store. I bought some onion sets for the fall garden Dwight would be planting soon; and as long as I was there, I also bought two impact screwdrivers. One for Dwight and one for Annie Sue, my electrician niece who's always griping about frozen screws.

Never too early to start Christmas shopping, right?

By the time I got out of that store, it was 1:20, so I scooted over to the Raynesford House and parked behind a black 1956 Cadillac convertible that had its top up. According to the nearby plaque, the white two-story house was built in 1813 by Enoch Raynesford and had been owned by Raynesfords ever since. Two broad wooden steps led up to a deep veranda that ran the width of the house and wrapped around one side. The shutters were painted black, and black wooden rocking chairs with colorful floral cushions were clustered along the veranda in groups of three and four.

Inside was the usual bed-and-breakfast display of old, though not necessarily antique, mahogany furniture—polished chests and sideboards and chairs upholstered in worn red velvet. Porcelain figurines sat on every surface and fake kerosene lamps shed soft electric light. I myself would rather stay at a modern impersonal motel than a historic B&B where a sudden move can send china doodads flying. I don't want to move eight ruffled pillows before I can get into bed and I certainly don't want to have to make polite conversation to strangers over my morning coffee.

A slender and very handsome middle-aged man came down the wide central hall to greet me when I entered. Except for a slight bump at the tip of his aquiline nose, he was almost classically beautiful and

must have set hearts aflutter in his youth. His warm
smile felt genuine, not something turned on and off for
paying guests, and I found myself smiling back just as
warmly.

"Judge Knott? I'm Walter Raynesford."

He had such long, thin fingers that I expected a
weak handshake. Instead it was pleasantly firm.

(*"Please remember just how green the grass is on
your side of the fence,"* chided my internal preacher.)

(His pragmatic roommate grinned. *"Doesn't mean
she can't appreciate the clover on the other side."*)

"Aunt Jo's in the sunroom," Raynesford said.
"Please come on back."

He led me into a large and unexpectedly modern
room, clearly a late addition. The whole rear wall seemed
made of glass and looked into a beautiful formal garden
with clipped hedges and beds of bright flowers.

Miss Josephine Raynesford stood as we entered.
Early eighties, I guessed, with her nephew's aristo-
cratic bearing and remnants of great beauty in her face.
She inclined her head graciously when he said, "Aunt
Jo, may I present Judge Knott?"

Her lips pursed. "I'm quite certain you've heard every clever comment that could possibly be made about
your name and title, Judge Knott, so I shall spare you."

"Thank you, and please call me Deborah."

She did smile then. "How prescient of your parents."

"Excuse me?"

"To name you Deborah. *'And Deborah judged Israel at that time.'* I believe she's the only female in the
whole Bible whose prominence did not derive from a
male relative."

I smiled back. "What about Esther?"

"Wife of a king and brought to his attention by her cousin Mordecai," she said scornfully.

"Ruth?"

"On the basis of that mawkish '*Entreat me not to leave thee*' speech, which was said not to a man but to her mother-in-law?"

I laughed. "Who promptly married her off to the richest man in the neighborhood."

"Exactly! Which eventually led to her becoming King David's great-grandmother, which is the main reason we remember her."

"You really are into genealogy, aren't you?" I said.

We beamed at each other and she gestured for me to be seated next to her on the sofa.

"Coffee, Aunt Jo? Or tea?" asked Mr. Raynesford.

"No, thank you, dear." She looked at me expectantly. "Something for you, Deborah?"

I shook my head and her nephew said, "Then if y'all will excuse me, one of our guests has booked a tour of the town for two o'clock."

"In that Cadillac convertible parked at the curb?" I asked.

He nodded. "My dad's first car. My son keeps trying to talk me out of it. I just hope I can keep it running till he's ready to take over the tours. Nice meeting you, Judge."

Miss Raynesford smiled indulgently as he left us. "I'm afraid New Bern's going to seem much too dull for young Walter after four years at Chapel Hill."

On the coffee table were several thick loose-leaf notebooks and she picked up one labeled *Raynesford 1850–1950*.

"My nephew tells me you're seeking information about a Walter Raynesford, who may have been killed in the Second World War. I've looked in my records, but the only Walter of that era came home safely and died in the eighties. There was a Herman Raynesford who was killed, but—"

"I'm sorry," I said. "I must not have made it clear to your nephew. Raynesford was the middle name of the man I was looking for, not his last. Walter Raynesford McIntyre."

"McIntyre?" She frowned. "We do have McIntyre cousins, but none in our direct line." She put aside the first notebook and began to leaf through one labeled *Collateral Raynesfords*. "Still, if his first name was Walter, then he must be closely connected. If we had his dates..."

As she turned the pages, I remembered the lighter, which I had dropped in my purse this morning "This was his. A birthday present from his girlfriend."

I pulled it apart and showed her the date engraved on the inner case: *11/11/1934*. "If this was his twenty-fifth birthday, then he must have been born in November 1909."

"November 1909," she murmured under her breath, her thin fingers running down lines of typescript. "Ah! Here he is. Walter Raynesford. Son and third child of Mary Elizabeth Raynesford and Gerald Scott McIntyre. Born November 11, 1909. Died 1974, Paris. No children."

"Paris? 1974?" That was unexpected. "He didn't die during the war?"

"Apparently not. The notation is my mother's handwriting and she was a stickler for accuracy. Is it important?"

"Not really, I guess."

"You haven't yet said why you're interested in him."

"It's sort of complicated," I said.

"Oh, good! I love complications!" She repositioned the cushions on the sofa and leaned back against them. "Tell me."

When I hesitated, she patted my arm. "I am very discreet, Deborah, and there aren't many complicated family stories I haven't heard over the years. The details may vary, but the broad outlines are often the same—love, hate, birth, death. How did you come to have my cousin's lighter?"

"He gave it to my mother before he went overseas. She was supposed to hold it for him till he came back, but he never came back or got in touch, so I think she assumed he'd died in action. She said he changed her life, but she didn't say how and I was too stupid to ask before she died."

I told her about Daddy and how Mother had been gently raised while he'd had to scrabble for everything he had.

"They were so happy together but I get the feeling that she wouldn't have let herself fall in love with him if it hadn't been for this Mac." I showed her the musical notes engraved under Leslie's name and hummed them aloud. "This may have been their song, but it was Mother and Daddy's song, too."

I sighed for all the questions that would never be answered. "I wonder why he didn't come back to New Bern?"

"Maybe it would have been too painful for him without his Leslie," she said. "Did your mother tell you why she killed herself?"

I had to shake my head. "And now we'll never know."

"People here have long memories, Deborah. If only you had that poor child's last name."

She looked down at the notebook still open on her lap. "Your Walter McIntyre had two siblings, a brother Gerald Junior and a sister Mamie. The brother died unmarried in 1983, but his sister…" She flipped over more pages and ran her fingers down the lists. "Here we are. Mamie McIntyre. She married a Lovick Middlewood. Middlewood? Hmmm. I wonder if that's Edgar Middlewood's father? If so, Edgar's right here in New Bern."

She pursed her lips. "I hadn't realized we were cousins."

"You sound as if it's not good news that you are."

Miss Raynesford smiled. "Very perceptive of you. Edgar and I used to attend the same church. We even served on the pulpit committee together. He wasn't happy when we welcomed black people into the congregation, but when a black man was made a deacon, he moved his membership to a more conservative church."

She closed the notebook and stood. "Let me give him a call."

CHAPTER

13

*Ye stiff-necked and uncircumcised in
heart and ears, ye do always resist
the Holy Spirit; as your fathers did,
so do you.*

— Acts 7:51

Jo Raynesford might have had misgivings when she
realized that Edgar Middlewood was a cousin, but he
seemed thrilled. Less than fifteen minutes after she
called, he was sitting happily on a chair in her sunroom.

"Cousins, you say, Jo? My Grandmother McIntyre
was a Raynesford? Well, well, well! Mother never
mentioned that but then she didn't ever talk much
about her family. Think of that!" he marveled. "Kin
to one of the oldest families in New Bern and she
never mentioned it."

He appeared to be a few years younger than Miss
Raynesford, but age had stooped him and, despite hearing aids in both ears, he was somewhat hard of hearing,

which is probably why his voice was louder than normal. He wore a blue bow tie with a buttoned-up blue-striped shirt and his eager dark eyes darted around the sunroom before coming to rest on some framed snapshots clustered on a side table next to his chair.

He picked one up for a closer look. "That's you with the mayor, isn't it? And here's you and Walter with the de Graffenreids the last time they came to New Bern. Was this the dance for them out at Tryon Palace? I heard it was a real fancy party. You visited them in Switzerland, didn't you? Did you stay at their mansion?"

Without waiting for her answer, he said, "Never been out of the country myself. Or even west of the Mississippi, for that matter."

His eyes had passed over me when he first entered even though Miss Raynesford had tried to introduce us. Now he all but shouted, "Sorry, ma'am, I didn't catch your name."

"Deborah Knott," I said, enunciating as clearly as I could.

"She's a judge, Edgar," said Miss Raynesford and his long narrow face rearranged itself into a respectful interest that had been missing before he heard my title.

"Didn't know I was being asked in to meet a judge," he boomed jovially. "She says you want to ask about my mother?"

"About your mother's *brother*," she corrected.

"Uncle Gerald? What about him?"

"Not Gerald. Walter."

Puzzled, he cupped a hand to his ear. "Water?"

I was nearer, so I said, "*Walter.* Walter Raynesford McIntyre."

"My Uncle Walter was named Raynesford?" He frowned and drew back as a sort of wariness came over him. "What about him?" he asked suspiciously.

"He was a friend of my mother's," I said. "Did you know him? Can you tell me about him?"

He glared at Miss Raynesford. "Is this some sort of a joke, Jo? Did you ask me here to insult me? To smear my family's good name?"

He jerked himself up from his chair and headed for the door.

"Edgar, no!" she cried. "We only wanted to ask you—"

He turned with so much anger that for a moment I thought he was going to hit her and I sprang up, too, to stop him, but he stepped back, as if suddenly remembering that he probably shouldn't hit a judge.

"We may not be as high and mighty as the Raynesfords, so ready to sit in judgment of God-fearing white Christians who follow God's commandments," he said to me. Then looking past me to Miss Raynesford, he snarled, "But I won't have you dragging my family through dirt. Walter *Raynesford* McIntyre!" His voice dripped venom. "I should've known that was his whole name. No wonder he went whoring off to Paris after the war. Ashamed to come back home even though you'd've welcomed him back to your church. Seated him on the front row next to some—some—! You people make me sick!"

And with that, he stomped out of the room and

down the hall where he slammed the front door so violently that I expected the glass to shatter.

Miss Raynesford let out the breath she'd been holding and gave me a wry smile. "Well, at least we now know why Walter Raynesford McIntyre didn't come home to the bosom of his loving family."

"Do we?" I asked.

"You heard him. 'God-fearing white Christians who follow God's commandments.' Back when we were taking a vote to elect a black deacon, Edgar got up and quoted scriptures that commanded servants—read *slaves*—to respect and serve their masters. And did you know that the takeaway lesson of the Tower of Babel was separation of the races? So they wouldn't mix?"

"Leslie was black?"

"This is the South, Deborah. If men like Edgar still foam at the mouth at the very thought of mixed marriages in this day and age, think what it was back then. Miscegenation. It was illegal for blacks and whites to marry in this state as late as the mid-sixties."

She sighed. "Even that song. The words were running through my head while we waited for Edgar to get here. It was popular when I was young and I remember that it kept asking whether or not two young people should fall in love. Maybe that's why your parents took it for their song, too. In some ways, from what you've told me, their social differences were almost as great as Walter and Leslie's. They had to wonder whether or not those differences should keep them apart. Maybe he encouraged your mother to follow her heart as he had."

"And Leslie killed herself because of that? Because their marriage would be impossible here in North Carolina?"

"Young people do a lot of foolish things for love." Her smile was sad. "Or when they think they've lost it. For all we know, he might have been the one to break it off."

I shook my head. "No. I can't believe that. He wouldn't have kept the lighter if he didn't love her."

"Guilt, maybe?"

It was a logical explanation. Not a satisfying one, but logical. And it would explain why he lived out his life in freewheeling Paris rather than return to uptight New Bern.

I stood to go and she accompanied me to the front door. "I'm sorry, Deborah. I wish I could have helped."

"You did help," I told her. "At least now I have a sense of why Mother seemed sad when she spoke of him. And not just because she thought he had died in the war."

After that emotional session, it felt anticlimactic to drive over to see Dr. Livingston.

As before, he was in his office when I opened the screen door and walked in. A ceiling fan high overhead stirred the air and a nearby floor fan helped make the room comfortable.

"Oh, good!" he said, and his leather swivel chair squeaked as he stood to welcome me. "I hoped that was you when I heard the door. I couldn't remember when you said you'd be back and we didn't exchange email addresses, did we?"

After the usual pleasantries, I said, "Did you find my mother?"

He was beaming. "And Captain McIntyre, too."

He sat down, picked up one of those red leather-bound diaries, and opened it to the entry he had book-marked. "Dad used a lot of abbreviations, so I'll just read it to you."

New girls at the USO club tonight. Two sisters and their roommate. One of them's that pretty little clerk-typist in Jim's office. Sue Stephen-son, from Dobbs. A real looker. Plays the pi-ano. Couldn't pry her loose to dance with me. Sally W. there, though, so the evening wasn't a total waste. She's always good for a laugh and a bit of—

Dr. Livingston gave an apologetic wave of his hand. "I *did* tell you that my father was as randy as a billy goat, didn't I?"

I smiled. "Does he get clinical?"

"I wish! No, it's just crude barnyard language. I'll spare you. This is from a few nights later." He turned back to the diary.

"*Finally got Sue S. to dance with me. Betty Grable gams, breasts like soft ripe peaches—*" From the sheepish look he gave me over the top of his glasses, I had a feeling that his father had used different words. "Sorry. He goes on to catalog your mother's beauty and her many physical charms and then says she just laughed at him when he tried to put the moves on her. She wasn't the first nor the last to resist him and he was usually pretty philosophical about it when he got turned down. Here's what he wrote about her when she slapped him down a week or two later: *With so much low-hanging fruit, a man would be a sap to let himself stay blue just because he can't take a bite out of every apple on the tree."*

"Poor man," I said.

He grinned. "Don't cry for him, Argentina. He got through a lot more apples than most men. I think he and your mother eventually became friends. Or maybe sparring partners would be more accurate. She teased him about being a sheep in wolf's clothing, because he never really forced himself on a woman. Just took advantage of any opportunities. But then I found this."

Sue's taken Captain Walter Raynesford McIntyre under her wing at the club. They sit and talk whenever she's not playing the piano. Anybody else and I'd be jealous because she'll dance with him but not with me because he doesn't try to feel her up.

He opened to a bookmarked page much deeper in the diary. "This is from three months later."

Saw Sue at the club tonight. She says Mac finally got the orders he wanted and flew out yesterday. Have to say the guy's got guts. I'll go if I'm sent, but I'm not volunteering. Sue's certain he'll be killed and under the circumstances, maybe that's what he wants. Wouldn't want to be him.

Dr. Livingston closed the diary. "There's only one more casual mention of her and none about McIntyre. Shortly after that, Dad was transferred to Walter Reed and finished out the war there."

"So even though he and Mac were both from New Bern, it doesn't sound as if they were particularly close."

He shrugged. "Well, he would have been a little older and he was probably upper-class town while my dad was a country nobody. Raynesfords ran the town a hundred years ago and set the tone for strict morality and civic responsibility. Defenders of the faith and all that."

"Really?" I was surprised. "I visited Josephine Raynesford right before I came here and that's not how she struck me. In fact, I gather that she wanted to open the faith to everybody."

"Oh, you heard about that, did you? Yes, she marched and demonstrated with the best of them in her day. Bet her ancestors almost rolled out of their marble mausoleums. All water under the bridge now and the name's pretty much died out except for Miss Jo and Walter. He's got a son, but the boy lives with Walter's ex wife up in Raleigh and I doubt if he'll ever come back in New Bern."

He placed the diary back on the bookshelf behind his chair. "Was Miss Jo related to Captain McIntyre?"

"I believe they were second or third cousins through his mother and she didn't know the name till I asked her, but she found him in a notebook her mother compiled."

"Did she have more information about him?"

"He wasn't killed in the war," I said, abruptly deciding not to bring Edgar Middlewood into it. "He died in Paris. That's all she could say for sure."

"Interesting."

We spoke a few minutes more and as I thanked him for his time, he said, "I hope you don't mind, but my father was so taken with your mother that I have to ask—was it a happy marriage?"

"Very happy," I said.

"You were lucky, then."

"His marriage wasn't?" I asked.

Dr. Livingston shrugged. "Don't ask me. They stayed together for fifty-two years and they were always polite to each other and kind to us kids. He was quite successful. Gave her anything she wanted except fidelity. She pretended not to know and eventually, I suppose she quit caring."

As I drove home with the afternoon sun in my eyes, I was okay with what I had and hadn't learned. Jo Raynesford might or might not be right about Leslie and why she had killed herself. I might never know Mac's whole story or precisely why Mother said he'd changed her life, but for the moment, that was no longer important to me. She and Daddy had loved each other utterly and completely and that love had spilled over to my brothers and me.

What else does any child really need to know?

CHAPTER

14

Thou shalt not steal.

— Exodus 20:15

DWIGHT BRYANT—TUESDAY, AUGUST 19

Breakfast that morning consisted of toasted bagels and sweet chunks of chilled cantaloupe from their garden, served with a side dish of fresh *Clarion* innuendos.

The lead story—"Victim's Uncle Questions Lack of Progress"—was based on an interview the paper's editor had conducted with Joby Earp.

"My nephew's body was found on what used to be our family's land till Kezzie Knott fast-talked my daddy out of it," Earp was quoted as saying. "How hard is the sheriff's department really looking at him and why is his son-in-law in charge of the investigation? Major Bryant asked me for my alibi. Did he ask for Knott's?"

Deborah's blue eyes flashed upon reading that aloud. "But you did ask him," she said.

"I know, shug, and so does the *Clarion*. They probably also know that Joby Earp's alibi is just as unsubstantiated as Mr. Kezzie's."

"What's unsubstantiated?" asked Cal.

"Means not proven. No one's confirmed that it's true," Deborah said.

"Why does Granddaddy need an alibi?"

"Because he and the Earps have had disagreements in the past," Dwight said.

"But Uncle Robert and Uncle Haywood didn't like that man that got killed either."

"Why do you say that, buddy?"

Cal shrugged and took another bite of his cantaloupe. Orange juice ran down his chin and Deborah handed him a fresh napkin before it could drip onto his T-shirt. "They were talking about him Sunday. I think they used to get in fights when they were kids. They said his uncle was a mean man, too. Uncle Haywood said he was always looking to yell at them."

Dwight grinned at him. "Maybe I ought to check *their* alibis."

"Oh, Dad!" And Cal went back to the comics while Dwight finished reading the *Clarion* story Deborah had abandoned.

Buried at the end of it was another appeal to the public for anyone with information about the death or the whereabouts of the victim's truck, which was described in detail.

When Dwight got to the office, Deputy Mayleen Diaz's freckled face was flushed with triumph.

"Jerome Williman was arrested in Buncombe County last night!"

"Great," Dwight said. "Now remind me who Jerome Williman is."

"Two weeks ago. The shaken baby case up near the Wake County line."

"Oh. Right. How's she doing?"

"Still in a coma on life support." Unconsciously, Mayleen touched her expanding waistline in a protective gesture. "No matter how many times we see it, I'll never understand why somebody can do that to a baby."

"How'd they catch him?"

"Expired registration sticker. He was parked at a Bojangles outside Asheville and a sheriff's deputy stopped by for a chicken biscuit. He noticed the sticker on his way out the door, ran the plate, and Williman popped right up on his computer."

"Good man," said Dwight. "Thank the Buncombe sheriff and ask if they want to ship him over to us or do we need to have somebody go fetch him."

A moment later, he had a call from the police chief down in Makely, about twenty-five minutes south of Dobbs. "Major Bryant? Jimmy Locklear here. I think we've found that red Ford pickup you're looking for."

"No joke?"

"No joke." He rattled off the license plate number and it matched Vick Earp's. "Guy from Cotton Grove said he read today's paper before driving down here to see his mother. He stopped to pick up some spark plugs at one of our auto repair shops and the truck was parked out front. He took pictures of the license plate and the windshield with the bullet hole on the passenger side and then drove right over to the station. Give me your email address and I'll send them to you."

"Is it still there?"

"Sorry. I drove past a few minutes ago, but it was gone and I didn't stop 'cause I figured you'd want to speak to the manager yourself."

"Thanks," Dwight said.

Without waiting for the pictures, he called to Ray McLamb and the two of them headed for Makely. Normally, Dwight drove a sedate four or five miles under the speed limit, but today it was flashing blue lights and a siren as he wove in and out of traffic in the unmarked sedan. Once inside the town limits, Dwight turned them off so as to approach inconspicuously. By then, Mayleen had relayed the pictures. Two men stood in front of the truck, but both had their backs to the camera.

Locklear had given him directions to the repair shop, part of a national chain. When they entered, no one was inside except a clerk who was stocking the shelves and the manager who was on his computer. He stood up briskly when they entered. "Help you, gentlemen?"

The name embroidered on the pocket of his green denim shirt was L. Roberts.

Dwight showed him his badge and then the picture on his phone. "This you, Mr. Roberts?"

Clearly it was. The same green shirt, the same khaki pants, same stocky build, same head of thick white hair.

"What's this about?" he asked in an accent that

sounded more like Chicago or Cleveland than Colleton County.

"We're looking for this truck and whoever's driving it."

"Because of that bullet hole?"

"That's part of it."

"Y'know, I had a feeling something wasn't right with that kid. Real antsy he was."

"You know his name?"

Roberts shook his head. "Never saw him before. He wanted an estimate for the windshield and a new paint job." He gestured toward the computer. "That's what I was looking up. Doubt if he can afford either one. Just another goofy kid. Doesn't look like his old man's name is Rockefeller either. I did get his number, though. Told him I'd call him and let him know how much it was gonna run."

"You think you could talk him into coming back in?" Dwight asked.

"You still didn't say why you want him."

"The truck belonged to a murder victim over in Cotton Grove."

"Really? Hmmm. Let me think." Roberts ran his hand through his prematurely white hair. "Okay. This might do it."

He touched the numbers on his cell phone and Dwight heard him say, "This is Les. You the guy that was in the repair shop about an hour ago? You wanted an estimate on some replacement glass for your F-150? It's your lucky day. I found what might work for you already here. Some guy ordered it and never picked it up. I was going to send it back by UPS this afternoon, but if it'll fit your truck and you can get over here before I pack it up, I can let you have it real cheap. Save me the cost of shipping."

He listened with a smile on his face and flashed Dwight and Ray the OK sign with his thumb and index finger. "Okay, pal. See you in twenty minutes."

His smile grew even broader as he clipped the phone back to his belt. "My girlfriend keeps telling me I ought to be a writer, all the stories I make up."

The skinny young white man who got out of Vick Earp's truck twenty-two minutes later had a bad case of acne and stringy yellow hair that brushed his shoulders. No more than seventeen or eighteen, Dwight decided, and still climbing Fool's Hill if he thought painting a red truck black would be enough to disguise it without a different license plate. He came bounding through the doorway and up to the counter with a happy smile of anticipation on his face, but as soon as Dwight tapped him on the shoulder and said, "Colleton County Sheriff's Department," he whirled around and raced back outside, straight into the arms of Deputy Ray McLamb, who had waited there in case he tried to run.

Dwight thanked the shop manager for his help and joined Ray in the parking lot.

"What's your name, son?"

With his hands cuffed behind him, the boy was defiant. "I don't have to tell y'all anything. I want a lawyer."

"Watch a lot of cop shows, huh?" said Ray. "Where you want him, boss?"

The rear of the unmarked car they'd driven down in was outfitted with bars and a divider for transporting suspects.

"Put him in the cage," said Dwight and he put in a call for a tow truck to take the pickup back to Dobbs.

The crime scene team was waiting when the tow truck made it to the department's parking lot and they went right to work on Vick Earp's truck.

In the interrogation room, the young truck thief had given them his name—Wayne Booker—but continued to insist he wanted an attorney.

"Good idea," Ray said easily. "Hope you can afford a smart one. Maybe he can get you off with life instead of a death sentence."

"Death?" Booker's voice went up two octaves and all the blood drained from his face. "I didn't kill nobody!"

"Wish you could tell us about it," said Dwight, regret in every syllable. "But we can't ask you anything till your attorney's present. Do you have one?"

Booker shook his head.

"Then you'll have to sit in jail till you can come before a judge who will appoint you one. In the meantime, Wayne Booker, I'm arresting you for the murder of Victor Earp. Anything you say—"

"Who the hell is Victor Earp?" the boy cried.

"The man whose truck you were driving. The man you carjacked."

"Carjacked? No! I didn't! I never! Honest! I found the truck."

"Book him," said Dwight.

"No! Wait! I take it back. I don't want a lawyer. I want to talk."

"You sure? You want to speak on the record of your own free will?"

Booker nodded.

"Okay, then. Turn on the recorder, Ray."

After the formalities were recorded, Dwight said, "Now then, Wayne Booker. Tell us how you came to be driving Victor Earp's pickup."

"I found it. I thought maybe it'd been abandoned because of the way the windshield was shot up."

"Found it where?"

"Down by the railroad tracks, near the creek. I live on the south side of Cotton Grove where Forty-eight and Old Forty-eight and the tracks all cross Possum Creek."

Although passenger service had been discontinued decades earlier, a freight line still bisected Cotton Grove on its way to Fuquay-Varina and points west. Trees and thick shrubbery hid most of the track from view and muffled the noises in summer, but in winter, when Dwight was a boy and the wind was right, the train whistle could be heard at night all the way out to the farm. A lonesome sound, yet somehow, oddly comforting.

"I cut through there on my bicycle all the time and I saw the truck backed up in the bushes last week."

"When?" asked Dwight. "What day?"

"Monday. I didn't think nothing about it. Thought someone was out on the creek fishing. But it was there on Tuesday, same exact spot. Wednesday I went fishing and it was still there. Hadn't been moved. It was unlocked and when I opened the door, the keys were just laying there on the seat, so I cranked it up. Half thought someone would come running and yell at me, but nobody did. There's a service track beside the railroad, so I put my bike in the back and drove it on down to an old shed I know and I left it there till today. I figured somebody might recognize it if I tried to get the windshield fixed there in town, so that's why I took it to Makely. How'd y'all find me so quick?"

"We've been asking people to keep an eye out for that truck," said Dwight. "I guess you don't read the newspaper."

"I don't read nothing. Get all my news offen the TV," Wayne Booker said with a scornful shrug of his thin shoulders. "Wait a minute, though! Is that the dude that got dumped out on Kezzie Knott's land?"

"You know Kezzie Knott?"

"Know who he is. My grandmother's brother used to make shine for him."

Dwight sighed. Sometimes he felt as if everybody in the whole damn county was connected to Mr. Kezzie one way or another through moonshine whiskey.

After lunch, with Wayne Booker fingerprinted and stashed in an interrogation room but not yet formally charged, Dwight and the team working on the case gathered to discuss what had been learned from Vick Earp's pickup.

"That must be how he was transported out to where he was dumped, Major," said Sam Dalton. "We found blood on the gas pedal and in the truck bed. Probably his. Crabtree's taken them out to Dr. Singh." He grinned. "She said she'd try to sweet-talk him into giving her a rough analysis right away."

Deputy Janice Crabtree was thirty-seven, blond, and attractive. She also had an associate degree in biology from the community college and loved to talk medical forensics with Dr. Singh, so there was a very good chance they could hear the results before the end of the day.

"We got the slug that went through the windshield." Dalton handed Dwight a small plastic bag. "Looks like a deer slug from a smooth-bore twelve-gauge shotgun just like the one we brought in from the brother. We can get a warrant for his ammo and do a test firing."

"Find any prints?" Dwight asked.

"The only useable ones in the cab are Booker's and the victim's. In fact, Booker's seemed to be on every surface—glove box, radio, CDs, mirror, GPS. I swear he was like a monkey looking for peanuts. We found a lot of Earp's prints but Booker's are the only clear ones on the steering wheel, gearshift, door handles, or the vinyl. His prints overlay all the others. Same with the latch on the tailgate."

"Maybe we can get something useful if the kid shows us where he found the truck," said Dwight.

"Earp was killed over a week ago," one of the team said dubiously.

"But it hasn't rained since then," Dalton reminded him. "We're supposed to get some tonight, though, so right now's probably our best chance."

"Get Booker," Dwight told McLamb.

Considering the amount of traffic on Highway 48—called "New 48" by longtime locals—and the old highway that followed the creek into Cotton Grove, the spot where the rails crossed under both roads was surprisingly isolated, a bit of waste ground made unattractive by the underpass, which sank the rails several feet lower than the surrounding ground level. Before the county built waste disposal sites twenty years ago, it had been an illegal dumping ground and an occasional refrigerator or box springs could still be seen rusting away under the weedy bushes.

They parked off the road near a break in the shrubbery that masked the railroad tracks. This was where Booker said he usually entered on his bike to get to the creek bank. Following along behind him, they cast their eyes right and left for any possible evidence that someone besides Wayne Booker had walked there. The ground was hard and baked dry by the last ten days of hot August sun. Even the wiregrass and sandspurs looked withered and half-dead.

"Yonder's where he probably drove in," said Booker, pointing to a rough dirt lane that led from Old 48 to the tracks.

Beyond that, around a bend in the service road that paralleled the tracks, was a stand of tall trashy shrubs: privet, wax myrtles, and sumac.

"And right here's where I found it," said Booker.

The bushes showed broken twigs with withered and dying leaves and several had been snapped off entirely. Tire tracks were still visible and there were faint tracks from Booker's bicycle. If the killer had left shoe prints when he got out of the truck, they were now scuffed over by the kid's sneakers.

Dalton paid particular attention to the twigs that

might have snagged a shirt or hair when the driver got out of the cab, but came up empty.

"You see?" said Booker. "Somebody backed it in here as far as it would go and just left it, so it wasn't really stealing. It's like when somebody leaves stuff out with the garbage and you take it off the curb. I got a guitar like that once. Nobody wanted it."

"And you really thought nobody wanted a two-year-old pickup in good running condition?" McLamb asked sarcastically.

Still trying to justify his actions, the boy was insistent. "Y'all saw that bullet hole in the windshield. Looked to me like somebody'd been trying to kill whoever's truck it was and he just didn't want to drive it anymore 'cause he was like a moving target, you know? That's why I was going to get it painted black. It was here at least three days. Maybe even longer, so it wasn't really stealing. Come on, you guys. I helped y'all. You know I did. You'd still be looking for it if I hadn't driven it down to Makely."

Dwight shook his head, amused by the boy's reasoning. "Next time you find a vehicle hidden away somewhere, call us first, okay?"

"I can go?" Booker asked hopefully.

They hadn't officially charged him, so he wasn't in the system yet and Dwight didn't see much point in hauling him into court for the slap on the wrist that he'd probably get.

"Yeah, you can go this time."

"Cool! Thanks, Major Bryant!" he said and loped back down the way they'd come, toward his home.

Turning to his deputies, Dwight said, "I'll go talk to

Mrs. Earp again and let her know that we've found the truck. Y'all spread out and canvass the houses along the tracks and on both sides of where the truck probably drove in. I know it's been at least ten days, but maybe someone will remember seeing something. Unless the killer had an accomplice, he probably left on foot."

"Or on a bicycle like Booker," McLamb said, wiping the sweat from his face. "Too bad the South got so air-conditioned. Not many people sitting out on their porches these evenings. They're all inside where it's cool, with their eyes glued on some screen or other."

As they walked back to their cars to begin the canvass, a freight train slowly rumbled past pulling dozens of flatcars, all loaded with pine logs harvested from tree farms down near the coast. McLamb turned to Dwight with a broad grin. "What d'you think, Major? Reckon our killer hitched a ride? Slow as it's going, it wouldn't be hard to grab on the side and step up on one of those bars."

"I don't know, Ray. At night?"

"Full moon that night," McLamb argued.

Just then, Dalton turned to Dwight with his phone to his ear.

"It's Crabtree, boss. Dr. Singh's done a quick and dirty and says it looks like Vick Earp's blood for both samples." He laughed at something Janice Crabtree must have said. "Singh wants to know if it's a tiger this time around."

"*What?* He found more cat blood?"

"That's what she says. From the bed *and* from the gas pedal."

They paused by Dwight's truck to discuss what this might mean.

"So maybe someone drove up in the yard while Vick Earp was picking up the broken glass," Dwight mused.

"Someone Earp'd pissed off," said Ray McLamb. "And the cat gets between 'em and one of them stomps it to death."

"Or maybe Earp killed it," Dalton suggested, "and the other person says, 'Hey, good idea!' and stomps Earp?"

"But where's the cat?" asked Dwight. "Why put it in the back of the truck? And cat blood on the gas pedal? When did Earp drive the truck after the cat was killed?"

"Maybe he wasn't the only one who stepped in the cat blood. It could've been whoever killed him and drove the truck out to the creek," said Dalton. "I don't know how we missed it unless some animal dragged it off, but we could go back out to where Earp was dumped and take another look for it."

Dwight nodded. "Get the canvass started, Ray, while I go talk to Mrs. Earp and I'll meet you and Dalton out there in an hour."

At the Earp house, Marisa Young's minivan was once again parked under the carport beside Mrs. Earp's car. As he walked up the drive a man was loading cardboard boxes into the back of the van. Sweat dampened the back of his gray T-shirt. The trunk and backseat of the car were packed with clothes and cartons of small kitchen appliances. The tool shed's double doors stood wide open and the shed was now crammed with tables, chairs, and some floor lamps. More boxes were stacked on the back porch.

The door was open, but before he could call or knock, Rosalee Earp came out with her arms full of men's clothing still on hangers.

"Tyler, you can— Oh! Major Bryant!"

Startled by his unexpected appearance, she stepped back and a winter jacket slid off the hanger to fall on the floor between them.

"I thought you were Tyler," she said.

"Sorry." He picked up the jacket. "I should have called first, let you know I was coming."

"That's okay." As the man came over to them, she said, "Do you know Vick's brother?"

"Dwight Bryant," he said. "Sheriff's Department. You're Tyler Earp?"

"Yeah. These for me, Rosy?"

When Mrs. Earp nodded, he took the clothes and carried them over to his truck.

Not only did the brothers have the same beefy build, thought Dwight, they both favored red Ford pickups. But whereas Vick's had been uncluttered and clean except for the blood, the back of Tyler's held an assortment of paint buckets, ladders, and some paint-smeared tarps. The cab had a gun rack over the rear window. Empty now.

"Tyler's helping me move," said Mrs. Earp, "and I'm giving him Vick's things."

She wore a sleeveless red tank top and knee-length beige shorts and her legs were surprisingly shapely. Her face was flushed from the heat, tendrils of graying brown hair had pulled loose from her ponytail and the humidity made them curl around her forehead, giving her a younger look.

"You're moving?"

She nodded. "I don't want to stay here any longer and Marisa's invited me to come live with her for now. See if we can stand each other. We're going to hold a yard sale this weekend."

"Rosy?" Miss Young came to the door. "What do you want to do with— Oh, hello, Major Bryant. Any news about Vick?"

She was perspiring even more than her cousin and wiped her hot face on the wristband of her long-sleeved tan T-shirt, before holding out a box of saucepans and colanders. "Yard sale or keep? You know I've got a ton of pots and pans."

"Yard sale, then," Mrs. Earp said. "But I do want to keep that iron skillet."

Miss Young handed her the skillet, then carried the box out to the tool shed.

"Come on in, Major," said Mrs. Earp. She set the skillet on the kitchen counter. "Everything's a mess, but we haven't dismantled the living room yet. Sorry about the heat, but with all this in and out, I've turned off the air-conditioning. No point trying to cool off the yard."

Despite the open doors and windows and some portable fans to stir the air, the house was hot and stuffy. She had spread white cotton sheets over the dark velour couch and chairs, which made them marginally cooler to sit on.

Dwight took a seat in front of a fan while Mrs. Earp

perched on the end of the couch where her cousin soon joined her.

"Don't need any living room furniture, do you?" Miss Young asked. "We could probably get Tyler to help you get it in your truck."

Dwight smiled. "Sorry. So, you're going to share a house?"

Miss Young smiled back. "I'm going to teach her how to be a slob."

"Oh, Marisa," Mrs. Earp protested. "You're not a slob."

"Not what Vick used to say."

"Oh well, you know Vick." She turned back to Dwight. "Is there any news? Have you found out who killed him?"

"Not yet, ma'am, but we did find his truck. Somebody tried to hide it down by the railroad tracks where it passes under Old Forty-eight."

"It wasn't wrecked, was it?" she asked.

"A little scratched up on the tailgate, but that's all."

"Good. The windshield Vick ordered has come in and they said I'd lose the deposit if I didn't take it. When can I get it back?"

"We'll bring it out to you when we're finished with it. Probably by tomorrow. I have to tell you, though— we found your husband's blood in the back."

Mrs. Earp's eyes widened.

"We think that's how his body got out to the country. He was probably attacked out there in your yard and then carried away in the truck to where he was left for dead."

When she didn't speak, Dwight said, "Have you

remembered anything more that might help us? Any enemies he had, people who might've had a grudge?"

She shook her head. "I told you, Major Bryant. Vick wasn't very social. He kept to himself, and didn't have any real friends. Didn't seem to need them. We never had anyone over except family. Marisa and Tyler and once in a long while his uncle. Joby and Earla. He said he got enough of people during the week and just wanted to work around the house or in the yard on the weekends."

"What about you, Mr. Earp?" Dwight said as Tyler Earp slowed in his walk down the hall.

The man scowled. "What about me?"

"Have any suggestions as to who might have killed your brother?"

He shrugged. "We didn't hang out together much. He thought he was better than me."

"That's not true, Tyler," Mrs. Earp said in a placating tone. "He just wanted you to make more of yourself."

"Whatever. Say, aren't you the deputy they talked about in the paper? Married to Kezzie Knott's daughter?"

"You know her?"

"Naw. Know who she is, though. We used to live out there when she was just a baby."

"I guess you feel he stole your land, too," Dwight said.

Tyler Earp shook his head with a sour laugh. "Me? No. That was Vick and Joby. They were the farmers in the family. Not me. I hated working in tobacco. Best day of my life up to then was when we moved off and

I didn't have to do it no more." He grinned at the two women. "Remember that time we went back out there for a picnic? How he almost cried talking about how great it was to work your own land?"

Miss Young nodded. "He sang that song every time anybody mentioned it. Got mad when you said that the only good thing about the place was swimming in the creek."

"He always wanted to farm," Mrs. Earp said softly.

"Won't much of a farmer," said Earp. "Him or Joby neither. Didn't break even some years."

"Yet to hear him tell it, they could have paid off the mortgage if Kezzie Knott had just given them another year," said Miss Young.

"And if you believe that, I got some oceanfront property in Arizona I'll sell you," he said scornfully. "Both of 'em sure hated Kezzie Knott, though. Blamed him for everything that went wrong out there. Blamed him for Joby going to jail this last time. Reckon you'd know better'n me how he felt about them, Major. Way I remember it, Kezzie Knott used to be real handy with his fists. With his gun, too. And that reminds me. When do I get my shotgun back?"

"Soon as we see if it fired the slug we recovered from your brother's truck. If it matches, you might owe Mrs. Earp for that windshield."

"Excuse me, Major," Mrs. Earp said timidly, "but can Tyler be charged with anything if nobody ever called the police? Vick never did and it was his truck."

"If you want your insurance to cover it, you'll need to file a police report," Dwight told her.

"I'll pay for it, Rosy," said Tyler. "It's not that much."

"We'll work something out ourselves, Major. Tyler's helping me move and he's going to help spruce up this house so it'll sell quickly."

"Yeah?"

Earp put his hand over his heart. "God's honest truth."

Dwight threw up his own hands in surrender. "All right. We'll let it drop if you're sure that's what you want?"

"It is," said Mrs. Earp.

"So when can I get it back?" asked Earp.

"I'll have someone drop it off," Dwight said.

As he reached the porch, the bloodstain on the step reminded him. "About your cat, ma'am..."

"Diesel?" Hope blossomed in her thin face. "You found him? Where is he? Is he hurt? Rusty said you told her he was dead."

"I'm afraid he is, ma'am." He pointed to the bloodstain. "He lost a lot of blood there, and we found more traces of it in the truck bed."

Mrs. Earp stared at the step, appalled. "In the *truck*? I don't understand. Someone killed Diesel and then carried him off in the truck, too? Why?" Her eyes filled with tears. "That poor sweetie. Everybody loved him."

"Not everybody, Rosy," said her cousin, handing her a tissue.

"Vick got impatient with him, yes, but he'd never do something like that. *Never!*"

She looked at them beseechingly. "Besides, even if he didn't like Diesel, he wouldn't let someone else hurt him. You know how he was."

Surprisingly, Tyler Earp agreed with her. "What was

his, was his and he'd never let anybody else mess with his things without a fight. Even things he didn't want. I remember out at the farm once, playing baseball. We were using a bat he'd whittled out of a tree limb and it split when he hit the ball. He threw it off in the bushes, but next day, one of the Knott twins—I think it was Haywood—had taped it up so it could still be used and I thought they were going to beat each other to death because Vick said it was his and Haywood kept saying 'Finders, keepers.' Robert had to pull 'em apart and make him give it back to Vick. Soon as we got home, though, Vick put it in the woodstove. He just didn't want somebody else to have what was his."

A classic dog in the manger, thought Dwight. But over a cat? A cat he didn't even like?

"I'll be in touch about the truck," he said and headed back to his own truck.

By the time Dwight got out to the farm lane where they'd found Vick Earp's body, Sam Dalton and Ray McLamb had already searched the area where the body had lain.

"No sign of the cat, Major, and I didn't see any buzzards or crows fly off when I drove up," Ray said. "You, Sam?"

The other deputy shook his head. "No, but the way coyotes are moving into the state, it could have been carried off deeper into the woods."

Nevertheless, a careful search up and down the edge of the branch did not give them any black cat fur.

"Weird," said Dalton. "Why dump it somewhere else?"

"For that matter, why kill it at all?" asked Ray.

Dwight told them what he'd learned from talking with Earp's wife and brother. "Maybe it really was a spur-of-the-moment burst of anger. Somebody hurts the cat and he goes off on them and winds up getting the worst of it."

They searched for another half hour before giving up and calling it a day.

CHAPTER

15

He causeth the vapors to ascend
from the ends of the earth; he maketh
lightnings for the rain.

— Psalms 135:7

I stepped out of the cool courthouse that afternoon into such brutal August heat, I could feel myself melting inside my sleeveless blue linen dress. The turquoise and green beads of my chunky necklace lay on my neck like a hot mule collar. Worse, the air was so heavy with humidity that I wondered if those dark clouds building on the western horizon meant we were in for something more than a summer thunderstorm. Our local NPR hadn't mentioned hurricanes in the morning report, but it sure felt like hurricane weather; and when Luther Parker stopped me on the sidewalk, all I wanted to do was keep walking to my car so I could crank up the AC and dry out.

Luther came to the bench a few months before me, our district's first black judge. We faced each other in

a runoff the first time we ran for judge and he won.
Not surprising, considering that I had just shot and
nearly killed one of Colleton County's more prominent
citizens, so I didn't hold it against him. But we have
adjoining offices upstairs.

Air-conditioned offices.

Why did we need to conference on a sidewalk hot
enough to scramble eggs when we could have talked in
comfort?

But then he said, "What can you tell me about Marcus Williams, Deborah?" and I stopped in dismay.

Marcus Williams is one of those kids who touch
my heart. He's seventeen and lives here in Dobbs with
his grandmother and two younger sisters. He's light-
fingered and can't resist stealing things for the girls,
things that his grandmother can't afford despite working two jobs, yet there's an inner core of sweetness
that reminds me of my favorite nephews and keeps me
from throwing the book at him. I hadn't seen him since
he helped Aunt Zell and me break into an empty house
back in May and I had hoped he was staying out of
trouble.

"Please don't tell me he was up before you today?"

"No, no," said Luther, "but that has to be the luck
of the draw considering how many times you've had
him."

"You looked up his record?"

"And asked your bailiff."

"Why?"

He handed me a cheaply printed business card. *Williams is willing...* was printed at the top followed by
Marcus's full name and a telephone number. Across

the bottom were small pictographs of basic mainte-
nance equipment: stepladder, paintbrush, lawn mower,
rake, clippers, and a bucket.

"He's started a handyman service?"

"And my sister wants to hire him. Her husband has
a heart condition and her son's interning in Washington—did I tell you? Cyl DeGraffenreid had an opening
in her firm up there."

Cyl used to be an assistant DA here before she
joined a prestigious black lobbyist firm in D.C. We
keep up with each other through Facebook, but I hadn't
talked to her in a couple of months. Much as I'd have
loved to hear more, it was too hot to linger out there in
the sun.

"Marcus Williams," I reminded Luther, returning
the boy's business card.

"Right. Anyhow, my sister needs someone depend-
able to do their yard work, which is why she asked me
to check out his reference. Is he honest, hardworking,
and worth fifteen dollars an hour?"

"I'm his reference?"

"Told my sister you knew he could be trusted to do
the right thing."

I had to laugh at that. But yes, he could have burned
through the credit card he used after I'd tried (and
failed) to jimmy that lock with it. I forgot to ask for
it back and he could have gone on a shopping spree.
Instead, he returned it the next day, along with Uncle
Ash's crowbar that Aunt Zell had brought with her as
a backup to my credit card.

"He's basically a good kid that's been handed the
short end of a stick," I said. "If he can finish school and

get a couple of breaks, he's bright enough to do any-thing he sets his mind to. Your sister needs to be real specific about what she wants him to do, but if he says he'll do it, I think he will."

"That's good enough for me," Luther said and headed for his own car.

Dwight's truck was parked by the back door when I got home, but there was no sign of him nor of Cal. A slight breeze stirred the tiny graceful limbs of a young wil-low near the garage. Not enough to cool, yet enough to bring me the smell of coming rain, along with the faint rumble of distant thunder.

Inside, I changed into cutoffs and a tank top, kicked off my blue slingback heels for slip-on straw sandals, then went looking for my menfolks.

They were nowhere in the house, but by the time I stepped outside, the wind had strengthened and I heard voices coming from the pond. I walked down the slope to see Cal out in the rowboat with Haywood and Robert, a few hundred feet from the pier where Dwight stood. Robert was bareheaded as usual, but Haywood had his porkpie hat pushed down on his forehead as he rowed for the pier.

"Hurry!" Dwight called and pointed to the thun-derheads, which were picking up speed. I watched as they blotted out the sun, making everything suddenly darker.

As lightning flashed across the sky, Haywood picked up his own pace with the oars.

The wind was gusting strongly now and there was less and less time between seeing the flash and hearing the thunder. I ran down to the pier, ready to help them out of the boat. As soon as they got close enough, Robert threw the rope to Dwight, who tied it around a post.

Robert handed me the fishing poles and climbed up the ladder while Dwight reached down for Cal's hands and swung him onto the pier just as the rain reached us. This was no soft, gentle rain. The drops were fat and heavy and hit my face and arms as if I were being pelted with small water balloons. With Haywood lumbering along behind, we ran for the house, but all five of us were drenched before we made it through the open garage door.

Safely under shelter now, we looked out and watched thick sheets of rain sweep across the yard. Thunder crashed all around us as lightning forked from the black sky and we all jumped when it struck a tall pine at the edge of the field on the far side of the pond. Cal immediately tucked himself under Dwight's arm in mingled fear and excitement. A moment later, hail began to bounce on the concrete apron outside the garage. Haywood would later swear the marble-sized hailstones were big as golf balls.

The worst of the storm passed as quickly as it had come. The hail stopped, but rain continued to pour down, sluicing off the eaves. We've never bothered with gutters because water seldom stands long in our sandy soil, so curtains of rainwater fell from the roof and the wind blew some of it in on us until Dwight lowered the doors. We went through the kitchen to chairs on the back porch, away from the wind, and I fetched towels to dry our hair. Thin clouds of steam rose in the fields beyond our yard as cool rain met with hot dirt and the temperature had dropped several degrees. I was even thinking about a sweater when Cal said, "My fish! Did anybody bring the bucket up?"

"Don't worry about 'em, son," Robert said. "They'll just keep swimming around in the bucket, although with this much rain, the bucket might overflow and they're liable to jump back in the pond."

"But we were going to have them for supper."

"Supper?" said Haywood, looking hopeful.

He and Robert had parked at the far end of the pond and I could hardly throw them out in such heavy rain.

"Call Isabel and Doris and tell them that you'll eat with us," I said.

I rummaged in the pantry and in less than thirty minutes, we sat down to tuna salad and sliced tomatoes with hot crispy rounds of cornbread on the side. Dwight drew four glasses of his homemade ale for us and poured milk for Cal.

The rain began to slack off as we finished eating, but it was still heavy enough that no one was anxious to retrieve a truck.

"A million-dollar rain," my brothers said, referring to all the crops that had been close to drying up in the field.

"Saved our garden," Dwight agreed, "although I hate to think what that wind may've done to the corn."

As we drifted back out to the porch rockers for coffee, Robert said, "Guess y'all still don't know who killed Vick Earp, do you?"

Haywood scowled at him. "We don't need to be talking about that."

Cal looked from one to the other, then said, "You gonna ask 'em about their alibis, Dad?"

"Huh?" said Haywood, easing his bulk into one of the rocking chairs.

From the next chair, Robert said, "Alibi for what?"

Dwight frowned at Cal. "Do you remember what I said about not repeating things to do with my work?"

Abashed, Cal dropped his head. "Sorry, Dad."

"I think you should go clean up the kitchen," he said mildly.

Grateful to escape so lightly, Cal disappeared inside.

"Alibis for what?" Robert's voice was more belligerent this time.

"Cal heard us talking about Daddy and what the *Clarion*'s been printing about Dwight not questioning him hard enough," I said, trying to pour oil on their troubled waters.

Dwight was more forthright. "Saturday, when I asked if any of y'all recognized Vick Earp, nobody said anything. We could've started questioning people and trying to find witnesses twenty-four hours earlier if you or Mr. Kezzie had said something right then, Haywood."

Haywood humphed and stared out into the rain, silent for once.

"Vick Earp's brother—Tyler Earp? He says y'all used to fight a lot when they lived out here and that there was bad blood between the Earps and the Knotts. I asked Mr. Kezzie about it and he admitted there had been run-ins between him and Joby Earp and that you boys used to get into it, too."

"Well, yeah," said Robert. "No secret about that." He gave Haywood a puzzled look. "Why didn't you speak up?"

"Won't my place," he said with a mulish look on his face. "Daddy didn't say nothing, so I didn't either."

"See, Dwight, the Earps always acted like there was something crooked about the way Daddy got their land," Robert said. "I was real little but I remember Mr. Sammy. He used to make whiskey for Daddy, back when Daddy was still into it real big. Before Mama Sue made him quit." He grinned. "Or Mama Sue *thought* he'd quit. Remember, Dwight?"

That got an answering grin from my husband. "Don't remember Sammy Earp or Joby either, but I do remember cutting firewood with you boys till Miss Sue caught on that we weren't doing it for people to heat their houses with."

"Well, Mr. Sammy was right good-natured but he'd start drinking on a Friday night and stay drunk till Monday. He used to run a tab at the store for months at a time, then he'd cut off a piece of his land to settle up till there were just a little scrap of it left for Joby when he died. Joby was mean as a snake, though. He and Miss Earla took in Vick and Tyler but that was her, not him. Did you know he shot at Daddy one time and almost hit Mama Sue?"

"Huh?" said Haywood. "When did that happen?"

I was equally surprised. "You knew about that? How come I never did?"

He gave a sheepish smile. "I guess it was like Cal just now. I heard some men at the store talking about how they had to pull Daddy offen Joby before he killed him. I spoke out of turn, just like Cal did and Daddy said I'd get a licking if I talked about it again, especially in front of Mama Sue. That was right around the time they got married and he didn't want her to know, so I never did. It happened so long ago, I pretty much forgot about it till Vick went and got hisself killed."

"So when's the last time you saw him?" Dwight asked.

"Last fall maybe. October or November. Remember, Haywood? We was hunting rabbits out where Black Gum Branch runs into Possum Creek and Vick was there. Just setting on the tailgate of his truck looking out toward the creek and— Wait a minute! Won't that where Daddy found him?"

Dwight nodded.

"Haywood asked him what he was doing there and he said it was none of our damn business and you said you'd make it our business, right, Haywood? For a minute, I thought he was gonna take us both on, but he just let loose with more cussing, got in his truck, and drove away."

"Spit at us first, though, and give us the finger," said Haywood. "He was always touchy as a hornet and after they moved off to town, it was tail up, stinger out every time he saw us."

"Anyhow," said Robert, "if you asked Daddy, you might as well ask us. Doris can tell you I was with her all that weekend and I reckon Bel can say the same for Haywood."

Haywood gave a short nod and stood up. "Rain's slacked off enough that I reckon we won't wash away if one of y'all'll run us over to our trucks."

Normally, he's the last one to mention leaving.

We all stood, but when Dwight pulled out his keys, I plucked them from his hand. "I'll take them," I said. "Why don't you go talk to Cal?"

"We'll come back tomorrow to get the boat," Robert told him.

I kicked off my sandals and splashed barefoot across the yard to Dwight's truck where I maneuvered them so that Haywood wound up sitting between us on the bench seat. When I got to the end of the Long Pond where their pickups were, Robert headed straight to his, gave a wave of his hand, and headed down a lane to his house. Before Haywood could follow, I put a hand on his arm.

"What?" he said.

"When did you last see Vick Earp?" I asked.

"Whatcha talkin' about, Deb'rah?" he blustered. "You heard Robert."

"Yeah, I heard Robert. I didn't hear you."

"And you think that makes me a killer? Thank you very much, little sister." And with that, he levered his bulk out into the rain, pulled his porkpie hat down firmly on his big square head, and stomped off to his truck.

Did I really think Haywood could kill? No.

Did I think he could do something stupid that would give people—people being Dwight—the wrong idea?

Oh yes.

CHAPTER

16

Children, obey your parents.

— Ephesians 6:1

When I got home, the dishwasher was running, the counters were tidy, and Dwight and Cal were playing cribbage at the kitchen table. Cal was half a street ahead and they were both talking trash to each other, which meant that everything was back to normal between them.

I poured myself a cup of coffee, kibitzed for a while, then took a long soaking bath. Cal was watching a baseball game and Dwight was working on his computer when I came out, so I checked my email. Two inspirational forwards from Doris, a bawdy joke from Bel, and a reminder from Seth's wife about a political lunch next week. Minnie's my campaign manager and keeps tabs on whether or not I'm holding up my end. Karen had sent pictures to all of us of Adam and their two sons out in California. She tries to keep the family links strong and would love to have the boys spend some real time here on the farm. Several of us have invited them to come for extended visits but they keep finding perfectly valid reasons why they just can't be away for more than a weekend. Karen regrets that they'll never feel connected to their Colleton County roots but realistically, I know their roots were never here. The farm she grew up on was sold last fall when her mother died and Adam will probably sell his share of the family holdings after Daddy's gone.

"That's fine with me," Daddy says. "I ain't gonna try to run things from the grave. His part'll be one of the outlying farms near town. None of y'all need to worry about having a housing development plunked down at your back door, 'lessen that's what you want."

Adam is Zach's twin and the family's success story if you count money as success. He started a company that develops computer programs and esoteric applications for the banking industry. Don't ask me what, though. My brain went numb the time he tried to explain it. As a child, he hated the heat and dirt of farming and his one ambition was to work with computers in an air-conditioned office. Despite his BMW, his big house, and his swimming pool, Haywood, Robert, and Andrew feel a little bit sorry for him. They and their wives have visited him out there and they all came home saying it was real nice "but you couldn't pay me to live out there. Too many people and not enough trees."

I looked long and hard at the pictures of Adam's sons. Almost strangers and yet so familiar. One of them had a smile like Zach's son, Lee, and his eyebrows could have been lifted from Haywood's Stevie. Eyes, chins, noses—they were our eyes, chins, and noses. I sighed and printed out the pictures for Daddy.

Rain continued through the night and even though cooler air was predicted, the front seemed to have stalled over us. Next morning found Pennsylvania enjoying cool dry air while we were subjected to more heat and still more humidity. I could almost feel mildew poised to attack the white posts and railings of the porch when we walked out to the garden through thick muggy air.

Cal immediately ran over to read the rain gauge. "Four and a quarter inches," he reported.

A few stalks of corn had blown over and I held them straight while Dwight pulled wet dirt back over the roots with his boot and tamped it down.

When we got to the pond to check on Cal's fish, the rowboat was almost swamped and would need bailing before anyone could use it again. The two fish he'd caught were still swimming around in the bucket, but they were so much smaller than he'd remembered that he decided to let them grow a little longer and upended the bucket back into the water.

Dwight checked his watch. "Time to get moving, buddy."

"Okay," Cal said, casting a wistful eye at the boat.

I followed them back to the house, watched them leave, and then got dressed for court, wishing all the while that Dwight and I could forget about work and spend the day out on the pond fishing with Cal.

*   *   *

The morning session brought a couple of cases of domestic violence. Both women had fresh bruises and cuts and were there to seek restraining orders against the men, but while the white woman came across as timorous and defeated, her black counterpoint was boiling mad.

"I been subjugated, dominated, intimidated, and humiliated but if he ever raises his hand to me again, he's gonna be castrated. I put up with his mess when he was drinking, but a dry drunk that's this flat-out mean? No, ma'am, I'm not taking it any longer."

At the afternoon break, I found Dwight seated at the desk in my office. "Any chance you'll finish early this afternoon?" he asked.

"I have an emancipation petition and a couple of divorces," I said. "Why?"

"I need to get Vick Earp's truck back to his widow and since we live out that way, I thought I could drive his truck, you could drive mine and then ride in with me tomorrow."

"Okay," I said.

He stood up to go, then paused and very deliberately closed my office door. "Remember the first time I came up here to your office after you said you'd marry me?"

I smiled. Did I remember? Oh yes.

I went into his arms and this kiss was just as wonderful as that one. He took his time, slow and thorough, and I felt myself melting into the smell of him, the taste of him. "We've got to stop meeting like this less often," I murmured as his hand caressed my body and sent my pulse racing.

He laughed and kissed me again. "Feel free to text me any time."

Back in the courtroom, I took care of all the routine proceedings first, mostly a matter of approving arrangements worked out by the parties involved, signing orders, and setting new court dates for continuances.

Then came the juvenile petition for emancipation of one Eva Jones, age fifteen, white, bright, and much taken with her own importance. She stated that she had been forced to live with her father and stepmother and she wanted to be emancipated so that she could live where she wanted.

The father was there in court to oppose her petition. I let Miss Jones speak first.

"My mom's remarried to a drug addict and she kicked me out of the house because she's jealous of me. Thinks I flirt with her loser husband. She's an alcoholic and we fight all the time, but my stepmother hates me, too, and she makes me share a room with her ten-year-old daughter. I get good grades in school and I work twenty hours a week so I can pretty much support myself until I finish high school."

And just where did she plan to live until then?

"My boyfriend's mom says I can live with them," she said cheerfully, pointing to the woman who sat on the front row behind her next to a young man with those Justin Bieber eyes that young girls seem to find so sexy. "He's totally responsible, too. He's got his GED, he works full-time, and he's never missed a single support payment."

"Support payment?" I asked.

"Yeah, he had a baby with his ex-girlfriend."

"Are you having sex with him?"

"We're going to get married as soon as I'm emancipated, but I'm using birth control. No babies for me till I graduate from college."

I hardly knew where to begin. "You're a minor, Miss Jones. Do you realize that he could be arrested for statutory rape?"

Behind her that young man's eyes widened with apprehension.

"*Rape?*" She was indignant. "How is it rape if I want it, too? I told you. We're going to get married."

I looked at her lawyer, not the brightest star in our district's judicial sky. "Mr. Whitbread, why is she here in my court taking up our time?"

"I've been hired to advise her, Your Honor, and she's a very determined young lady."

"Who hired you?"

"Miss Jones."

I turned back to the petitioner. "Where did you get the money to hire an attorney, Miss Jones?"

"My boyfriend's mother lent it to me. I'm going to pay her back when I get my inheritance."

"Inheritance?"

"Yes, ma'am. My grandfather left me fifteen thousand dollars to go to college but I can't get it till then." She paused and looked at me speculatively. "Or if I'm emancipated, maybe I could get it right away?"

I spent the next ten minutes trying to explain the law to Miss Jones.

"You can't get emancipated just because you don't want to obey your parents or share a bedroom with your stepsister or because you want to have sex with someone who's obligated to support another woman's child until that child is eighteen. As for your inheritance, depending on your grandfather's will, you may not be able to spend that fifteen thousand on anything except college."

"That's not fair!" she exclaimed.

"When you're fifteen, life seldom is," I said bluntly. "I suggest that you make peace with your father and stepmother, finish high school, go to college, and find someone to marry who hasn't already made half his life choices by fathering a child while he's still living at home with his mother. Your petition for emancipation is denied."

Furious, the girl whirled away from her seat and stomped out of the courtroom, followed by Sexy Eyes and his mother.

"Thank you, Your Honor," said her father.

"Good luck," I told him and turned to the two divorces.

The first was simple and uncontested. All the formalities had been taken care of and both parties had signed all the necessary forms. All they needed was my signature.

The second had a property issue they hadn't yet settled. It had been to mediation and was now back to me. The Bumgardners were mid-forties and childless. He was an accountant, she taught high school math.

They'd already had their ED hearing in which their marital possessions had been, in layman's terms, equitably divided between them. That had been accomplished without major arguments or delays. Now it was just a matter of who would get custody of their dog, a two-year-old King Charles spaniel named Bertie.

They had not brought Bertie to court, but they had brought pictures and for the record, yes, he was adorable. He had been bought with their joint credit card and the credit card bill paid for from their joint bank account. I did not sense any anger between the two humans, just a strong attachment to the animal. Neither disputed the other's affection for the dog or claimed that it liked one of them better than the other, but Mrs. Bumgardner argued that she was the one who had found him at a reputable kennel, that she walked him most of the time, and, since she was retaining the Colleton County house with its large yard, that it would be less traumatic for Bertie to live with her rather than in her ex-husband's Raleigh apartment.

Mr. Bumgardner argued that he was the one who had driven to Tennessee to fetch the dog from the kennel and that the only reason she walked him more was because her teaching schedule gave her the summer off and allowed her to get home earlier every afternoon during the school year. "I take him out every morning and I give him his evening walk if she hasn't already done it. Bertie's an indoor dog, Your Honor. We've never let him out in the yard alone. Besides, my apartment's next to a park with a fenced-in dog area if he wants to run off the leash. And yes, she got the house, but she's been talking about moving to Virginia and that will be just as traumatic for him."

"Is this true?" I asked.

"I haven't made up my mind, Your Honor," she said. "But Virginia pays its teachers a lot better than North Carolina does. Better than South Carolina and Georgia, too, for that matter."

That made me wince. Our state used to lead the area in education. Now we're ranked forty-eighth in the nation for per capita public school spending. Virginia beats us by miles. And it isn't just education but the court system as well. We're understaffed and underfunded and we took more deep cuts this past year.

"I can sympathize, Mrs. Bumgardner," I said now, "but if I decide on joint custody, how would you get Bertie back here when it's Mr. Bumgardner's turn?"

In the end, I gave them joint custody. Every Friday afternoon, whoever had Bertie would take him to a shopping mall in Garner, halfway between their two abodes, to make the exchange at six o'clock. "If you want to agree on a different time, fine, but repeated failure to get there within the agreed-upon hour will be grounds for the other to come back to court. If one of you moves out of the area, we can revisit the schedule. Maybe extend the time to two or three months."

After a few months of this, one of them might cave and buy another dog, but I didn't count on it.

In dividing up possessions in a divorce, there are various categories. Among them are items that both agree are marital and belong to both of them, items that clearly belong to one or the other exclusively, items of disputed ownership, items of value, items of no value, and items that neither spouse wants. I once handled a divorce in which both spouses listed their special needs child in that last category.

I have never had a pet listed there.

The Bumgardners were not happy with my decision, but half of something is still better than all of nothing, so they agreed to live with it for the time being.

By now it was 5:23. I adjourned and met Dwight, who'd already let Kate know we'd be running a little late. Because of my family's connection to the Earps, we had discussed the case in fairly comprehensive detail, so I knew who Marisa Young was and why he was delivering Vick Earp's truck with its spiderwebbed windshield over there.

As I followed him out to Cotton Grove, I couldn't help thinking about Daddy and Haywood. Not for one moment did I think either of them could have had anything to do with the murder, but I could understand why the *Clarion*, pushed by Joby Earp, kept insinuating that Daddy was getting special treatment by Sheriff Bo Poole's department.

Vick Earp was, by all accounts, a loner who pretty much kept to himself, which limited the pool of suspects. Yes, it might have been a spur-of-the-moment thing, a sudden rush of anger from some homicidal maniac whose buttons got pushed, but let's face it: homicidal maniacs are more the stuff of fiction than real life. In most cases, you have to know a person, interact with him, be enraged or thwarted by him to take that irreversible step.

Daddy said he'd wanted to kill Joby Earp. *Would*

have killed him if people hadn't pulled him off. But Joby Earp had almost killed the woman Daddy had fallen in love with. No one was suggesting anything similar for Vick Earp.

(*"But let us not forget that whoever killed him knew his fixation on the land his grandfather had lost and was familiar enough with the place to dump his body there,"* said my mental preacher, who has a way of remembering unpleasant truths.)

(*"Haywood? Don't be silly,"* said the pragmatist from the other side of my brain. *"Haywood would have left him where it happened, not driven him all the way out to the farm."*)

(*"And what if he was killed there, not driven there?"* said the preacher.)

Before I could panic over that thought, I remembered the cat. And the fact that blood from both of them had been found in the truck bed.

Everything seemed to indicate that the murder had taken place in Cotton Grove. The truck had been used to dump the body and then driven back.

Why?

Because the killer needed to get back to his own vehicle?

So we needed someone who knew him, someone who needed to move the body and who also knew about Black Gum Branch.

Joby Earp?

Dwight said there had been hostility between the two of them, mitigated by Joby's wife, who was like a mother to Vick and his brother Tyler. He certainly knew the lanes that crisscrossed the farm. His wife was his alibi, but Dwight said she was so firmly under his thumb that she'd probably say anything he wanted.

And what about Tyler Earp?

He'd shot up Vick's pickup and was angry because he was owed money for a paint job that was never going to be paid. He knew the farm and while I wasn't sure exactly where he lived in relation to where the truck was found, Cotton Grove's not that big. He might could have walked home from the murder site if his own truck wasn't nearby. His roommate said that they'd been together all night and into midmorning, and that Tyler had passed out in front of the TV. But the roommate had been drinking, too. Would he have heard Tyler leave and return?

Which brought me to Vick's wife, Rosalee. Dwight only had her word for when Vick hit her or that he was still alive when she left. She certainly knew about Black Gum Branch. Had parked there when they were courting and picnicked there over the years. Again, I didn't know how far the Earp house was from the railroad track, but if she was on foot, surely someone would have seen her because it was still daylight when she got to her cousin's house.

The cousin? Marisa Young? She told Dwight that she'd doctored Rosalee's cuts and bruises and put her to bed. Would she have been angry enough on her cousin's behalf to go looking for Vick, kill him, and then dispose of his truck? She and Tyler had picnicked out there at Black Gum Branch, so she knew the spot. But Rosalee could alibi her for the first part of Friday night and then again Saturday morning. On the other hand, if she'd given Rosalee a sleeping pill...?

So who did that leave?

What about the neighbor who shared a cat with Rosalee Earp? Rusty Somebody-or-other? What if she saw Vick trying to kill her cat and just grabbed up the first thing at hand to stop him? But was she familiar with the farm?

The main problem in all of this, so far as I could see, was that there was no knowing when or where the blow that killed him had been delivered. Dr. Singh said he'd been hit three times, but he hadn't actually died until shortly before Daddy found him. All that blood in the truck bed certainly indicated that he hadn't died immediately. He could have been hit hours before he was found or only minutes. By the time the truck was located, the blood had been baked dry by the August sun.

We were now entering Cotton Grove on Old Forty-eight. A few blocks in, Dwight put on his turn signal and soon he had pulled into the driveway of a small neat brick house. I followed him up the drive and around to the back.

CHAPTER

17

Can a man take fire in his bosom,
and his clothes not be burned?

— Proverbs 6:27

Marisa Young's front yard was narrow but quite deep. Undeveloped woods were on the left of a long graveled driveway that led to a turnaround at the back between an unexpectedly spacious porch and a small one-car garage. Two vehicles were parked back there, a Toyota sedan and an SUV with a bicycle rack on the back. Both were packed with cardboard boxes. The garage door was rolled up and two middle-aged women were toiling there, stacking boxes on the floor. A bicycle hung on hooks at the back of the garage.

Dwight got out of Vick Earp's truck and I joined him in the shade of the nearest tree. The humid heat of the late afternoon was like a sauna.

According to Mother and Aunt Zell, their mother had been impervious to heat. "Horses sweat, men perspire, ladies glow" was her mantra. Right now, I was glowing like one of my neon signs. That stalled cold front couldn't get here fast enough for me.

I had never met the sturdily built woman who wore khaki slacks and a loose black blouse with three-quarter sleeves and black sneakers, but the smaller woman, dressed in blue denim shorts and a coral tank top, had a familiar face, and I knew she must be Rosalee Earp, the woman who had petitioned me for a restraining order against her husband last year after he left her bruised and battered. There was a scab on her chin from where he'd hit her Friday last week, but the bruises on her arm were almost gone and her black eye was fading, too.

She seemed to recognize me, and came forward with a smile that carried a tinge of sadness when Dwight introduced me.

"I'm so sorry about your husband," I said. A platitude I know, but what else can you say in a situation like this?

"Thank you," she said. "You warned me that he might hurt me really bad someday. We didn't know that he'd be the one to get hurt."

"My husband tells me that you and your cousin are going to live together now?"

"For the time being. We may wind up moving to the D.C. area. That's where my daughters are. It would be nice to live closer to them and they'll never come back to Cotton Grove." She gestured to the boxes. "I won't unpack my things until we decide."

She called to the other woman. "Marisa. Come meet Judge Knott."

We murmured pleasantries to each other and we both mopped perspiration from our faces as Dwight gave Earp's keys back to Mrs. Earp. I was ready to get back in the truck—Dwight's air-conditioned truck— but he wanted to go over a few details with the women again and Mrs. Earp suggested we go onto the porch where she had a pitcher of freshly made iced tea.

The porch was screened on three sides, shaded by oaks and made more bearable by a large paddle fan in the ceiling. The tea was icy cold and lightly sugared, just the way I like it. I drained the glass in a few greedy gulps and said, "Oh yes, please" when offered a refill.

"You're a bird-watcher?" I asked Miss Young, sipping my second glass more slowly.

A rhetorical question. Suet cages hung from the eaves of the house and I saw nuthatches, tufted titmice, and a downy woodpecker perch to feed. Hummingbirds darted in and out and hovered over the little red plastic flowers on at least a half-dozen nectar tubes and no sooner had we come inside, than towhees, wrens, and brown thrashers lined up to splash in the two large concrete birdbaths set amid the flower beds that rimmed the porch. A decorative cardinal carved from stone perched on a low post by the porch steps.

"In this hot weather, I have to fill the birdbaths twice a day," said Miss Young. "I thought the rain would cool us off but today feels even worse."

"Did you find Vick's wallet, Major Bryant?" asked Mrs. Earp. "He got paid every other Friday and he would have had a couple of hundred dollars in cash on him."

"Sorry," Dwight said. "There was nothing in his pockets except a few coins."

"Don't worry, Rosy," her cousin said. "Rusty said she'd help you switch his bank account over to your name and I'll lend you as much as you need."

"There's so much to think about and do," Mrs. Earp said wanly and I nodded, thinking of the many legal hoops my cousin Sally has jumped through after Aunt Rachel died this spring.

"You mentioned Mrs. Reynolds," said Dwight. "How did your husband get along with her?"

"Rusty? Fine, I guess. Not that she ever came over except to ask about Diesel. Vick and her husband didn't take to each other the one time they met. If it hadn't been for the cat, Rusty and I probably wouldn't have become friends." She sighed. "Poor Diesel. I guess we'll never know what happened to him."

"Did she ever picnic with you out at Black Gum Branch?" Dwight asked.

"No."

"What about your other neighbors? He ever have any disagreements with them?"

She shook her head. "I told you. Vick was a loner and I quit trying to change that. It was easier just to keep to ourselves."

It sounded like a bleak life to me, but maybe she had friends at work.

Our tea glasses were leaving small puddles on the table and she handed us some paper napkins, which the overhead fan promptly blew to the floor while I scrambled to catch them.

She looked up at the fan. "I can't reach the chain, Marisa. Could you turn it down a notch?"

Dwight said, "Let me," but Miss Young was already standing. When she reached up for it, the loose sleeve of her blouse slipped back and I saw a large bruise on her upper arm.

"You got quite a knock there," I said.

She hastily pulled her sleeve into place. "Yeah, I banged it when we were moving the boxes yesterday."

Mrs. Earp looked contrite. "I'm sorry, Marisa. Was it when we moved that chest?"

Now I can't claim any great insight or *aha!* moment, but I've seen enough battered women to know about bruises and this one was not acquired yesterday. Why would she lie about it? Unless...?

"Are you sure it was only yesterday?" I asked. "To me, it looks as old as Mrs. Earp's bruises. Like you got it about ten days ago."

"I—I fell," she said. "You're right. That one's from last week."

"May I see?" Dwight asked politely.

She tried to bluff her way out of it, but with all three of us looking at her now, she pushed her sleeves up and there were fading bruises on both arms. "I took a tumble out there in the yard. No big deal."

Dwight wasn't buying it. "The thermometer's been stuck near a hundred all week, yet every time I've seen you, you've had on long sleeves. Why've you been hiding those bruises, Miss Young?"

She looked stricken but didn't answer.

"Marisa?" said her cousin. "Did Vick come over here that night?"

There was a long silence, then all the starch went out of her and she nodded.

"I thought he was going to kill me. I didn't have a choice. Honest! It was self-defense."

"Self-defense?" Dwight asked skeptically. "Then why didn't you call the police?"

"Because I wasn't sure!"

"Not sure?" Mrs. Earp moved her chair closer to her cousin and made her take a swallow of her tea. "What happened, Marisa?"

"He did come here," Miss Young said. "About ten-thirty. You were sound asleep, Rosy, but I was still so riled up I couldn't sleep. It had cooled off a little, so I put on the yard lights and went out to deadhead the flowers. I was about to come inside when he drove up. He was so drunk he could hardly walk and I told him to leave or I'd get my gun. I thought he was walking back around to get in his truck when all of a sudden, he reached into the bed and threw Diesel at me. I was shocked and didn't know at first if he was dead or alive. When I bent down to pick him up, Vick kicked me. Hard. I thought he'd broken my arm, it hurt so bad."

She touched the spot where the toe of his boot had landed.

"He came at me again and I grabbed up that stone cardinal and smashed the side of his head and he went down like a rock. Blood all over his face."

"Oh, Marisa, honey!" Mrs. Earp said. "Why didn't you call me?"

"I wasn't thinking straight, Rosy, and my arm hurt so bad I almost cried. I went in the kitchen to make an ice pack for it and to try to think what to do. I was going to call 911," she told Dwight. "Honest. But before I could get back to the yard, I heard the truck start up and he was gone. So I thought maybe I hadn't hurt him as bad as it looked and by next morning, before you came, I thought he must be okay or we would have heard something."

"You're sure that's what happened, Miss Young?" Dwight said. "You didn't put him in the bed of the truck with your bicycle and take him out to where he was found, then hide the truck and pedal back here?"

"What? *No!* My bicycle's had a broken chain since June. I was waiting for cooler weather to take it in to get fixed."

"She's telling the truth, Major," Mrs. Earp said. "We haven't ridden in ages."

"You have a bicycle, too?"

She nodded. "Didn't you see it in the tool shed? Behind the mower?"

Clearly he hadn't and I could see the wheels turning in his head, trying to make sense of two bikes and come up with an alternate theory that might involve her.

"Diesel?" asked Mrs. Earp.

Miss Young pointed to the birdbath at the end of the porch. "He was dead, Rosy. I buried him in the flower bed there. Underneath the zinnias." She straightened her shoulders and faced him squarely. "Am I under arrest, Major Bryant?"

"Not until we figure out who dumped his body and drove his truck back to Cotton Grove. But you'll have to come in and sign a statement."

"Do I need to bring a lawyer with me?"

"Up to you, ma'am," he said. "You've already told us your story in front of witnesses, though."

Okay, I'll admit it. As we headed out of town, I was rather pleased with myself for having noticed Marisa Young's bruise, which cleared up the mystery of the cat and maybe eliminated one suspect, but I'd barely begun to crow when Dwight's phone rang. He had it on speaker mode, so I heard Cotton Grove's no-nonsense police chief come straight to the point.

"You still looking for that red pickup, Major?"

"No, some kid found it down by the railroad tracks. Why?"

"I've got a couple here who say they saw it on their way out of town on the evening of the eighth. Wasn't that the night of the murder?"

"Sometime between six-thirty that night and mid-morning the next day."

"Well, this was around eleven."

"And they waited till now to speak up?"

"As I said, they were on their way out of town, heading up to Richmond to stay with their daughter for a few days after their first grandbaby got itself born. They just got back yesterday and started catching up on the *Clarion*—all the obituaries. You know how some old people are. Want to make sure they haven't missed somebody's funeral. Anyhow, they saw the appeal for any sightings of that truck, so they came in."

"They're still there? I'll be right over. Any more details?"

"It was stopped near a Lincoln Town Car with a flat

tire. He thinks it was black, she says it was dark green. And there were two men. One was waving a wrench at the other one. Tall and fat and wearing a porkpie hat. The other guy was shorter."

My heart stopped. There are lots of tall fat men around, but how many of them would be driving a dark green Lincoln Town Car with a porkpie hat on his head?

Haywood?

CHAPTER

18

*Behold, how good and how pleasant
it is for brethren to dwell together in
unity!*

— Psalms 133:1

**DWIGHT BRYANT—WEDNESDAY EVENING,
AUGUST 20**

At the Cotton Grove police station, Dwight discovered that the Mangums, David and Sunny, characterized by the police chief as old people who read the obituaries, were probably only in their late fifties.

Old is a relative term, he thought, and he guessed the chief's own age as maybe thirty.

Chief Creech had made the Mangums comfortable in his office and an extra chair was brought in for Dwight. After introductions, he asked for permission to record the interview and they agreed. Prompted by

Creech, the couple repeated their story for him, interrupting each other amiably as long-married couples do.

They had received a call from their son-in-law around 9:45 on Friday, August 8.

"He said our daughter had gone into labor," said Mr. Mangum, "so we packed up and got on the road as soon as we could. That would have been around ten-thirty or a quarter to eleven."

"Ten-fifty-five, because you forgot to set the alarm and had to go back in," said his wife. "David was driving, which is why I'm the one that really noticed everything."

"We took the shortcut out of town to get to Forty-eight," said Mangum.

"Where exactly?" Dwight asked and between them, the Mangums described a back road that led from their house to Old 48 and then to 48 proper. Not all that far from where the Booker kid had found Earp's pickup.

"We'd just turned onto Old Forty-eight when I saw this Lincoln Town Car with a flat tire. A black Lincoln," said Mr. Mangum.

"No, honey, I told you. It was dark green," she said.

"Whichever."

"How were they headed?" Dwight asked. "North toward New Forty-eight or south on the old road?"

"South," Mangum said promptly. "I slowed down because I was going to stop and help."

"But I asked him not to this time because I was in a hurry to get to Richmond," said his wife, "and besides, someone else had already stopped. A red pickup with a cracked windshield."

"A Ford," Mangum said.

"A Ford," she agreed. "There were two men standing by the side of the road, but I thought they looked like trouble and I didn't want us to get involved."

"Why did you think there was trouble?" Dwight asked.

"Something about the way they were standing. Sort of faced off like they were ready to go at each other."

"They were under a streetlight and David had slowed down enough that I got a good look at them."

"Could you describe them for me?"

"Both of them were our age at least. The short one was probably about my height. I'm five-six. The one waving a lug wrench was taller, more like you, Major Bryant."

"A lug wrench?"

She nodded. "I thought maybe he was going to hit the other man."

"Can you describe him a little more?"

"Like I told Chief Creech here, he looked like he was really mad about something. He was big and tall and he was wearing one of those silly little hats like my dad wears. I don't remember what else he was wearing. Dark pants, maybe?"

She looked at her husband, who shrugged.

"The other man had on a light shirt. Light blue or green, I think. And he was holding a towel or something to his head. He might have been bleeding but I couldn't tell. That's really all we saw. He was the one who got killed, though, wasn't he?"

"Sounds like it," Dwight admitted.

"You think it was the man in the porkpie hat?"

"Not necessarily. Right now, though, he's the last one on record to see Vick Earp alive."

"So if we'd stopped like I wanted to," said Mangum, "this Earp guy might still be alive?"

Dwight shrugged. "Or you two might be the last ones on record to see him."

Mrs. Mangum shook her head. "Well, I'm sorry he's dead, but I'm glad I didn't miss getting to see our granddaughter get born." She scrolled through some pictures on her phone. "Here she is just six minutes old."

"Real cute," said Dwight, to whom all newborns looked the same. He took down the Mangums' contact information and thanked them for coming forward.

The interview had been recorded digitally and Chief Creech promised to forward it to the address Dwight gave him.

Back in the truck, he put it in gear and eased away from the curb.

"Was it Haywood?" Deborah asked.

"'Fraid so, shug. Big and tall? Green Lincoln? Porkpie hat?"

"You can't seriously think that Haywood's capable of—"

"Vick Earp was holding a cloth to his head like he was bleeding. Probably where Miss Young hit him. And your brother had a lug wrench in his hand, Deb'rah. I can't ignore that and you can't ignore that their confrontation was on Old Forty-eight, not very far from where Earp's truck was stashed. If he was the one who dumped the body, he could have walked from the railroad tracks back to his car in just a few minutes."

"I don't care how much opportunity he had," Deborah said hotly, "and I know Haywood's done some stupid things in his time, but he would *not* have killed someone and brought the body back to the farm. He just wouldn't, Dwight."

Dwight grinned. "Even for Haywood, that would be real stupid."

Her relief was palpable. "Then you don't think he did it?"

"What I think is that I need to go have a talk with him and before you ask, no, you can't come with me."

"I wasn't going to ask that."

"Oh yeah?"

"I was going to ask if you wanted to have supper at the barbecue house. Haywood and Bel will be there. Third Wednesday night," she reminded him. "Cal asked me this morning if we could go and he's already there. Aunt Sister picked him up on her way."

The date had slipped his mind. Vinegar-based pork barbecue is like mother's milk in eastern North Carolina and members of the extended Knott family usually gathered at a cousin's nearby restaurant once or twice a month for supper and to play and sing together informally afterwards. Always on the third Wednesday night and often on a fifth Wednesday should one fall in that month, although any Wednesday night might find some relatives there with instruments in the trunk of their car. Everybody was welcome to sit in. Cal had learned how to play the harmonica at these gatherings, Deborah strummed along on her guitar, and even though he didn't play, Dwight usually sang with the others. Haywood seldom missed a chance to rosin up his fiddle and loved to chime in with what he called "my big gross voice," a rich deep bass that could roll like thunder.

"Well, maybe I'll ride along and see if I can cut him out of the herd," Dwight said.

It was after eight before they got there. Most of the players had finished eating and were tuning up their fiddles and guitars. Cal was happily running scales on his harmonica and when Mr. Kezzie cut loose on "Shady Grove," Aunt Sister fell right in behind him on her dulcimer. Herman's daughter Annie Sue doesn't play an instrument per se, but she's an electrician and she keeps boxes of loose screws and wire nuts on her truck and passes them out to anyone who wants to help her keep the beat. Her brother Reese was the one who gave Cal the harmonica and the two of them were blowing harmony, while Haywood's wife Isabel played the banjo.

Deborah's foot was tapping as she ate and she quickly downed a barbecue sandwich so she could join them. Dwight took his time over his plate of barbecue, coleslaw, and hushpuppies and when the players paused to refill their tea glasses, he edged over to Haywood and said, "Talk to you outside for a minute?"

There were chairs and benches on the side porch and Dwight brought his own glass of tea along.

"What's up, bo?" Haywood asked as he settled into one of the chairs.

"I need you to tell me about your fight with Vick Earp."

Haywood made a face. "Which one? We been fighting since we was young'uns."

"The one you had with him Friday night a week ago. The night he was killed."

"Wha'chu talking about?" he blustered, almost rising out of the chair.

"You were seen in Cotton Grove waving a lug wrench at him, Haywood. Did you hit him with it?"

"*No!* I never! And if somebody says I did, he's lying."

"Like you were lying when you said you didn't recognize him on Saturday? Or when Robert said y'all hadn't seen him since last fall?"

The indignation went out of him. "I didn't lie," he said truculently. "I might not've said nothing, but I didn't lie."

"Tell me," said Dwight.

"I'd been over to Fuquay to see a man about a John Deere 60 he wanted to sell us for parts. He's got a whole shed full of old tractors and stuff. You wouldn't believe all the things he's got. A 1923 Farmall that looks like it just rolled off the line and a 1939 Allis Chalmers. Real pretty. Anyhow, we got to talking and time got away with me. You know how it is."

Dwight nodded. He did indeed know how much time this particular brother-in-law could spend talking. Haywood had the curiosity of a cat and was so easily distracted that he was an endless source of exasperation to Robert or Andrew, who constantly had to prod him to keep to the task at hand.

"So it was well after ten before you started for home?"

"That's right! How'd you know?"

"You were seen, remember?"

"Oh yeah. Right. Well, I was headed for home through Cotton Grove and out Old Forty-eight when I got a flat tire. I got out and was changing it when Vick Earp come along. High as a kite and spoiling for a fight. I told him I won't in no mood to get into it with him right then and besides, it looked like he'd already got the worst of it in a fight with somebody else. He was mopping up blood from the side of his face. There was a bullet hole through the windshield of his truck and I thought at first maybe he'd been shot, but then I seen the hole was on the passenger side, so that won't it."

Haywood took a swallow of tea and shook the ice around in the bottom of his glass.

"He stood there cussing me and every Knott that ever walked the earth. Said if he had a gun, he'd shoot that wrench right out of my hand and I said it was a good thing he didn't have a gun, but if he didn't get back in his truck and get the heck away from me, I was gonna show him what else a lug wrench was good for."

"And did he?"

Haywood nodded. "Almost ran me down when he pulled out, though. He turned at the next corner and I thought at first he was gonna go around the block and come at me again, but he didn't. I finished changing the tire and come on home. Bel was still up and fussed at me for staying out so late. But she had our phone 'cause she went to Raleigh Friday. We're gonna have to get us another one so we can call each other if we're both out."

"What time did you get home?"

"'Bout eleven-thirty?"

"And Bel will swear to that?"

Haywood chuckled. "Now, Dwight, you know Bel don't swear. But yeah, she'll tell you that's when I come in. We finished here? I want me some of Miss Ila's peach cobbler before it all gets gone."

"Sounds like a good idea," Dwight said.

Not that he really thought Haywood had murdered Vick Earp, but it was good to have proof. If the Mangums had seen Earp alive around 11 and Haywood was home by 11:30, he did not have time to drive the body out to the farm and then take the truck back to Cotton Grove.

CHAPTER

19

A brother is born for adversity.

— Proverbs 17:17

Lying in bed that night after he had told Deborah about his talks with both Haywood and the Mangums, Dwight was nearly asleep when she turned to him and said, "Tell me again where Vick Earp lived?"

Yawning, he said, "North side of town. Why?"

"And Marisa Young lives on the east side, right?"

"You were there, shug," he answered sleepily.

"So where was Vick Earp going at eleven o'clock at night?" she asked. "Not back to Miss Young's house and not back to his own. Practically everything's closed at that hour. So where was he going?"

Whereupon, she promptly fell asleep leaving him to stare into the darkness with possibilities tumbling through his head.

*   *   *

Next morning dawned bright and clear, a high-pressure day that brought dryer air and cooler temperatures. The predicted high was only 86 degrees with humidity expected to stay at 38 percent. Their slugabed cold front had finally arrived.

At work, Dwight looked at everything they'd collected on Vick Earp's murder, including pictures of the dead man's head wounds taken the day he was found. He drove out to the hospital with the pictures and tracked Dr. Singh down in his lab. Singh frowned when Dwight asked his questions.

"Look, Bryant, you know I'm just a part-time ME. If you didn't think the manner of the man's death was straightforward, you should have sent the body to Chapel Hill. It's not my fault if the state doesn't want to pay for all the autopsies they used to do. They knew they were setting themselves up for something like this the minute they cut funding for state labs."

"I'm not second-guessing you, Doctor. You said he died from a blow to the head. All I'm asking is which blow?"

He spread the close-ups of Vick Earp's head wounds across Singh's lab bench and pointed to the one of Earp's upper left temple. "This is where a woman hit him with a concrete bird about the size of a baseball a little before eleven the night before he was found. She said it dazed him, but he was still able to get up and drive away."

"So?"

"So then he was hit twice more, right?"

Singh nodded, looking closely at the photographs.

"The woman who hit him thought she'd killed him, but witnesses saw him a few minutes later and although he was bleeding, he was still functioning."

"So what's your question?"

"Which one killed him? The one on the side of his head or the ones in back?"

"Well, not this one," Singh said, pointing to one of the pictures. "This looked as if he took a whack from something like a flat board." He looked at his notations. "Yeah, something flat. About four or five inches wide. He could have been standing or sitting. His head was upright, anyhow. His heart continued to beat after this blow because I saw severe bruising, but it didn't break the skin."

He picked up another picture. "This is the one that did the most damage. It looked to me more like a downward thrust. Like he was lying facedown and something came straight down. Hard. Broke his skull. This wound was around thirteen centimeters wide by about a centimeter long and at least a half-centimeter deep. If the first blow was from a thin board, then this wound could be the end of that board."

"And that's the one that actually killed him?"

"I wouldn't go to court and swear it, but nobody walks around too long with a skull crushed in like that. You said that when he was first found, they thought both wounds were still oozing blood?"

Dwight nodded.

"The primary cause of death *was* loss of blood. He simply bled out. I doubt if the one in the temple would have killed him by itself, but combined with the other two? If he'd gotten treatment right away—? Hell, Bryant! I don't know."

He shook his head. "A pretty problem, isn't it? He might have survived one blow, but all three? And if he was moved around so that the wounds were re-opened? All I can tell you is the time of death. Your witnesses said the blood was still oozing at ten o'clock. The EMTs said he was dead when they got there at ten-thirty and that's consistent with when they got him here to me. His heart probably stopped beating about ninety minutes before I saw him and that's all I can tell you."

"One thing more," Dwight said. "Take a look at this scraping. Is it Vick Earp's blood?"

Singh looked at his watch. "Sorry, Bryant. I have to leave in exactly twelve minutes."

"Come on, Singh. How long can it take to do a rough comparison? You must have kept the slides. Just tell me if it looks like his blood or if it's that damn cat again."

"So what do you think, boss?" asked Deputy Ray McLamb when Dwight returned from the hospital.

Before he could answer, Mayleen Diaz came to the door. "Tyler Earp's at the front desk. Wants to know why we're keeping his gun when his brother wasn't shot."

McLamb made a face. "Cares more about that gun than his brother."

"Then why don't we give it back to him?" said Dwight. "Show him in, Mayleen."

                    *   *   *

Tyler Earp's broad beefy face lit up when he saw the
twelve-gauge shotgun lying across Dwight's desk.
"'Bout time," he said happily and ran his work-worn
hand along the sleek, smooth stock.

Watching him, Dwight tried to peer past the bulging
waistline, graying hair, and lined face to see the boy he
must have been when Earps still owned part of Mr.
Kezzie's farm, but he could dredge up no memories and
both of those boys had been enough older that he
wouldn't have overlapped them in school or on the
school bus. With his own father dead and his mother trying to hold on to the farm while she went back to school
for a teaching degree, he had hung out with the Knott
brothers whenever he could. Mr. Kezzie treated him like
another son and Miss Sue gave him a woman's sympathetic attention when he needed to talk.

Now he wondered if they had tried to tame the Earp
brothers, too, or had Joby Earp made that impossible
by firing that first shot?

Without thinking, he said, "Did you know Kezzie
Knott's wife?"

Surprised, Tyler Earp said, "Miss Sue? Can't say I
really knew her, but I knew who she was. Joby didn't
ever have a good thing to say about either one of 'em,
but they never acted ugly to me. And they sure were
good to those boys. I remember once when we were
playing baseball after work one hot as hell day. Miss
Sue brought an ice-cold watermelon out to the field
where we were playing. And she brought a bucket of
water and some rags so we could wipe our faces when
we finished."

There was such wistfulness in his tone that Dwight had a sudden sense of how emotionally bleak Earp's childhood must have been that the memory of a cold watermelon and a bucket of water could have lasted this long.

He sighed and said, "This *is* your shotgun, isn't it, Mr. Earp?"

"Well, of course it is. Your deputy here took it off my wall. You trying to say it's not?"

"No, sir. Just making sure. You ever lend it to anybody? Your uncle, say? Or your brother?"

Earp shook his head. "Joby's got his own guns and Vick thought they were a big waste of good money."

"So do you want to tell us what you did with this gun on the night your brother was killed?"

Earp took a step backward. "Wha'chu mean?"

"He came to your house that night, didn't he? Bleeding. Maybe looking for a fight?"

"No! I told you. Rocky told you. We went to the Lillie Pad and then we came home and went straight to bed."

Dwight made a show of picking up his notepad. "Actually, Rocky went to bed, but he left you snoring in front of the television. Yet you were in your own bed at ten o'clock the next morning."

"I had to take a leak during the night. I woke up, turned off the TV, and went to the bedroom."

"But not right away. Not till you'd disposed of Vick's body. You had quite a busy night, didn't you?"

"You're crazy. Vick wasn't shot. You said so."

"It's a beautiful gun, Earp. Nice wood stock. You keep it nice and clean, too."

Confused, Earp said, "Yeah, well, a dirty gun's asking for trouble."

"Unfortunately, you missed a place." Dwight took a straight pin from his desk drawer and ran it along the joint where the narrow metal butt plate met the heavy wooden stock.

Tyler Earp watched wide-eyed as a tiny speck of dark brown gunk fell onto the white sheet of paper Dwight had placed underneath that end of the gun.

"That's Vick's blood. Our medical examiner just confirmed it." His voice was gentle. "You didn't shoot him. You clubbed him with the stock and while he was lying facedown on the ground, you just rammed down with the butt plate and broke his skull."

"Oh God!" Earp moaned. "Oh, God in heaven!"

He sank down in the nearest chair and put his head in his hands. "I didn't mean to. It was an accident."

"Tell me," Dwight said quietly.

With his head still in his hands, Earp's words came slowly at first. "It was like you said. I was sleeping it off in my La-Z-Boy when I woke up and Vick was there. I keep this gun on a rack over the front door and he was taking it down. I asked him what the hell he thought he was doing and he said he was taking it in payment for his fucking windshield and then he walked right out the door with it. I jumped up and went after him and pushed him as he was going down the steps. He rolled out into the yard and dropped my gun. Must've hit his head, I guess, because he came up all bloody. Said he was gonna beat my brains out. I grabbed the gun and smacked him with the stock and when he went down again, I just—I just—"

Shoulders still slumped, his hands clasped between his legs, he lifted his head and looked at Dwight remorsefully. "He was a shitty brother but I didn't want him dead. Honest. But he was stealing my gun and he was gonna beat up on me again just like he's done my whole life."

"Why did you take him out to Black Gum Branch?" Dwight asked.

"Was the only place he was ever happy," Earp said bitterly. "He was always bitching and moaning about losing the land, so I thought he might as well spend the rest of his days there. I rolled him into the bushes, then drove his truck back to town, hid it down by the railroad tracks, and walked home."

He stood up, resignation in every inch of his body. "I guess I'm under arrest, huh?"

"'Fraid so," Dwight said.

"No crowing," Dwight said when Deborah got home that afternoon, "but if you hadn't asked where Vick was headed that night, we might have given Tyler back his gun before it occurred to us that he wasn't heading out here to the farm."

"No crowing," she agreed, "but what happens now?"

"Well, Bo's dumped it all in Kevin Foster's lap. He's gonna let our DA figure out who's really to blame for Vick Earp's death and what the charges should be. Miss Young said she hit him in self-defense and I believe her, but he might not have died from what his brother did if he hadn't already lost so much blood."

"One thing for sure—no jury of his peers is going to

blame Tyler Earp for defending his shotgun," Deborah said dryly. "I'd better go let Daddy know that he can quit worrying about Haywood and Robert."

"Robert? I never thought Robert was involved."

"Daddy did, though. You know how Robert always cleans up Haywood's messes."

CHAPTER

20

There are three things which are too
wonderful for me, yea, four which I
know not: The way of an eagle in the
air; the way of a serpent upon a rock;
the way of a ship in the midst of the
sea; and the way of a man with a
woman.

— Proverbs 30:18–19

I left Dwight and Cal digging for worms in the compost pile. They swore we were going to have pan fish for supper.

At the homeplace, Daddy's truck was gone, but Maidie sat on the back porch shelling butter beans. "Not real sure where he's gone, Deb'rah," she said. "He'll be back 'fore long, though. He knows I'm making spareribs and corn fritters for supper and he ain't gonna miss that."

I joined her on the porch and began helping her shell.

"Y'all getting all the butter beans you want?" she asked. "'Cause Cletus and Mr. Kezzie's got plenty to spare if one of y'all want to come pick them."

"We're fine for beans," I said. "You know Dwight. He overplants just like everybody else on this farm."

"Don't never hurt to have some extra to share," Maidie said comfortably. "I sent some to Will and Amy this morning and Bel says Herman and Nadine will be out tomorrow to pick over at their place." She sighed. "Does seem so hard that that boy's still in a wheelchair."

Herman is Haywood's twin and barely survived arsenic poisoning a few years back. With his walker, he can manage to get to the bathroom, but his motorized wheelchair is easier for most of his day-to-day activities.

We shelled in companionable silence as the sun sank toward the treetops. Maidie's about fifteen years older than me and I realized she might know things about Mother and Daddy that I didn't.

"Remind me again how old you were when you started keeping house here?"

"I was sixteen when I come. You won't even walking good. Not that you needed to walk. Them boys acted like you was their play toy and they'd've carried you around on their shoulders till you was grown if Miss Sue hadn't made them put you down. But I won't housekeeper, I was just extra help for your mama and Aunt Essie. You remember her, don't you?"

"Oh yes," I said. We all loved Aunt Essie. Daddy had hired her after his first wife died and she had stayed on after he married Mother. Mother wasn't afraid of hard work, but she had no intention of killing herself with it. Everyone said Annie Sue had worked from first light till last dark, but if she found time to play with the boys or walk out to look at the land for pure pleasure, I never heard about it. Mother loved her life out here on the farm and she wanted to take time to savor it, which is why she paid a washerwoman to come do the laundry. She also kept Aunt Essie on to help her with the other household chores so that she wasn't too tired at night to read to us or play the piano while Daddy played his fiddle and we all joined in on the singing.

Aunt Essie stayed with us till she went up to Philadelphia for the birth of her first grandchild where she met and married a Philadelphia policeman.

By then, some of the older boys had married and moved out of the house, so Mother and Maidie managed alone. Aunt Essie used to bring her grandchildren down to visit in the summer and Maidie still gets Christmas cards from that daughter.

"Did Mother ever talk much about how she and Daddy met and wound up getting married?" I asked.

"She didn't have to, honey. Aunt Essie was here the first time she came out to the farm. After Frank and Robert fell through the ice. And then she helped Frank save his mama's footprints. You know that story."

"Yes, but those stories are about Mother and the boys. What about Daddy?"

"He loved her better than Peter loved the Lord. You know that, too."

"But did she ever talk about how he proposed or how she decided to say yes?"

Maidie thought a minute and then shook her head. "Now that you mention it, I don't think so. It was like they were the two matching halves to something whole and you couldn't think of one being without the other. Didn't take 'em long, though. Aunt Essie said they met around Christmas and got married in May, right after Miss Zell and Mr. Ash did."

"Did she ever mention a man named Mac? A pilot that she met during the war?"

"No, not that I ever heard. Who was he?"

"She told me that he changed her life, but she never said exactly how. I thought maybe she told you."

Maidie smiled. "No. All she ever said was how lucky she was to find Mr. Kezzie and the boys. She used to tease him that she fell in love with them first and that the only reason she married him was for his fiddle-playing."

That made me smile, too.

"If it's fretting you, how come you don't just ask him?"

"Oh, you know how he gets when he thinks we're prying into his private business."

"Seems to me like he's not as touchy about that as he used to be. The children have been over a lot lately, asking him about what it was like when he was young and he's been telling them, so I reckon he'd talk to you."

"Really? Which children?"

She rattled off the names and it was basically the kids who still live on the farm and who want to stay here and work the land. They've been trying various crops to replace tobacco. The prettiest were the four acres of sunflowers and another two acres of fragrant white tuberoses. I forget what else they're trying, but if they really want to farm, it's going to take a lot of hard work. I was disappointed to see them growing so much corn, but cows have to eat, I guess.

I had brought along the pictures of Adam and Karen's boys and, like me, Maidie noticed all the family resemblances. She, too, sighed to think how they would never come back from California. Would never feel a part of life on this land.

She went inside to wash the beans and put them on to cook. I had about decided I needed to go back home myself when Daddy drove up in his truck.

"Well, hey, shug," he said as I walked out into the yard to meet him. "If I'd've knowed you was here, I'd've come back quicker. Your menfolks with you?"

"No, they're probably out on the pond right now, trying to catch our supper."

"You're welcome to stay and eat with me. Maidie's making spareribs and corn fritters."

"Sounds good," I said, standing on tiptoe to kiss his stubbly cheek, "but I've got my mouth set for pan fish. I just thought I'd come and tell you that Tyler Earp's been arrested for killing his brother."

He wanted to hear the details, so we went back up on the porch and Maidie came out to hear, too.

When I finished, Maidie stood up and said she'd be getting on over to her house with her and Cletus's supper. "The ribs and the beans are done and I left the batter all made up, Deb'rah. All you have to do is fry it."

I knew she was leaving so I could ask Daddy the things that had been "fretting" me, as she put it. I kissed her smooth brown cheek and whispered, "Thanks, Maidie."

"Here, now," Daddy said. "You don't need to be cooking my supper."

"Don't be selfish," I teased. "Maidie knows how I like corn fritters and I'm sure she made enough for you to share."

We went into the kitchen and I turned the gas on under Mother's favorite black iron griddle and added a little olive oil. While it heated, I fixed Daddy a plate of boiled ribs and butter beans with diced onions and tomatoes, then dropped batter by the spoonfuls onto the sizzling hot griddle. Minutes later, the first were ready for Daddy's plate.

He didn't stand on ceremony. Hot and crispy corn fritters are delicious. Cold ones? Not so much.

After I'd made as many as he thought he could eat, I poured the rest of the batter into a jar to take home to Dwight and Cal. They would go great with fish.

While Daddy ate, I nibbled on a fritter and showed him the pictures of his West Coast grandsons.

"Real nice-looking boys," he said. "Bet they can't drive a tractor good as Cal, though."

I laughed. "Bet they don't want to, either."

When he'd finished eating and I'd stuck the leftovers in the refrigerator, he said, "Let's go back on the porch. Gonna be a real pretty evening and Maidie's started fussing if I smoke up her kitchen too much."

He reached for his pack of Marlboros and I used Mother's Zippo to light his cigarette. He took it from me and turned it in his hands as if it were something precious. "Will give you this?"

I nodded. "She ever talk to you about the man who gave it to her?"

"Mac? Yeah, she did." He pulled the lighter apart and ran his index finger across the inscription. "About Leslie, too."

"I know it's really none of my business, Daddy, and you don't need to tell me if you don't want to, but right near the end, she told me that he changed her life. She was fixing to tell me how, but somebody—I think it was Aunt Zell—came in about then and we never got back around to that story."

"And you want to know how a man that went and got hisself killed in the war told Sue it was all right to marry somebody like me?"

"Is that what he did?"

Daddy took a long drag on his cigarette and leaned back in the squeaky glider. "How much you know about him?"

So I told him about my sessions in New Bern and how I'd talked to Dr. Livingston's son and Mac's cousin and how he hadn't died in the war but lived another thirty years in Paris.

"Yeah? Wish your mama could've knowed that."

I also told him how Mac's nephew had exploded in anger when I asked about Mac.

Daddy gave a sour laugh. "Yeah, I reckon he did."

"People are such bigots," I said hotly, "but you'd think he'd be over it by now. It's been legal for blacks and whites to marry in this state since 1971."

Daddy frowned. "Who told you Leslie was a black woman?"

January 10, 1946

Loosely wrapped in a warm blanket, Sue sits cross-legged on the pallet and watches Kezzie throw another log on the fire. She never tires of looking at his naked body. He's tall and thin, but there's strength in the muscles of his arms and long legs. She's glad he's not hairy and loves running her fingers across his smooth chest until his nipples harden and he goes down on her.

In the last two weeks, they have almost turned this end of the ruined house into a real room. He has framed a partition across the open end and tacked burlap bags on both sides of the uprights to cut the chill January wind and hide themselves from any prying eyes. More boards serve as a table and bench and she now stashes extra quilts and blankets in the trunk of her car to cushion the tarp he has laid across the rough planks of the floor.

No one knows where she goes almost every morning, or even that she does go. Her mother never gets up before ten and has little interest in what either daughter does as long as it doesn't embarrass her. Her father is in his office by eight and Zell is caught up in wedding plans and furnishing the house where she and Ash will live after the wedding.

Out in the kitchen, Mary notices when Miss Sue wraps three or four sausage biscuits in waxed paper and fills the thermos bottle with coffee. She suspects there is a man, but no one asks her what Miss Sue does and Mary doesn't speak out of turn. She just fries up extra sausage patties and makes sure that a few biscuits never make it to the breakfast table.

Kezzie turns now and sees her watching him. He's still a little shy about exposing his body and is soon back under the quilts again. She drops the blanket from her own bare shoulders and slips in next to him. After the urgency of their first needs, this is when they just hold each other. If they do make love a second time, it's slower. Sweeter.

Eventually, he sighs, kisses her again, and turns to get dressed. She will go back to Dobbs to be a dutiful daughter and sister while he goes back to earning a living for his small sons. (She knows what he does but this is the one thing they do not discuss.)

Today though, she continues to lie there watching as he pulls on his pants, buttons his shirt, and ties the laces on his brogans.

"What?" he says when she props her head up on one elbow.

"I've been thinking about if we get married."

"Huh?"

"Zell's marrying Ash the first week in May and I'm her maid of honor. If you and I got married a week or two later, she'd be back from the honeymoon. I could wear her gown and she could wear my brides-maid dress, so that would save a lot of money. I don't care about having a lot of bridesmaids."

"Now wait a minute," he says.

"I know you probably don't want a church wedding, but Mother will absolutely curl up and die if we don't, and I can't do that to her."

"We ain't getting married."

"Why? Don't you love me?"

"Love's got nothing to do with it, shug."

"How can you say that? Love's got everything to do with it." She looks at him almost shyly. "You do love me, don't you? I certainly love you and your little boys, too. You need a wife and they need a mother."

"We ain't even knowed each other a whole month."

"If you count the Christmas dance, it'll be a full month on Saturday and I know all I need to know about you. You're a good man, Kezzie Knott, and a good father." She smiles, her eyes dancing with mischief. "And much as I love being out here like this with you, come summer and mosquitoes—"

He doesn't smile back. "We ain't getting married, Sue. We're too different. You've been to college, I ain't even been to high school."

"I quit after one semester and yes, I've read a couple of Shakespeare's plays and I took a year of geometry in high school." Her voice turns coaxing. "But you can make sense out of a complicated deed, you turn a profit with that store you own, and I watched you build that burlap wall without knowing a thing about the Pythagorean theorem."

"The what?"

"Pythagoras. A Greek mathematician who figured out how to make a right angle." She waves Pythagoras away impatiently. "I may have book learning but you know how to do things, build things. Think how much we can teach the boys."

He shakes his head. "Your daddy ain't gonna let his daughter marry a bootlegger."

There it is. Finally out in the open, yet she brushes his admission aside with no more concern than if he's said he's a Fuller Brush Man.

"I don't need anybody's permission," she says firmly. "I hope he'll give us his blessing, but I'll marry you without it if I have to. Besides, you might be surprised. Dad respects you."

Surprised is too weak a word. "He does?"

She nods. "He does."

He turns that over in his head, then sighs. "All the same, you can't marry me. You need somebody like him A lawyer or a doctor."

"I don't want a lawyer or a doctor." Rebellion flashes in her eyes. "I want the father of my baby. I'm pregnant, Kezzie."

He's shocked. "You ain't!" His own eyes go to the shiny little packet that lies next to their pallet. "You can't be."

He picks up the packet and waves it at her. "I used one of these every time."

"Not every time, darling. Not those first two times."

He groans and sinks down beside her. "Oh Lordy, Sue."

When he tries to put his arms around her, she turns away in tears. "You really *don't* love me, do you?"

He pulls her to him and kisses her until she yields to his embrace. "It scares me how much I love you, but I'm not right for you. Why can't you see that?" He pushes the hair back from her face and his blue eyes are sad. "I can't give you all the things you're used to. You're a town girl, honey, and running a farm's hard work. Besides, them boys ain't gonna keep acting like little angels once they get used to you."

"I'm not afraid of hard work, Kezzie. Don't you see? I want it. I *need* it. I can't stay in town and twiddle my thumbs and pretend I'm doing something with my life. Out here is real. The boys are real. The land is real. *You're* real. This is what I want."

"Are you sure, Sue? Really sure?"

"I've never been more sure of anything in my whole life."

She hasn't realized how tense he is until she feels his arms relax around her and he finally smiles.

"Another baby, huh? Well! Maybe this one will be a girl. I always did want a little girl."

She stops smiling. Guilt floods through her veins and the look on her face puzzles him.

"What's wrong?"

Her eyes are brimming with tears again.

Alarmed, he says, "What? Tell me!"

"Promise you won't be mad at me, Kezzie?"

"Mad at you? Mad about what?"

"I'm not really pregnant," she confesses. "I was going to trick you. Make you think you *had* to marry me. But I can't do that to you. If you don't love me enough to marry me before God and my friends and my father, then—"

He laughs out loud and hugs her to him tighter than ever. "Oh, honey! I even love you enough to marry you in front of your mama, poor lady."

He folds up the quilts and blankets while she dresses. "Second week of May, huh?"

Her smile is radiant. "Second week of May."

"Reckon I'll have to buy me a new suit. And new clothes for the boys."

He takes a pack of cigarettes from the pocket of his jacket and offers her one. "Still can't figure where you get the nerve to do this. Not much scares me, Miss Stephenson, but you got me beat by miles on this one."

Before he can strike a match, she pulls out Mac's lighter, hesitates, then hands it to him.

He turns it in his fingers. "Who's W.R.M.?"

"Walter Raynesford McIntyre."

"Old boyfriend?" He flips back the lid of the Zippo and lights their cigarettes. "Do I need to be jealous?"

"No, he's a friend who didn't come back from the war. But he's why I know I'm right to follow my heart. He's the one who showed me what happens to people when they don't."

She pulls apart the lighter so he can read the hidden inscription. "Let me tell you about Mac and Leslie."

CHAPTER

21

Thy mother is like a vine in thy
blood, planted by the waters.

— Ezekiel 19:10

I was puzzled. "If Leslie wasn't black, then what was the big deal? Was she a Lumbee Indian? Jewish?" I tried to think what other prejudices were rampant in those days.

Daddy shook his head. "Leslie won't a black woman, honey. Leslie was a white man. And he killed hisself because Mac won't man enough to speak up for him when the word got out about him in New Bern. Nobody knowed Mac was like that, but when they found out Leslie was, they beat him up and tied him naked to a fencepost in the middle of town with a sign around his neck. Thought it was a big joke. Somebody brought him a blanket and cut him loose—not Mac— and that night he shot hisself."

I was stunned.

"Mac told your mama that Leslie was dead 'cause

he was a coward. They couldn't live together in New Bern and they couldn't go to Paris but they could've gone to New York or California or some big city. Found a place where people would let 'em live like they wanted to."

He slid the engraved case back into place, closed the lighter, and handed it to me. "It happened a few weeks after he give Mac this lighter and Mac never quit grieving. He liked your mama and before he went overseas, he made her promise that she'd be braver than he was. That she'd break the rules and not care what people thought was right or wrong for her. 'Follow your heart,' he told her. When I tried to tell her we couldn't get married, that we was too different, that people would say she was throwing herself away on me, she wouldn't listen. She said we was right for each other and we was, won't we?"

"Oh yes!" I said. "*Yes!*"

"Real funny, ain't it, how things work? People finally getting used to the idea that we are how we are and we can't change the way we was made." He smiled. "You might not even be here if it won't for Walter Raynesford McIntyre. Nor Will and the little twins neither."

"Don't count on it," I said. "Aunt Zell says Mother was always pretty headstrong. The promise might've made it easier, but promise or no promise, I bet she would've married you anyhow."

He stretched his long legs straight out and there was something downright prideful about the smile on his face. "Yeah, I reckon she would've."

The rusty old green glider barely squeaked with

the gentle push of his foot. "Just wish she could've knowed what's about to happen with the grandchildren."

"The grandchildren?"

"Ain't they told you yet?"

"Told me what?"

"That's right. They wanted to keep it a secret. You gotta pretend you're real surprised when they tell you."

"Tell me *what*?" I said again.

"You know how your mama never did like me messing with whiskey?"

I nodded.

"Just about the only thing I ever lied to her about."

"So?"

"Them young'uns been plaguing me to death this summer, making me tell 'em how to make it, wanting my best recipes."

"What?"

"Ain't you wondered how come they planted so much corn this year? They're gonna have me making corn liquor again, honey, only this time, it's gonna be legal. They already started the paperwork. Full circle, Deb'rah. Full circle."

Please turn the page for a sneak peek at Margaret Maron's new novel featuring NYPD homicide detective Sigrid Harald, coming in August 2017.

Near the lower end of Sixth Avenue, on a corner where the windowless side of one building pulls back eight feet further from the other, an opportunistic sycamore tree shelters a long metal park bench anchored in cement. The space isn't big enough to be called a park—no grass, no flowers, but it's a shady place to sit in the summer and, with cardboard scraps to cover its slats in winter, the bench makes a warmer bed than the icy sidewalk, sheltered as it is on two sides by brick walls. Despite periodic efforts to rid the homeless from the streets of New York, the bench does seem to invite them. The nearest bus stop is a block away and the storefronts on the other side of the street are not for browsing but strictly utilitarian—an electrician, a shoe repair, a locksmith, and a dry cleaners. Locals seldom use the bench and they don't complain about the street people who do.

Live and let live.

Except when they don't.

That mild summer morning, a patrol car on the beat stopped at the corner. When the officer got out to prod the sleeping bum onto his feet, the man was dead. No blood and no obvious sign of violence. This was not a first for the young officer, nor even a second. Living on the streets too often meant dying on the streets. Too much rotgut whiskey, too many drugs, or an untreated medical condition, who knew?

Not his problem.

Ordinarily, he would have called it in, waited for the wagon to come take the body off his hands, made a note of it in his daily report, and that would have been that.

What made this death different was finding a second body under a dingy comforter at the far end of the bench.

"I thought it was the first guy's belongings," the officer told Lt. Sigrid Harald when the homicide team arrived. He pointed to the take-out cartons strewn under the bench where ants and yellow jackets were working on the food scraps. A crumpled bag bore the logo of a nearby Italian restaurant. "It's like he had supper and then lay down and went to sleep, but then when I saw the other one..."

Sigrid watched the ME swab the mouths of the dead men. Both wore jeans, T-shirts, and lightweight hoodies. Both were white. The first man was at least seventy. His long white hair was worn in a single braid, his short white Santa Claus beard looked hand-trimmed. His clothes were cleaner and marginally newer than those of his companion in death and he wore scuffed leather moccasins without socks. The other man wore ragged sneakers. His graying hair was close-cropped and he appeared to be in his early forties, but he had the sunken cheeks and ashy skin of an addict so he could have been much younger.

His immediate examination finished, Dr. Cohen stood and indicated that the detectives could begin searching the bodies.

"Overdose?" Sigrid asked him.

The ME shrugged. "The younger guy's got the teeth of a methhead, but the other one? No sign of meth and no tracks on his arms. Time of death for both of them was probably sometime between midnight and six a.m."

"Food poisoning?" she asked.

"Botulism or ptomaine?" He cast a doubtful eye over the two bodies. "Won't know till I open them up. No vomit though and it does look as if they had a good final meal if that Giuseppone bag means anything. I'll take samples, but you know how long it takes to run a tox screen if it's not something common."

After sending some officers to canvass shops and houses in the immediate area, Sigrid walked over to Detective Albee, an attractive blonde in her mid-thirties, just as Albee pulled a roll of fifties and twenties from the older man's pocket.

"Four hundred eighty," Albee said as she finished counting and slid the money into an evidence bag.

"No ID?"

"Sorry, Lieutenant. Just a Duane Reade receipt—the one on Ninth and Forty-Third—for a bottle of aspirins, a MetroCard, two ones, and some change in that other pocket. Nothing else except these two keys."

The keys could have been for a door, but there were no identifying names or numbers.

Detective Jim Lowry had finished with the grocery cart parked behind the bench. It held an umbrella, a half-used roll of paper towels, a box of crackers, and some articles of dirty clothing, but nothing to identify the owner.

"Probably belonged to the methhead," Lowry said, "since he's the one with the blanket."

Detective Tildon had turned out the pockets of the younger man and he held up a small nondescript switchblade with a bone handle. "Just big enough to make someone back off," he said. "No ID, but he's got a flyer for a soup kitchen two blocks down and a crisp new twenty that could've been peeled off the old guy's roll."

A few years older than Albee, Tillie was Sigrid's most trusted team member even though he occasionally tried her patience with his excessively detailed reports. Now he carefully bent down with his cell phone and took a picture of the younger man's face, then turned and did the same with the older one. "Want us to go talk to the staff at the soup kitchen? See if they recognize either of them?"

She nodded as one of the uniforms rounded the corner. Holding on to his arm for support was an elderly white-haired woman who barely topped his elbow and who seemed to move with difficulty. A small crowd had collected behind the yellow tape that marked off the benches.

"Lieutenant?" the officer called. "This lady may know one of them."

Sigrid motioned them forward.

"Mrs. Brunieri," he said. "She lives just down the block. A guy in the diner says he saw her come this way with takeout last night."

Until then, Sigrid had not paid attention to their precise location. Now she looked more closely at the direction from which Mrs. Brunieri had come and recognized the diner where she and Elliot Buntrock had eaten supper with Rudy Gottfried last week. And unless she was mistaken, this was the same woman who had entered the house across the street.

Seen up close, the old woman had a small wrinkled face overshadowed by thick eyebrows of coarse wiry white hair that almost met over the bridge of her nose. She ignored Sigrid's outstretched hand and shuffled straight over to the bodies still on the bench. Albee pulled back the paper sheets that covered them.

"That one I see many times," she said with a distinct Italian accent. After looking at the older man, she gave a half nod. "Him, only once. Last night."

"You brought them food?" Sigrid asked.

Those bushy eyebrows drew together over a frown and she nodded with obvious reluctance. "Most places give too much food for two old women and when there are leftovers, we give to the homeless. If no one is here, I leave it on the bench. Someone always takes it."

"And these two men were here last night?"

The woman pointed to the body of the older man. "Just him."

Both of the open foam cartons on the ground under the benches bore smears of red tomato sauce, white cheese, and scraps of pasta, but the one under the meth addict seemed to have less of the red sauce than the box lying closer to the other body. Mrs. Brunieri pointed to the first box. "That was ours. Fettuccine alfredo. Not the lasagna."

"You brought it in that Giusepponi bag?"

"No, but others leave food here, too."

"What time did you come?" Sigrid asked.

"About eight thirty. Maybe a few minutes before."

"And the older man was here?"

She nodded.

"But you knew the other man?"

"Not to *know*," the woman said. She gestured to the meth addict. "Him I see many times. Not the other one."

"So when did you last see him?"

From further up the block, a fire engine pulled out into the street with lights flashing and siren blasting, so that Sigrid had to repeat the question.

Mrs. Brunieri beetled her thick gray eyebrows, then shrugged. "Last week. We ordered from the Chinese that day and my signora sent me with the sushi we had left over."

"But last night, it was just the man with the beard?"

She nodded. "I asked if he'd seen Mattie—" She looked at Sigrid in sudden consternation.

"Who's Mattie?" the lieutenant asked.

"One of the bums that's sometimes here."

Sigrid fixed her with skeptical gray eyes. "You sure it's not the other dead man?"

Mrs. Brunieri dropped her own eyes.

"You might as well tell us the truth, Mrs. Brunieri. I have a feeling we'll find out anyhow as soon as we run his fingerprints."

The older woman sighed. "He's Mattie. Mattie DelVecchio."

When Buntrock first described some of his neighbors along this short block, he'd said that one of them was the widow of a Mafia don who had been gunned down in this very street thirty years ago. He hadn't mentioned the man's name and she had not bothered to ask.

"Benito DelVecchio's widow is your employer?"

Again the reluctant nod.

"And this man?"

"Benny's cousin. His mother was a good friend to my signora. He broke her heart and she died." In a mixture of sadness and scorn, she told them how Mrs. DelVecchio had tried to help the young man break free of drugs, but when that failed, she washed her hands of him and forbade him to come to her house again. "A disgrace to the family, but still family. She does not talk to him and she does not give him money, but every Tuesday, she pretends she's very hungry and then there is too much food to throw away, so I bring it to this bench. Every Tuesday. Usually, he's here, sometimes not."

"And the other man?"

"I do not know, Lieutenant. I told him the fettuccine was for Mattie and he laughed. Said he was having

Italian that night, too. Said all that was missing were the mandolins and a full moon hitting the sike."

"The 'sike'?"

Again she shrugged. "I did not ask."

Sigrid looked at Tillie, whose face echoed Mrs. Brunieri's unfamiliarity with the word.

Giuseppone di Napoli was a popular neighborhood restaurant and when questioned by Detectives Albee and Lowry, the manager rolled his eyes. "Lasagna? Do you know how many of our customers order that? And half of 'em take some home with them." But he thumbed through the receipts from the night before. "Twelve lasagnas served onsite, and two takeouts, both of those on credit cards."

Within the hour, Sigrid's team had names and addresses for those two. One was a woman, who lived two blocks over on Prince Street. The other lived half a block up on Sixth. For once they got lucky. Both customers were home and both still had their takeout boxes. The woman's was in her garbage pail, the elderly man's was in his refrigerator. "One order of Giuseppone's lasagna lasts me three meals," he told them.

They came up empty on the neighborhood canvass, but Sigrid gave orders for officers to come back after five to try finding people who were not at home now.

"Albee, you and Lowry stop by the restaurant later and see if any of last night's waiters can remember who took lasagna home with them."

A volunteer at the soup kitchen recognized Mattie DelVecchio's picture on Tillie's phone, but the other victim's picture drew only shrugs and headshakes.

Having run out of reasons to put it off any longer, Sigrid signaled to Tillie. As a rule, she kept her emotions so firmly in check that most of the department assumed she had none. They would have been surprised by the cold anger building inside her as she and Tillie walked down the side street, past Rudy Gottfried's basement apartment.

Number 406 was a well-maintained private home. It was period Federalist on the outside, but when Mrs. Brunieri answered the door and showed them into the living room, Sigrid was instantly reminded of her Grandmother Lattimore's early-twentieth-century home down in North Carolina. Polished mahogany chests and tables held tasteful keepsakes. The chairs were upholstered in harmonizing colors and Oriental rugs lay on the hardwood floors.

All bought with money from organized crime, thought Sigrid.

Like her grandmother, Mrs. DelVecchio's wrinkled face held traces of youthful beauty. She did not rise when they entered and was clearly accustomed to deference. She sat in a high-backed wing chair like a contessa on a throne and she did not smile in welcome. No sooner had Mrs. Brunieri announced them than she fixed Sigrid with an arrogant dark eye.

"Where have they taken the boy's body and when will it be released?"

"Are you Mattie DelVecchio's next of kin?" Sigrid's voice was equally hard and she did not offer the customary words of sympathy. Nor did she wait to be invited to sit. Instead, she took the nearer armchair and gestured for Tillie to sit as well. She saw Mrs. DelVecchio register the presumption with a further tightening of those thin lips.

"I will be responsible for his burial."

"We'll leave a number you can call. When did you last see him?"

Mrs. DelVecchio frowned and glanced at the woman who seemed as much her companion as her housekeeper.

"Two years ago," the other woman said promptly. "The Easter after his mother died, God rest her soul."

"What about you yourself, Mrs. Brunieri?" Sigrid.

"A week ago. I took him some chicken and rice."

"And last night?"

"I told you. I left fettuccine on the bench beside that other man."

"Where did he live?"

"On the street. That grocery cart. Everything he owned was in it."

"It was his choice," said Mrs. DelVecchio. "He—"

She paused at the sound of a key turning in the outer door, and they watched as a heavyset man of late middle age let himself into the foyer. Just under six feet tall, he had a broad flat face that was pitted with old acne scars. Without removing his sunglasses, he let the door slam behind him and lumbered into the room.

"Caterina! I came as fast as I could. A fender bender had traffic on the bridge backed up. Are you all right?"

He bent over the seated Mrs. DelVecchio and his thick fingers clasped the slender hand she offered him.

"Now that you are here, yes," she said. "These are police officers, George."

His glasses finished turning from dark to clear as he straightened to face them and behind the lenses, his brown eyes widened. "Lieutenant Harald, isn't it?"

"I'm sorry," Sigrid said, rising from her chair. "Have we met?"

"Only informally." He held out his hand. "George Edwards. It was at that gawd-awful opening for one of Hal DiPietro's artists. Last spring. Right before he was killed. Didn't you handle that case?"

Sigrid nodded, remembering now that this was the man who had helped the receptionist pick up the slides Rudy Gottfried had slung at DiPietro. "You're an attorney, aren't you?"

"Yes. Caterina—Mrs. DelVecchio—called me as soon as she heard that her nephew was found dead next to another body. Something about the fettuccine Brunie took him?"

"We don't have a cause of death yet, Mr. Edwards. We're just here to learn more about him. Do you know any of his friends? Where he lived?"

"No. I helped him get into rehab two years ago and he didn't have a fixed address then. That's the last time I saw him."

He gave them the name of the facility. "They might know something. They were supposed to do a follow-up."

Mrs. DelVecchio gave an impatient wave of her hand.

"If there are no further questions for my clients—"

"Just one," said Sigrid. "Mrs. Brunieri, you said that others leave food on that bench, too. Who?"

"Different ones," the housekeeper replied. "The

woman next to the red-door place most often and sometimes the boy from the diner. Maybe others from the street. I do not keep watch."

As Sigrid and Tillie rose to go, George Edwards gave them his card. "If you need to speak to them again, please call me first."

Back outside, Tillie spotted the red door on what looked like a warehouse at the opposite end of the street. There was no professional signage on the front of the three-story building, but there were steps leading down to the basement. A homemade board wired to the iron handrail announced that jazz played there nightly from 8:30 till 2:00, Wednesday through Saturday. They crossed, rang the bell at the house next door, and were answered by a tall athletic-looking woman who wore her brown hair in a single side braid across her shoulder and cocked her head in amusement.

"You're not the plumbers, are you?"

When they showed her their badges and introduced themselves, the woman frowned. "Somebody complained again?"

"Complained?" Sigrid asked. "Complained about what?"

"Oh, people are always complaining about something," the woman said smoothly, leaning against the doorframe. She was barefooted and wore a red shirt and white capris. Her toenails were painted a pale green. "I'm Janis Jennings. How can I help you?"

"We're investigating the deaths at the end of this block, down on Sixth."

"Oh, is that why all the police cars and people are down there? I was wondering. Who died?"

"Two men. We don't have any identification on them yet and are hoping you can help us, Miss Jennings," Sigrid said.

"*Mrs.* Jennings," the woman corrected cheerfully. "Just don't ask me where *Mr.* Jennings is. Haven't seen him in four years. He went down to the diner for coffee one morning and never came back."

"You file a missing persons report?" Tillie asked.

Mrs. Jennings hooted with laughter and her braid bobbed up and down against her red shirt. "God, no! Good riddance. He took his clothes and our dog and cleaned out our bank account. I wouldn't mind having the dog back, though. She was good company."

Tillie pulled up the pictures of the two dead men on his phone. "Do you know either of these?"

Mrs. Jennings cupped her hands around the screen to shade it from the overhead sun. "Never saw this guy," she said of the older man.

She swiped her finger across the screen for the second picture. "Awww! Poor Mattie! Oh, jeez. That's too bad. Did he finally overdose?"

"You know him?"

"Know who he is. He's been hanging around the neighborhood ever since I got here. Liked to brag about being connected."

"Connected?"

"To the Mafia guy who used to live over there." She pointed down the block to Number 406, the Del-Vecchio house. "Said he was keeping an eye on his widow. Protecting her."

"Protecting her from what?" asked Tillie.

Mrs. Jennings shrugged. "Who knows? I thought it was all in his head till somebody at the diner told me that some Mafia guy was gunned down right in front of his house there. I felt sorry for Mattie. Used to give him a freebie once in a while."

"Freebie?" asked Sigrid.

"You know. A free meal, a couple of dollars."

"You took food to him?"

"If I saw him down at that bench." She grinned. "He told me the widow didn't like him hanging around, so if he was there when I was passing, I'd give him my doggie bag if I had one. A few bucks now and then."

"I take it you don't care for the widow?" said Sigrid.

"I don't care for hypocrites. That house wasn't bought with clean money, was it? Drugs, too, probably. Yet she could turn up her nose at poor Mattie and complain about—"

"About you?" Sigrid asked when the woman changed her mind about whatever it was that she started to say.

"Me and anybody else on the block that annoyed her. If we left our trash barrels out at the curb too long. If we were having a party or the jazz club got too loud on a Saturday night."

A plumber's van pulled up to the curb. The man behind the wheel rolled down his window and called, "Jennings?"

"You got it, honey," she said happily. "Sorry, Lieutenant, but I've got a leak in my washer line."

On their way back to the park bench, Tillie stopped to ask questions at the diner, while Sigrid crossed over to Gottfried's apartment but the artist did not respond to the doorbell.

By now, the bodies had been removed and the beat officer who had called it in was rolling up the yellow tape. The foam food cartons had been bagged and tagged and there was nothing left except Mattie DelVecchio's grocery cart.

"Might as well bring that in, too," Sigrid said. "And get the other guy's clothes from the ME, Albee. Maybe you missed something the first time. And check for fingerprints on his bankroll."

Before heading back to her office, she left orders for the officers who would come back for a second canvass to see if they could learn who had brought lasagna to that park bench.